For Duty

The Antaran Legacy, Book 1

The Antaran Legacy: For Duty ♦ 2

This is a work of fiction. Names, characters, places and events portrayed in this book are either products of the author's imagination or are used fictitiously. Any character resemblance to actual persons, living or dead, is entirely coincidental.

The Antaran Legacy, Book 1: For Duty

Copyright © 2011 by Matthew C. Plourde

All rights reserved. Except for use in any review, the reproduction or utilization of this work, or portions thereof, in any form is forbidden without the written permission of the author.

An "Antaran Legacy" novel by Matthew C. Plourde
http://matthewcplourde.wordpress.com/

Cover artwork by Axel Torvenius
Edited by Jennifer Blessing Miceli

ISBN: 1456514431

EAN-13: 978-1456514433

First Edition: February 2011
Second Edition: November 2011

For my daughter Jenna.

I would bring the stars to you if you wished it.

"Seven paths aloft men say they take;

Yet six alone are viewed by mortal eyes.

From Zeus' abode no star unknown is lost

Since first from birth we heard, but thus the tale is told…"

- 270 B.C. by Aratos, *Greek Astronomer*

Chapter 1

"Welcome to Olympus Hospital," the bald man said as he waddled forward. When he realized with whom he was speaking, his eyes widened and he gestured a sign of veneration before he continued. "Forgive the chaos, most esteemed High Lady. I am Esodus, administrator of this facility and chief surgeon. The Humans who crashed are in good health and their leader is anxious to speak with you." The administrator's voice trailed off as he stooped in reverence to the eldest daughter of Emperor Agreios.

Though annoyance welled in her throat, Lady Helena didn't allow the emotion to break over her painted face. The sharp blue lines and sweeping curves of her facial markings stirred not a millimeter as she gazed at her reflection upon Esodus' scalp. While the hospital administrator genuflected on the ground, Helena silently cursed her father for turning her family into an idol of worship. Centuries ago this man would have simply lowered his head in respect. This day, however, Esodus caused a pedestrian traffic jam in the middle of the bustling hospital corridor.

"Rise, Administrator Esodus." Helena made a lifting motion with her white-gloved hand as she spoke. Like a puppet on a string, Esodus stood. Helena's grey eyes fixed upon the administrator, but the stare was not returned. When she spoke, everyone in the corridor froze and listened in awe.

"I am here on behalf of the Senate and the emperor. You are all to be commended for your healing skills and for your compassion towards the off-worlders." Her azure robe shifted as she stepped forward and spoke to the administrator, choosing to disregard his title. "Can the Humans be moved, Esodus?"

Still refusing to meet her gaze, her responded, "Y-yes My Lady. Well, most of them, that is. As you know, the ship crashed only yesterday. Some of the survivors will require more surgery."

Yes, she did indeed know when the crash occurred as she was right in the middle of it. New Olympus was the largest city on Antares, and the Human vessel plunged into the side of the mountain that gave the city its midday shade. Superheated debris rained down from the mountainside killing thousands. Helena spent the previous day attending to wounded off-worlders and Antarans alike at the smaller Tiberius Hospital which was closer to the crash site. This morning she was prepared to do the same, until her father contacted her with new orders.

"Well," she said, "a Human ambassador is en route to transport the off-worlders home." Relaxing, she brushed a strand of raven hair off her shoulder and gestured to Esodus. "Take me to them."

As they walked, she sensed his desire to say something more - something about the condition of the off-worlders. However he didn't speak. Helena could've delved deeper into the man's thoughts, but she decided to refrain. More important matters occupied her mind. She couldn't decipher the wisdom behind her father's decision to involve the Antaran people in the Human-Proxan War. What good could come of it?

They stopped beside a titanium door. Before the administrator could open his mouth to speak, Helena knew where they were.

"The Human captain is in here," she said.

"My Lady knows the truth before it is possible to be known," Esodus bowed again and closed his eyes in prayer.

"You will introduce me as *Lady Helena*, nothing more." She tapped her toe in frustration and Esodus snapped out of his trance.

"Understood?" she said as she attacked each of his eyes with a cold stare.

"As you w-wish, My Lady," he said as he placed his palm upon the reader.

With a *whoosh* the door glided into the floor and the two praetorians standing guard jerked to attention. Helena sensed their awe as they averted their gaze. The antechamber was large enough to hold a table on one side, a closet on the other, two guards at the far security door and little else.

"Administrator," one of the praetorians said, "the off-worlder requested communications. Again."

Esodus' mouth was open before the praetorian finished. "Of course, My Lady, we have followed protocol and denied interstellar communications to the off-worlders."

Protocol. Protocol stemmed from tradition. And tradition from custom. Helena's favorite childhood story depicted the struggles of a young princess as she defied her father to follow her heart. Protocol demanded Helena obey her emperor's command. Tradition required a child to trust in her father's wisdom, as it is greater than the child's. Why would she question her orders? Did she harbor more venom for Humans than she first thought?

Trust your emperor, she repeated in her head.

She planted her stare upon the senior praetorian. "Open this door, Praetorian. Only Esodus and I will enter, unless you are called for."

The praetorian nodded and opened the door without further acknowledgement. He resumed his post within an instant, hand at the hilt of his sword.

Helena took a step and then stopped to glance at the praetorian. "You adherence to protocol is impressive. Your Centurion will hear of it."

If her father was remembered for anything, it would be his ability to train disciplined royal guards. Helena sensed the deadliness in these two men. They kept their emotions well below the surface, a place she could only probe with considerable effort. They were here to guard the emperor's eldest daughter and heir on her visit to Olympus Hospital. And since Helena had never been face-to-face with an off-worlder before, she was thankful for their presence.

As they entered the room, Esodus announced, "Captain Connor. Lady Helena is here to see you."

The Human turned his head to the pair. His emotions were painted on his face as clearly as Helena's blue tattoos. He was annoyed.

"Why can't I contact my admiral? Why am I confined to this room? Where is my crew? Why..?"

Helena raised her hand and settled her gaze upon the off-worlder. To her surprise, he stared back at her as he crossed his arms. He was more muscled than an Antaran male, and his skin held richer color and thicker hair. Antaran skin tended towards pale gray or near white. Tangles of brown hair extended to below his ears and his jaw was covered with the shadow of a beard. Bandages encased his left forearm and entire right leg, but he wasn't as wounded as some of the survivors Helena tended at Tiberius Hospital. For the most part, Humans resembled Antarans. That fact supported the Antaran legends suggesting a similar heritage between the two races.

He seemed surprised by her apparent age as he was expecting someone older. A quick probe into his mind told her that they had both seen about the same number of years. Apparently, her people held their youth longer than Humans.

She didn't need to delve deeper into his thoughts to know he was angry. She could also sense Esodus' surprise. The way the off-worlder spoke to the emperor's heir was probably unfathomable to the hospital administrator.

"Your ambassador is heading to Antares now. He sends this communication," Helena said as she lifted a small datapad from the folds in her robe and handed it to Esodus.

Captain Connor took the datapad from the administrator and asked, "Can I have some privacy?"

"We have already examined the message and we are aware of its contents," Helena said. "It is devoid of secret code and, in fact, has instructions for you. The Antaran Senate has been in contact with your government since the crash. My people, the Antarans, wish nothing more than to see your crew well and able to journey home."

Captain Connor examined the datapad and then to his two visitors. He smiled and asked, "How do I turn this thing on?"

Esodus suppressed a laugh and leaned over to activate the datapad. Though Helena couldn't see the image from where she was standing, she watched it enough to know the face of the Human on the screen.

Captain Connor, the message intoned, *this is Admiral Glycin. The Antarans limit my message length, so this will be brief. You and your crew are safe for now. An ambassador is en route with a transport to bring you to The Median. Until then, you are Earth's ambassador to the Antaran people. Potential alliance is in the works, extend them some Human hospitality. Rest-up and review your chess strategies.*"

Before the screen flickered to black, Captain Connor furrowed his brow and asked, "Chess?"

"Yes, Captain. Chess," Helena responded as she walked to the far wall. "Do you wish to know what you are playing for?"

The Human planted his fists on the mattress of the bed and raised himself forward. The bed responded to his actions and lifted to support his back.

After a grimace of pain he said, "Helena, right? Your name is Helena?"

"Animal!" Esodus said as he took a step towards the bed. "You will address the Lady-"

"Esodus. Perhaps you should return to your duties," Helena said with practiced restraint in her tone. "Be sure to prepare the Human survivors for their trip home. You have two weeks."

She sensed the despair and confusion boiling together in the administrator's thoughts. Then, he regained his composure and responded within the proper protocol, "As you command."

Helena's eyes followed the hospital administrator as he left the room and she caught the praetorian looking sideways into the room – a place which saw raised voices a moment ago. As expected, they were paying attention. Helena doubted she would need their assistance if the off-worlder became hostile, but their presence was comforting nonetheless.

"My apologies, Captain," she said, returning her gaze to the Human in the bed. "Esodus is not a diplomat."

"Neither am I," Captain Connor grumbled as he tossed the datapad to the table beside his bed. After crossing his arms again, he took a moment to give her a long visual examination. She waited. Then he said, "You're more than just a diplomat."

"Very perceptive of you. However, I am here on diplomatic duties, so we will concentrate upon that end."

"This has to do chess somehow?"

"In a roundabout way, yes," she said. "Your war against the Proxans has claimed far too many Antaran lives. While I understand you are just soldiers in that war, my people are dying as you fight over resources on the far side of *my* planet."

"We have orders to leave your civilization alone."

"And what good are those orders when starships crash into our cities?"

"Believe me," he said, "I had no intention of crashing my ship. You must tell me – how is my crew?"

Helena sensed a genuine concern in his emotions. He was worried for his shipmates. This fact intrigued her because her data suggested that Humans were little more than barbaric warmongers. Was there more to the captain's exotic exterior? True, their species shared many commonalities, but the mere fact that he was born on a different planet branded him *alien* to her.

Realizing her pause was too long she said, "We are tending to your crew and the survivors will be allowed to leave. You may also take your deceased as well, if you wish. However, I will discuss all of that with your ambassador."

"Not my crew," he said. "The ambassador will not make any decisions about my crew. Got it?"

"Those are choices to be made by your ambassador, you should-"

"Listen," he said as he rose from the bed. Helena scanned his thoughts and didn't find any violence there. Though if anything changed, she was prepared to subdue him. "I don't know this ambassador from Jack, okay? He might not put my people ahead of his political goals. There are good people in my crew. Fine folk fighting a war for survival. Don't blame them for what happened yesterday. They fought with honor and bravery. And they fought to keep that ship from crashing into your city. If you have to release your hatred on anyone, release it on me. Not my crew."

Exhausted from his exertion, he fell back into his bed. Helena sensed pain and sorrow from the off-worlder. His first priority was his crew and not his own life. Scolding herself for making preemptive judgments, she softened her tone.

"Very well," she said, "if there is punishment to be dealt, I will recommend you receive it in full. However, may I make a suggestion?"

In-between labored breaths, he asked, "What?"

"Follow your admiral's advice and rest. We play chess in two weeks."

Chapter 2

Helena didn't sleep that night. Instead, she spent her time at Tiberius Hospital. She was accustomed to occasional long shifts, but these hours were marred with a grief that lurked on the outskirts of her heart. As heir, she couldn't allow that grief to take hold. Instead, she wore her usual mask of stone on her face.

Her last patient was a boy named Cispius. After three hours in a white room, Helena couldn't save him. She had lost many patients over the past few hours, but this one threatened to overwhelm her. After he was gone, she rushed from the white room and ripped her surgical vest from her body. The decontamination shower rained its chemicals over her face and naked body. Without reapplying her tattoos, she locked herself in the adjoining preparation chamber.

How many more of her people had to die before the Humans and Proxans ended their war? This boy, Cispius, was a miracle to his family. His parents were the last hope for the family to continue their bloodline. As they aged, the possibility of a successful pregnancy waned and the family prepared to turn their histories over to the Archives – another Antaran light extinguished in the dwindling population. Then, Cispius was born. Helena shared the family's joy through Cispius' memories as she operated on him. The boy's family was a respected one. They shouldn't have suffered such a monumental loss. Cispius was their treasured son. He was strong, intelligent, happy and healthy.

After a few moments, Helena retrieved her Gima tattoo brush and absently swept the fine bristles across her face. The boy's parents were at the hospital. Helena sensed their anticipation and fear. They would want to know everything, including how Cispius *felt* at the time of his injury and death.

Helena prepared herself for her next ordeal by looking into the mirror and reminding herself of her responsibilities. Sure, her father allowed her to play doctor from time to time, but her true duty was to her people. Duty. She found safety there. Warm in her sanctuary of aged tradition, she maneuvered the corridors until she arrived in the waiting room. Deflecting the anguish she sensed in the parents' hearts, she smiled for them.

"Cispius was valiant in his final hours," she said, "but his wounds were too deep. You may see him now, if you wish."

After a few solemn moments between husband and wife the father asked, "Did any of the other students survive?"

Helena marveled at Calator's control. Though he just learned of his son's death, he was worried about the other children. Calator was a fine citizen.

"Yes," she said, "including young Livia."

Livia was the daughter of Calator's friend and business partner. She was very close to Cispius.

Though Calator and Paulina controlled their emotions, Helena sensed their despair. Cispius was the end of their family, the last son. All their hopes were on his small shoulders. They foresaw a bright future for their child, but now they were left with the grief of knowing Cispius wouldn't taste the same joys they had experienced. The loss crushed them in a way Helena couldn't understand, as she had no children of her own.

"We must make preparations," Calator said, his mind safe in the coming regimen of his son's funeral. He didn't want to focus on the oppressive hole in his life.

"A representative from my office will contact you for assistance," Helena said, "if you require."

Paulina nodded and said, "Thank you, My Lady. You are most gracious in our hour of darkness."

"I live to serve," Helena said, reciting the rote she learned at an early age.

"Will you speak?" Calator said. "I mean, at his service. Will you tell our family what you told us? About his bravery?"

"It cannot be tonight, as I must return to the palace now," Helena said. "However, it would be my honor to speak over his body before you give him to the fire. Tomorrow morning?"

Paulina forced a smile and said, "We will wait until tomorrow."

Exhausted and drained, Helena boarded her aircar and absently peered from the back window as the driver sped her toward the palace. The nighttime glow from the Antares sun painted the city a deep red. Spires from numerous buildings stretched into the incomplete darkness, lights flickering at their peaks. Her gaze wandered north to the plumes of smoke still visible near the mountain. Stunted trees extended towards the scar of the crash site. The terraforming efforts around Olympus were dealt another complication. They'd have to start over again in some areas.

Like the smoke, her thoughts were carried to distant places by the winds of doubt in her mind. Were her people destined for continued suffering at the feet of these galactic wars? How many more children must she bury? Was there nothing she could do?

As she wrestled with those questions, she sensed a plan in her father's mind. Even at such a great distance, she felt his determination and fear. His plan weighed heavily on him, but Helena didn't dare attempt to invade his memories. He would detect her.

Her curiosity piqued, she spoke into the intercom to the aircar driver. "Praetorian, we must reach the palace with the utmost haste."

The soldier-driver nodded and lifted into the clouds. The vehicle buffeted against the increased speed as the clouds rocketed past the windows. In the distance, an energy storm's lights licked the edge of the haze. A few moments later, they arrived safely on a palace landing pad.

Helena's sisters were already assembled when she arrived at the war council. Taking her seat next to her father, the emperor, she sensed his anxiety. Now that she was closer, she was shocked at the intensity of his emotions.

"Heir Helena," the emperor said, "thank you for your prompt report. Your firsthand accounts from the hospitals have proven very informative."

Helena nodded.

"I have called you all to this summit to discuss my plans with the Humans," Emperor Agreios said. "We will make peace with them."

"Father," Helena said, suddenly unable to read his emotions, "I know it is not my place to question, but why are we helping the Humans? They have waged war in our skies for far too long."

Agreios looked at his eldest daughter and said, "Far, far too long..."

"We should be sentencing them for their crimes, not negotiating peace!" Valeria, the second eldest sister rose in her chair and allowed her emotions to take hold - again. Helena failed to teach Valeria that serenity was superior to fury. Her sister was tragically set in her ways.

Helena's other sisters – Justina, Marcella, Claudia, Prisca, and Terentia – obeyed protocol and didn't speak. Though they were alone with their father, the younger sisters were only allowed to respond to inquiries. They weren't afforded free reign.

Of course, Valeria considered herself an exception. "We should send a clear message to the Humans of Terra, or whatever they call their swampy hole of a planet," Valeria said. "When the ambassador arrives, we should hold him as well."

"Valeria," Helena said, "you speak from your heart, not your mind. Listen to your own words and you will see the folly in them."

"Don't tell me how to think, sister," Valeria said with venom on the surface of her thoughts and words.

Terentia, the youngest sister, came to Helena's defense as always. "Helena was just trying to-"

"What do you know of anything?" Valeria said. "Go back to your books and talk to me when you have seen eighteen seasons."

"Now then," Agreios said, "there is no need to be rude to your sister."

"She has no place at a war council," Valeria said. "She's never even been in battle!"

"Battle," Agreios said with a defeated exhale. "None of us have seen real battle. We have lived, sheltered, on this little planet since our colonization. The Humans and Proxans do battle. We *write* of battle, we *train* for battle, but we do not *know* battle – not like they do. No, we are an insignificant speck in an endless ocean of stars. Do you think the Humans care if we live or die? Do you think we can threaten them when we have no warships? Tell me, Valeria, with what would you threaten the mighty Human Confederation? Your ill attitude?"

Marcella and Claudia suppressed laughs. Helena considered shooting a scolding look in their direction, but she decided to make an exception at the expense of the hotheaded Valeria. She could always reprimand them later, if she remembered. Again, exceptions could be made.

"And tell me, Helena, what would you have me do?" the emperor asked. "Continue ignoring the exploitation of our planet by these warmongers? Allow more ships to crash into our cities and kill our people? What alternative do you see?"

Knowing her father didn't want a response, Helena met his gaze and awaited his next words.

"Fine then," he said. "Now that we've all had our little moment to rant let me tell you of my plan, for it involves great risk to us all. And I see no other path."

Emperor Agreios rose and paced in front of the windows, which overlooked the shining buildings and sky bridges of New Olympus. "I have meditated long about this and I have reached this conclusion: we will not survive this war if we continue to ignore it. Since we cannot fight *nor forgive* the Humans or Proxans, I must pursue other means to secure our civilization's safety."

After a long pause, he turned to look upon each of his seven daughters. Tears were in his eyes and Helena wondered why he allowed his emotions to loiter so close to the surface. A quick probe of his surface thoughts uncovered fear again. What was he afraid of?

"I love you all," he said, "which is why this is a difficult decision for me. I plan to crush the Humans and Proxans to such an extreme that they would not have the capacity to build another battleship. Then, and only then, will they be unable to bring their war to our world. To accomplish this, I need all six of you."

In answer to several looks of confusion, Agreios said, "No, Terentia, you are not old enough for this mission. I am sorry."

Terentia lowered her head. Helena suppressed pity for her youngest sister, as she recognized the wisdom in her father's decision. If Terentia wasn't to be included, then Helena trusted her father had valid reasons.

"The plan is complex and will require all your ability, courage and dedication," Agreios said. "You may not know this, but the resources required to build a battleship are immense and, more importantly, finite."

The emperor clicked a button on his datapad and the table surface illuminated displaying a solar system. "Here is where the Humans and Proxans mine their precious tellium – the gas which makes their engines possible. This is their main battleground, but since neither side can afford to lose a true battleship, only minor skirmishes are fought there. You see, each side only has a handful of the big cruisers that allow for hyper-fast travel and massive engagements. Replacing each battleship takes decades. We will destroy both the ships and the star which produces tellium. That is my plan."

Emperor Agreios changed the view to a scientific readout of a star. "Humans and Proxans mine opposite sides of this enormous star. The mining process is delicate and time-consuming. Once the gas is collected, it is shipped to faraway vaults where it is processed and stored."

The view changed again to a technical readout of a huge battleship. "The engines of these ships are carefully constructed to house the gas in a perpetual hyperdrive which can propel the vehicle at beyond-light speeds. When a battleship is destroyed, the explosion alters the very fabric of the surrounding space. According to our research, if a battleship was flown into the center of this tellium sun, the sun would collapse."

A virtual demonstration of the collapse played on the table's surface. Well-schooled in astrophysics, Helena recognized the potential validity of the demonstration. Her father's plan had merit.

"Here's the difficult part," Agreios said as he dimmed the table. "I need each of you to secure a tactical position on six of the eight known Human battleships. You will use your skill and mental ability to advise the Human captains and guide them to victory over the Proxans. Then, at the planned time, you will gain control of your vessel and send it into the nearest star. Helena's target ship – their flagship called *Jupiter* – will be sent into the tellium sun to destroy it."

Helena nodded, showing her approval and acceptance of her father's decision to send his eldest daughter to accomplish the most important part of the mission.

"To that end, I have opened diplomatic channels with the Human government," Agreios said. "I told them that our greatest resource is our people, not the crude metal on the dark side of the planet. They have agreed to evaluate our usefulness over a game of chess with one of their captains."

"What's chess?" Terentia asked, forgetting her discipline.

"Apparently," Agreios said, "it is a game of tactical acumen with a limited scope and known parameters. The Humans have agreed to hear our representative – which would naturally be Helena in this situation – if she can defeat one of their captains at this game. Apparently, Human captains study the game so completely, that they are unbeatable, even to other captains. Games between them end in draws. Since my offer rests solely on our ability to provide the Humans with tactical assistance, the Humans wanted to evaluate my claim that we are better tacticians."

"Are we?" Helena asked, not sure she'd been exposed to enough warfare subject matter to count herself an expert.

"Do not forget your training," he said. "As long as your enemy has a mind, you can best that enemy. Neither the Humans nor Proxans command the mental disciplines we Antarans do. This captain should be no match for you, Helena. Once you defeat him, you will travel back to their homeworld to negotiate our alliance. Secure yourself and your sisters on their battleships and the rest of the plan may unfold. We will, at last, be free of these wars."

Helena performed some quick math and probability analytics in her head. The exercise took only seconds and she said, "We need Terentia on this mission. My analysis returns an eighty-five percent success rate and a twelve percent loss rate in our war against the Proxans. Without Terentia, the Humans will have two or three battleships remaining after we destroy the tellium sun. That is not enough for success. We need to leave them with only one battleship if we are to ensure a complete victory."

Agreios frowned and said, "Yes, I came to that same conclusion."

"Then it is agreed," Helena said.

"No," he said. "We will conduct the mission without Terentia. Unfortunately, I cannot send someone else, as you all are the best trained and most naturally gifted in our mental disciplines. We cannot risk detection until the plan reaches its conclusion. Terentia will *not* go."

"Father, may I speak to you alone?" Helena asked, prepared to sway him with her logic. Why couldn't he accept the truth of the numbers? Numbers were pure and inscrutable.

The emperor nodded.

Terentia stopped next to Helena on her way from the conference room.

"Thank you," she said. "I belong on this mission."

"I did not do this so you could prove your worth to the family," Helena said. "In my analysis, you are not likely to succeed. However, I see the truth of father's plan. We must do this to ensure our survival."

Terentia bit her lip but didn't respond. As Terentia exited, Helena allowed her eyes to linger upon her younger sister. The days of their carefree youth were lost to the thickness of time. Helena raised Terentia after their mother died and they shared a special bond. Were her words too harsh? Helena sometimes lost herself in her role as heir to the throne, and a spark of regret formed deep in her heart. Before that spark could ignite into the flame of emotion, she suppressed her thoughts and closed the door behind her sisters.

"What does my eldest daughter wish to speak with me about?" Agreios asked.

Noticing her father didn't address her royal title as heir, Helena almost lost her composure. He omitted her title on purpose as he wasn't pleased with her.

"Emperor, your plan is a good one and I appreciate all you must sacrifice," Helena said, proud of her father for his determination and cleverness. "The Histories will remember your wisdom and courage."

Agreios sank into his chair and looked at his daughter. Tears formed in his eyes again. "Courage? Do you think there is *courage* in my plan?"

Helena sat next to him and touched his forearm. She studied his wrinkled, yet strong face – a face that appeared as if it was carved in stone. Why were his emotions so readable? Was he losing control?

"Are you alright, Father?"

"Helena, my dear, I love you all so much. I don't know if I've said it enough lately… But you are all so precious to me."

"You are precious to us as well, Father." Helena avoided the word "love." Though she studied the word in her literature, she wasn't sure it was an emotion afforded to royalty. Memories of her mother threatened her emotional barriers. Did she love her mother? Why was her mother taken from her at such a young age? No. Those thoughts were dangerous. Helena closed her eyes and recited the serenity chant in her mind:

> *I shall not despair,*
> *The walls of reason ground me – I find my center.*
> *From my center I collect strength, wisdom and clarity.*
> *There is no chaos, only serenity.*

When she opened her eyes, her father was looking at her. He knew the chant and he probably realized Helena was using it. She hoped she didn't give away her reasons for using the chant more than usual lately. Grief over the loss of a loved one was weakness and the heir to the Antaran throne couldn't afford any imperfections.

"This is difficult for me," Agreios said, "to send my daughters into battle like this. I fear I may never see you again."

"We will succeed."

Agreios smiled and said, "I never doubt you, Heir to Antares. Since the day you were born, you have proven yourself dependable and dutiful. I know you will not fail me. However, that is not why I shed these tears."

"I will not speak of your tears, not even to my sisters."

He waved his hand. "Such things do not concern me anymore. Too late, I realize that I missed the most important parts of life. Logic, tradition, rulership – I would trade it all to relive my days with my daughters. I would have very much liked to be the one to comfort you when you cried, to cheer you when you succeeded and to read you those bedtime stories. Xyla was an excellent proxy, but as your father, *I* should have done those things. I should have *watched* you grow, rather than review the reports of your status on my datapad each morning. Regrets. Regrets fill my mind these days, dear daughter."

Shocked by the emperor's words – her own father's words – Helena couldn't speak. Was this regret clouding his vision? She reviewed his plan again and found it to be in sound logical shape. What was happening to him? Why couldn't he push aside his emotions and embrace the cold truths?

"I know why you are here," he said. "You are here to convince me that Terentia needs to be on the mission."

She nodded.

"Not this time, Helena. I have done the math, same as you, and our success is likely. I will not send Terentia into battle and that is final."

Recognizing the resolution in his face, she didn't push the matter. However, her math came to the same conclusion time and again. Failure was more likely than she was comfortable with.

Chapter 3

After another busy night with no sleep, Helena kept her promise to speak at Cispius' funeral. The orange sun cast the faces of the grieving family in the usual Antaran glow. Helena restrained herself from reaching into their minds – their mood was contagious and she couldn't afford a swing of depression.

"Though I only knew Cispius for the brief time he was in my care," Helena said, "I was instantly impressed by his good nature. We needed to keep him unconscious, but I was able to travel through his memories. His thoughts were warm and safe. I feel I know you all so well, as his thoughts centered on his family life. A life he adored. In the end, he honored his family by being the dutiful citizen you trained him to be. He held the door open for his classmates as his school burned. This responsibility was his, and he welcomed the chance to show his peers that he was ready to sacrifice for them. Though you did not know it, Cispius was named Class Protector a few months ago. This honor was one he shouldered with great enthusiasm, yet he didn't want to appear prideful. So, he did not tell you."

Helena paused to gaze upon the still form of Cispius under his shroud on the pyre. He deserved a future. All Antarans did.

"That is how he died," she continued, "as a good citizen and friend to his classmates. I touched his mind during his last few minutes in this world, and he wanted me to tell you all about this. Not because he wanted to be remembered as a hero. Instead, he wanted you to know how much of an honor it was to be a part of this family. In his death, like in life, Cispius honors you all. I will personally add this to your family record for its storage in the Archives."

After Helena's words, she touched the pyre and closed her eyes. Though she wasn't as religious as her sister, Justina, Helena hoped Cispius was enjoying a life beyond this one. The innocent boy had earned it.

In turn, each family member followed Helena's motions until they formed a ring around the pyre. Calator ignited the torch and smiled one last time at his son in the flesh before setting the pyre ablaze.

Through the years, Helena had attended and spoken at many funerals. However, those other funerals seemed like the faint light of the stars behind the growing pyre flames. The family's grief choked the air as much as the smoke from the pyre. Why was she unable to block their feelings from invading her heart? What was so different *now*?

Perhaps she was more sensitive because she was on the precipice of something monumental. Whatever the outcome of her mission to Terra, the course of her people had been altered. She wanted to tell the family that everything would be made *right*. The Humans and Proxans would pay for their crimes, as Valeria had said at the war council. However, Helena felt her words would be hollow. No amount of vengeance could fill the hole in their lives now. Success or failure, Cispius was extinguished from their world.

After the fire had faded to a smoldering glow, Paulina sat beside Helena and said, "Thank you, My Lady. Those were very kind words. We all thank you for staying with us to the end."

Without looking into the grieving mother's eyes, Helena said, "I always remain until the end. It is only proper."

"You are so important," Paulina said, "to us all. We understand if you must return to the palace or to the hospital."

"Your son was my last patient," Helena said distantly, "for quite some time, possibly."

"Oh," Paulina said, her mind embattled between curiosity and protocol. She knew she wasn't allowed to ask a question out of curiosity alone.

Helena decided to spare the woman. "I am leaving for the Human homeworld of Terra soon," she said, "to negotiate peace. My father wishes to end the suffering to our people."

"The emperor is wise," Paulina said.

Before she saw her, Helena sensed Terentia approach. The family rose to their feet, eyes open with wonderment.

"My sister," Terentia said, "I come on behalf of the emperor."

Helena stood and accepted her sister's greeting in the formal way. "Welcome to our somber ceremony, my sister," she said.

Terentia turned to Paulina and handed the grieving mother a bouquet of crag roses. "From the palace," she said. "Know that we all mourn with your family."

Helena's heart swelled. Her sister had transformed from a bratty kid into a poised young woman. Perhaps her father was right. In the end, Terentia must be spared. The rest of them had fallen into some trap of nobility or adulthood. However Terentia embodied all that was pure about youth and royalty. She was the shining beacon amongst the daughters of Agreios, though she didn't realize that fact herself.

"On behalf of my entire family, we thank the daughters of Emperor Agreios."

Terentia smiled and said, "If you'll allow it, may I sing for Cispius' soul?"

Calator stepped forward to put an arm around his wife. "We would be honored."

Renowned for her singing voice, Terentia hummed an inspirational tune from the ancient days of Antares. Some of the gathered family members recognized the melody and wept quietly to themselves. Peace settled over them as Terentia's notes carried into the streets and above the nearby buildings.

Helena defocused from the song and concentrated on her next ordeal. Was she ready to leave her planet and conceal her intent towards the Humans long enough for success? What if she was discovered? Were a funeral pyre and song of lament already waiting for her in the near future?

Chapter 4

Helena sat in front of her mirror. Using a gima-wrap, she tied her black hair into a single tail as was customary for diplomatic sessions. Streaks of silver marred the perfect darkness of her hair, but Helena didn't mind. Her mother had silver hair.

"No, Helena."

She attempted to push the memories of her mother aside again, so she focused on her gima-tattoos.

As she painted the sweeping blue marking across her face to signify her station, Helena recalled the story of her people and the Gima. If nothing else, the diversion kept the memories of her mother buried.

The first tribes to settle Antares arrived on crude starships. Originally from the same planet, the Humans, Proxans, and Antarans were forced to abandon their dying world. Unified at first, the massive fleet of ships sailed towards the promise land – an Eden in the stars. But as decades turned into centuries, the people began to quibble and splinter. Two large factions arose from the infighting and the Humans were the first to settle. They found a planet much like their home world, but with more tropical temperatures. Then, the Proxans settled on a hard, rocky planet. The remaining settlers were left to live on their ships or suffer on inhospitable planets. The Antarans settled for one such desolate planet.

Too close to a red giant, Antares was a brutal place to live. The first Antarans (named "Gima," for the little fleet's flagship) found themselves altered after a few thousand years on the surface. Their mental discipline formed into a religion of science and engineering. They discovered a way to calm the red giant and return it to a life-giving star.

Through the millennia, the astro-psychic effects of the planet had subsided. Only a few bloodlines were still strong in the discipline, and Helena's family possessed the same level of power as the ancient Gima.

Today, two weeks after the crash, the ambassador from Terra had arrived on Antares. Following tradition, Helena wore the blue facial tattoos and ceremonial robe of a Gima heir. According to Gima customs, off-worlders weren't permitted to directly gaze upon royalty.

Helena reached for her white silk gloves. Her mother's gloves. As she slid the ends to her elbows, she focused on her diplomatic mission. Everything rested on the outcome of her actions. She couldn't allow room for failure.

Helena joined her sisters at the senate house. Marked with the gima-tattoos, Helena thought they looked impressive. All seven of them rarely gathered in one place. The emperor was also adorned in the trappings of the ancient Gima and he quieted the crowd by raising his arm.

An older Human man sat next to the emperor, and Helena looked to one of the praetorians behind her father. Helena sensed the guard's tensed muscles, ready for action at an instant. Her father's personal guards weren't relaxing.

Then, Helena spotted Captain Connor. Dressed in a dark blue uniform with shiny medals, the captain appeared much different than when Helena met him at the hospital. With his wounds healed and face shaven, Helena suppressed the natural attraction she felt for the off-worlder.

As the emperor welcomed their guests, Terentia leaned close to Helena and said, "Did you see them?"

Lowering her voice Helena said, "You mean the Humans?"

"Yes. They are… different."

Helena nodded. "I met one of their captains at Olympus Hospital. Very interesting people."

Terentia giggled and Helena logged a mental note to reprimand her younger sister at a later time. This was not the venue for foolery.

"One of them is very cute. Strong too, like the pictures from our legends," Terentia said.

As Helena gazed at Captain Connor, she decided the encounter with the off-worlder wasn't entirely unpleasant. She scanned his surface thoughts and found his mind suddenly on alert. He looked in her direction. Confusion followed by recognition flooded though his mind and he smiled. Was he smiling at her?

Helena looked away and whispered to her sister. "Listen to father."

After a few more pleasantries were exchanged between the emperor and the Humans, Terentia leaned towards Helena again. "Did you study this game called chess?"

"Yes," Helena said, "I reviewed the material sent to us by the Humans and found the game simple."

"You can win?"

"With minimal effort, I believe," Helena said, surprised to find Captain Connor looking in her direction again. She sensed his mind filling with pleasure when he looked at her. These Humans were simple creatures.

"And now," Emperor Agreios said, "my daughter and heir will present the terms of our offer."

Helena stood as the eyes of the gathered senators, dignitaries, and Human visitors turned in her direction. Before she began, she noticed surprise in Captain Connor's mind. He didn't expect her to be of such high station. Possibilities ran though his mind at such tremendous velocity, Helena couldn't keep pace. Why did she focus on him?

Clearing her thoughts and betraying no emotion on her face, Helena said, "Welcome old friends, new friends, and family to this remarkable day. The proud Antaran people offer a formal request for alliance with the Human Confederation. In exchange for protection, the Antarans offer exclusive mining rights to the ores on the dark side of the planet. We also offer the wisdom of our people to help in the war against the Proxans. My sisters, the emperor, and I hope this will begin a new era. One where Human and Antaran call each other *friend*."

Nods of approval returned from the gathered crowd. Helena delved into the Human ambassador's mind and she found amusement there. He thought the Antarans insignificant and not worthy of consideration.

"I understand," Helena said, settling her gaze upon the ambassador, "that the Human Confederation will accept our offer upon a condition? Please state that condition now."

The Human ambassador, Bergem, rose from his chair and smiled at Helena. She sensed his annoyance with the whole affair. He wanted to return to whatever task he was focused on before his detour to Antares. But Helena couldn't discover the details of that unfinished task. Dealing with the Antarans wasn't important to him. Helena didn't smile back, and she imagined what his face would look like after he learned of the destruction of his fleet. Perhaps then, the Antarans would be the ones making the demands.

Bergem said, "Honorable Heir, Emperor, and gathered senators – we are most pleased to discuss an alliance with the Antarans. However, we already mine from Antares, as we do not recognize the Antaran claim of sovereignty. I speak for my leaders when I say we cannot commit forces to protect Antares – the war consumes all our resources. However, if the Antarans can prove the validity of their claim that their tacticians are of value in our efforts against the Proxans, then we will open ourselves to further discussion on Terra."

Helena had her rehearsed question ready, even though she knew the answer. This show was more for the senators and dignitaries. The emperor had already negotiated this deal.

"How can we prove this claim?" Helena asked.

"Human captains are picked from amongst the brightest officers," Bergem said. "They have mastered tactics and this expertise can be tested in a game we call chess. If an Antaran can defeat a Human captain in this test of tactical skill, we will open ourselves to further diplomacy."

"Thank you, Ambassador," Helena said. "We have received your data on this game of tactics, and we are prepared to prove our claim after dinner."

♦

The Humans, senate chiefs, and high dignitaries joined the emperor and his daughters at the head table. Helena noticed her sister, Terentia, glance at Captain Conner from time to time. Had Helena not taught her sister, she would've thought Terentia possessed as little self control as the Humans.

"This is fantastic," Captain Connor said as he popped another red potato in his mouth. "Much better than on Terra."

Helena sensed the captain was telling the truth. Interested in learning more about this man she said, "Do you have potatoes on Terra?"

"Yes," he said, "we do have potatoes, but it's more of a forced agricultural experiment than an actual food."

"That's interesting," she said.

"I might have to take some of these home with me," he said, still focused on the nourishing red orbs.

Amused by the captain's childlike enthrallment with his food, Helena smiled and said, "I'm sure my sister will not charge you for them."

"Claudia is quite proficient in the palace gardens." Agreios said, "I believe these are yours, my dear. Correct?"

Claudia smiled at Captain Connor. Then she nodded and said, "Yes, Father."

Had all her sisters lost their discipline while in the company of the off-worlders? Perhaps Helena was too lax in their studies. She decided to address the matter, if they survived their dangerous missions.

"Helena, right?" Captain Connor said as he addressed the emperor's eldest daughter again.

Turning her eyes to the captain, Helena said, "Yes, Captain?" Her heart flinched when his eyes stared back at her. His face was *alive* and curious.

"We met at the hospital?"

Helena nodded.

Captain Connor traced circles in the air in front of his face and said, "I recognize the… the markings."

Helena sensed panic in the captain's thoughts. Why would he panic? "That is very observant of you," Helena said, not certain what he was trying to achieve.

Valeria huffed. "My sister has a talent for stating the obvious," she said. "I am Valeria, High Vizier to the Palace and daughter of Emperor Agreios. We welcome you to Antares."

"That's quite a title," Captain Connor said.

"Do you mock me?" Valeria said, her eyes as cold as the dark side of their planet.

"No… I-"

"Valeria," Helena said, "the off-worlders mean no disrespect. They do not know our ways."

Hoping her sister could contain her anger towards the Humans, Helena prepared to interrupt Valeria at the slightest sign of impropriety. Before the summit, Valeria vowed to challenge the Humans on their war policy which resulted in countless Antaran deaths. The emperor forbade Valeria from confronting them and jeopardizing the mission. Now, it appeared Valeria was ready to defy her father.

Helena attempted to read her sister's intentions, but Valeria had prepared the requisite mental blocks. She couldn't pierce her sister's mind.

"Do you think," Valeria said, "that your war has not affected us?"

"What Valeria means," Helena said, "is we assume you have weighed the Antaran cost already paid as a result of your war. If you require specific numbers, my office can provide those for you."

This time, Helena was able read her sister. Valeria fumed.

"We don't need your numbers," Ambassador Bergem said. "What you forget is the Human Confederation claimed this planet before your ships landed. Be thankful we have no use for the settled side."

"That sounds like a threat," Valeria said, her ire now directed at the ambassador.

"No threats," Bergem said. "Merely observations to take into consideration."

Helena turned her attention to Ambassador Bergem, who had only poked at his food. His mood revolved around boredom and annoyance and he didn't like Antaran food. True, most everything grew in the rocky soil, so variety of flavor wasn't as prominent as it was in Human food. As Helena probed further into Bergem's mind, she sensed he wasn't just an ambassador. Something more sinister lurked in the shadows of his subconscious.

"Be careful, Ambassador," Agreios said, "the old tiger who lay in the grass should not be provoked. He still has teeth."

Captain Connor turned to the ambassador and said, "Aren't you on a diplomatic mission? This is no way to treat our hosts."

Ambassador Bergem slammed his napkin on the table and said, "Emperor, we thank you for your hospitality, but I must get the captain and his men home. Let us skip to the match and we'll be on our way."

Helena focused more intently on the ambassador but couldn't penetrate his thoughts. His rudeness made little sense given his diplomatic mission. What was he hiding?

With his eyes on Bergem and his voice steady as Mount Olympus, Agreios motioned towards Helena and said, "Your opponent is ready whenever you are, Ambassador."

Chapter 5

Prisca approached Helena and said, "Do you think you're ready?"

Helena nodded. "Yes, however... something bothers me about the ambassador. I'll need everything I've got to focus on the captain. Keep tabs on the ambassador's mind. I don't trust him."

Prisca, Helena's anchor in times of need, nodded and eyed Bergem. Helena smiled to herself as she watched her sister probe the off-worlder's mind. Though the second youngest, Prisca was a natural prodigy when it came to reading minds. Helena taught her sister everything she knew, and then Prisca taught Helena a few tricks.

"I will discover his secrets," Prisca said, her eyes still locked on Bergem as she took her seat.

Dependable Prisca. Helena wished she could have Prisca at her side on the diplomatic mission to Terra. But her sisters needed time to deepen their training before the mission – a final focus study before their plan was executed.

"Very well," Marcella said. "If everyone would kindly take their seats, we can begin."

Marcella enjoyed the spotlight. Sure, she was beautiful beyond words, but she was also quite empathic. Her ability to read a crowd and shifting emotions made her the perfect mistress of ceremonies and public relations officer for the emperor. Even Helena couldn't resist her urge to smile when

Marcella was talking. Her melodious voice brought joy and comfort.

"Captain Connor from Terra," Marcella said, motioning her hand towards the off-worlder. Then, Helena took a seat opposite the captain at the chess table. "And Heir Helena," Marcella said. "A duel of wits is in accord, with the fate of the Human-Antaran alliance in the balance. Heir Helena has never been defeated in Jocca, but this game is called Chess – a Human game. Captain Connor is undefeated in the game to be played. Captain Connor is also a decorated ship commander in the Human Confederation Navy. Bets are not allowed for this match, as the highest wager is already in place."

Leave it to Marcella to add drama to an already tense situation.

Emperor Agreios stood and smiled at Helena. "Begin," he said.

Helena sensed a great amount of love from her father, but she was forced to concentrate on her opponent as Captain Connor moved a pawn two spaces forward. From what she remembered of the Human material, he performed a standard opening that allowed several of his pieces an avenue to escape from the back row. The goal was to control the center of the board. She sensed that he preferred to use that move as an opening in most of his matches.

Helena countered with a pawn of her own and Captain Connor smiled.

"I hope you're not just following a known strategy," he said as he moved a knight over his row of pawns.

Scanning his thoughts to see what his next move would be, Helena moved a knight of her own into position. "I studied many of the strategies known to work," Helena said, "but I found them shortsighted."

Captain Connor laughed, moved a bishop next to Helena's knight and said, "Really?"

He was enjoying himself. Why was he so unconcerned with the match? Surely he cared if he won or lost.

Helena moved another piece and studied her opponent. "Do you not agree?"

Captain Connor shrugged. "There's a reason they've worked for thousands of years."

"This game is that old?" she said, intrigued by Human history.

Claiming a piece, he said, "Yes. Chess dates back to our home planet, from what I understand."

Helena focused and attempted to follow her opponent's many strands of thought. He was considering several different ways to defeat her.

After Helena countered his move, Captain Connor said, "How are you making these moves so fast?"

She mimicked his shrug, though she wasn't sure why. "It's simple math, really," she said.

The captain paused and looked into her eyes. Helena's heart fluttered and she chided herself. Why was she so distracted around this off-worlder? Physical attraction shouldn't be enough to give her pause. Yet, here was a dashing outsider, charming his way into her heart where only her love for her family and country should reside. He had no place there.

"Math, you say?" Captain Connor said. "What if I make this move?"

Immediately after the captain's play, Helena calculated her best move based on his strategy and shifted a piece to counter.

"Wow," he said. "That's pretty good. You've never played this before?"

Helena shook her head. "We have other games, but I've never heard of this one."

Captain Connor grinned. "You're just pulling my leg, aren't you? What if I do this?"

Again, after the captain moved his piece, Helena countered. This time, Captain Connor examined the move and leaned back in his chair. He released a low whistle and glanced at the ambassador.

"Okay..." Captain Connor said. "That wasn't nice."

Helena stared at her opponent and said, "While this may be just a game to you, Captain, my peoples' lives hang in the balance. Can we speed this along so I can accompany you to Terra?"

A laugh escaped Captain Connor's mouth followed by a few more laughs. Each one was an individual sound.

"Is something funny?" Helena asked.

"Yes," Captain Connor said after he moved a piece and was immediately countered again. "You're not playing fair."

Afraid her mental invasion was detected, Helena retreated from his mind and said, "How do you mean?"

Smiling, he said, "You're kicking my ass."

Helena took another piece after the captain made his move. Like his seat was crawling with biting beetles, Ambassador Bergem bolted from his chair and approached the table.

"Only the contestants are-" Marcella never finished her sentence as the ambassador maneuvered around her.

"What are you doing, Captain?" Bergem said. "Are you throwing the match?"

Captain Connor raised his eyebrows and exhaled. "No, sir. She's a freak."

He moved another piece, and Helena crept back into the captain's mind. Sensing his plan to recover from her assault, Helena countered.

"See?" Captain Connor said, chuckling again. "It's like she's reading my mind."

The captain's mood remained jovial, almost in awe at Helena's skill. She decided he was just cracking a joke and not making an accusation. Humans remained oblivious to the Antaran mental discipline.

"Stop playing around, Captain," Bergem said. "Just finish her."

After claiming another piece, Captain Connor put his palms to the sky and said, "You're saying that like I have a choice."

Helena detected distaste in Captain Connor's mind for the ambassador. She hoped Prisca had gleaned some useful information.

"Dammit, Captain," Bergem said as he returned to his seat. "I'll have you demoted if you lose."

Captain Connor leaned close to Helena and said, "You're not making me look good in front of my ambassador."

"My responsibilities do not include improving your public image," Helena said.

"Listen," Captain Connor said, "I might not get another chance to talk to you, so I'm sorry about what happened. The crash. Please know that I tried my best to avoid your city."

Helena secured a better position with her queen and said, "You failed."

The off-worlder seemed genuinely remorseful, and Helena regretted her words. Her mother warned her of the dangers of embracing logic to an extreme, but Helena didn't have her mother's guiding voice in her life any longer. Had she gone too far? Would her mother disapprove? No, Helena decided her path had allowed her to take control of important events in her life. Like this one.

"Well," Captain Connor said, "Even if you won't accept my apology, I'm sorry anyway."

"The problem with your apology is simple, Captain. It is not enough," Helena said, maneuvering her knight for a decisive strike. "Thousands of my people have died because of your war. A war the Antarans have no interest in. No, Captain, I cannot accept your apology. Check."

Marcella translated the move to the Antaran audience, as they weren't familiar with the game. "Helena has just forced Captain Connor into a very disadvantageous position," she said.

Ambassador Bergem rose from his chair again and scowled at him.

"Well," Captain Connor said, "I'm not apologizing for the whole war. I'm just sorry my ship went down and killed innocent people. That's all."

The captain moved his king, just as Helena anticipated.

"Perhaps you will do better next time," Helena said, referencing both the crash and the chess match. She wondered if the off-worlder's simple brain recognized the barb. "Check."

"Damn," Captain Connor said.

"Captain?" Bergem said.

Captain Connor huffed. "Settle down, Ambassador. I have a few tricks left."

Surprised at the captain's tactic to remove the immediate danger, Helena nodded to her opponent. "Nicely played, Captain." She probed his thoughts to find he reverted to long dormant chess knowledge buried below the surface of his thoughts. Perhaps these Humans had more depth than Helena originally assumed.

"But," Helena said as she countered, "you must see your fate, even now."

Captain Connor smiled. "My Lady, you are a formidable opponent."

Scanning his thoughts as he decided his next move, Helena found the captain to be a jumble of emotion. He seemed surprised to be losing, annoyed with the ambassador, aroused on an epic level by Marcella and intrigued by Helena. How could he even *think* with so much noise?

"All right," he said, "let's try this."

Captain Connor attacked with his rook and Helena realized she had him. She moved her pawn into place and a knowing look spread over the captain's face. He had lost.

"Shall we call it, Captain?" Helena said, giving her opponent the opportunity for a graceful defeat.

Captain Connor scanned the game board. However, he knew he was finished. "You know, My Lady, *surrender* isn't in my box of tricks."

He captured an irrelevant piece, but seemed satisfied to cause some destruction in his death throes.

"Interesting," Helena said as she positioned her rook to contain the enemy king. "Check."

"I know," Captain Connor said. "But I can take a few more pawns before it's over."

True to his promise, Captain Connor maneuvered away from check and captured a pawn. However, the game was over.

"Check," Helena said.

"One more," Captain Connor said.

"Checkmate," Helena said as she toppled the captain's king by moving adjacent with her queen.

Chapter 6

"How about this?" Terentia asked, holding aloft a shimmering silver robe.

Helena examined the garment and said, "I doubt I will be attending any dances while on Terra."

"I don't know," Terentia said, "Captain Connor is quite handsome. Perhaps-"

"My dear," Helena said as she folded another gown, "are you reading those trashy romance stories again?"

"I know what you're thinking," Terentia said. "And I promise to focus entirely on my studies over the next few months. I'll be ready for my duties here on Antares while you are away."

"I have faith in you," Helena said. "And besides, the captain had eyes for Marcella."

"What man doesn't?"

Prisca entered Helena's private chambers and smiled. "I see you two are discussing important matters of state."

"Helena's social life is of the utmost importance," Terentia said. "Well, to me anyway."

"Social life? What's that?" Helena said.

"I doubt any of us will ever know," Prisca said as she sat on the edge of Helena's bed. "Except maybe Marcella. How did she get the best job?"

"Have you *looked* at your sister lately?" Helena said. "She rivals Galeria from the Legend of Arrius."

After sharing a laugh, Prisca turned serious. "Helena, I'm sorry I wasn't successful with the ambassador."

Helena waved her hand and said, "I told you before, your apology is not necessary. That man is not easy to read."

"Do you think he's dangerous?" Terentia asked.

Helena nodded. "I'm sure of it."

Terentia bit her lower lip. A habit Helena failed to break. "Be careful, please."

"Do not fear for me," Helena said as she placed her hand on her sister's cheek. "Mother trained me well for this mission."

"I miss her," Prisca said, wiping tears from her eyes.

Helena hugged Prisca and said, "Me too."

Terentia rose to leave the room, as she usually did when they discussed their mother. Guilt burdened Terentia, as their mother, Vipsania, died giving birth to her.

"No, Terentia," Helena said. "I've watched you carry your guilt for too long now. None of us blame you for Mother's death."

Lips quivering, Terentia said, "Valeria does."

Helena and Prisca gathered their younger sister in their embrace.

"How many times do I need to tell you?" Helena said. "Valeria is a bitch."

Terentia giggled in between sobs.

Prisca kissed Helena on her cheek and said, "We will miss you."

"I'll miss you both as well," Helena said. "But now, I must go speak with Justina."

Prisca eyed her and said, "How long has it been?"

"Since we've spoken at anything other than an official function?" Helena said. "Too long."

"I haven't seen her in a while either," Terentia said. "Tell her I send along my best wishes?"

Helena nodded. "Of course."

As usual, Helena found her sister, Justina, at the Chapel of Light. Since their mother's death, Justina had turned to prayer. Now a high priestess of their faith, Justina spent most of her time at the central chapel in Olympus. Helena watched with pride as her sister finished the evening mass.

"Very moving," Helena said as she sat opposite her sister in the chapel's antechamber.

"I thought it fitting," Justina said. "Reminding the people about *family* when my sister is about to leave."

"I'm sorry I missed the beginning… I was-"

"No need," Justina said. "We both know your path is not a spiritual one."

"My world is numbers and-" Helena paused. "We've been over this before. I don't think we need an old wound reopened. I am, of course, here to say goodbye."

Justina nodded and said, "My prayers will go with you, my sister. And-" Her voice wavered slightly. Enough for Helena to notice. "And, I wish you to take this."

Unraveling her prayer beads from her wrist, Justina held them towards her sister.

"These are-" Helena gasped, surprised at her inability to control her reaction.

"Yes," Justina said. "These are Mother's beads. I think she would want you to have them on this journey, even if you don't have faith in the Light."

Stunned by her sister's generosity, Helena allowed her emotions to creep towards the surface.

"I will return them to you when I am finished. And I know I haven't been involved in your life lately, but…"

"Again," Justina said, "apologies between us aren't necessary. We have different lives. You at the palace and me serving my faith. However, I think we have said all we need to say. You don't approve of my decision to follow my faith and I tolerate Father's mockery of our religion. As you said, we don't need to reopen that wound."

"When we're done with this, I want things to be different between us," Helena said. "I... I miss you."

Helena scolded herself, this time for allowing her feelings free reign. Perhaps her father's emotional weakness had spread to her heart as well.

Justina smiled. "Facing death has a way of softening the soul. Things will be no different when you return, though I wish it otherwise."

Despite her one moment of weakness at the mention of their mother, Justina hadn't softened. Helena took comfort in her sister's strength.

"I must go see the emperor," Helena said. "It was nice talking with you, my sister."

"Go with peace in your heart and clarity in your mind, dear sister."

As Helena departed the chapel, she wondered why she always left so many things unspoken with Justina. She wanted to apologize for judging her so harshly when she turned away from palace life and towards the waiting embrace of the church. She wanted to tell her sister that her public criticism of Justina's sect was a political action, not a personal one. She wanted to tell her that she envied her for finding peace in her life when Helena only knew stress.

Maybe next time, Helena lied to herself.

Absorbed in her own thoughts after another aircar trip, Helena hadn't noticed Valeria.

"Going to see Father?" Valeria said, stepping in front of her sister.

Helena met Valeria's dark green eyes and said, "Yes."

Sensing Valeria had just come from the emperor, Helena wondered how far Valeria's dagger was planted in her back.

"Let me guess," Helena said, "Father denied your request to replace me on this mission."

"You know the math," Valeria said. "My skill surpasses yours. I should be the one to negotiate with the filthy Humans. Father is not acting logically."

"Do you think *skill* is all that factors into the equation?" Helena said. "You have yet to learn so much, little sister."

As Valeria's anger exploded she said, "You are favored for now, and I will support you in this, our time of war. However, once we are rid of the Humans and Proxans, I will show Father the truth. You are unfit for rule."

Helena studied her sister. Where did she go wrong? As second oldest, Valeria was taught as much by their mother as by Helena. Why did Valeria not embrace logic? Why must everything with her be a battle? Where did her anger live and grow? For many years, Helena had asked herself these questions.

Without betraying her sadness and frustration, Helena said, "Our final words should not be in wrath. I will see you again after my negotiations, sister. May logic guide you."

Valeria smiled. "Always the dutiful daughter, saying the things you should say. Very well, I can play that game too. May logic guide you as well, dear sister."

After the last word, Valeria stormed away. The praetorians at the emperor's chamber door remained motionless throughout the exchange. Through the years, they had witnessed many such fights between Helena and Valeria. To the guards, the room was still undisturbed – life as normal at the Antaran palace.

Helena passed through the gilded doors and found her father on the balcony, his favorite spot. He smiled when he saw his daughter.

"Heir Helena," Agreios said. "My heart is warmed by your presence."

"Father," Helena said with a slight nod of her head. "I hope the afternoon finds you well."

Agreios returned his gaze to the city below the balcony and said, "Someday, my dear daughter, you will have children. Only then, will you understand what I feel in my heart when I know how few of you are likely to return from this dreadful task. My heart is rife with guilt."

Refusing to be drawn into her compassion for her father, Helena said, "I have meditated on your strategy, Father. There may be a problem."

"Nothing escapes your sharpened eye, does it?"

"You know, then?"

Agreios nodded. "I know."

Voicing her concern, Helena said, "If we do not succeed, then the Humans will come for everyone. The destruction will be worse than it is now."

"Yes. That is an awful risk."

Helena approached her father and said, "Is it *too much* risk?"

After a lengthy pause Agreios said, "Do you recall the Legend of Arrius?"

Helena nodded and sat next to her father. For a few moments, they gazed upon the orange Antaran sun. She enjoyed her conversations with her father, though she felt this could be her last such experience for quite some time.

"Well, you know the tale," Agreios said. "The radiation from the sun was killing our ancestors, the Gima, yet not all of the city-domes were affected. The queen at the time, Galeria, arranged for her people to relocate to the healthy domes. Though she was under enormous pressure from the politicians and senators to quarantine the afflicted city-domes, the queen did not waver. She decided that the entire Gima people would live or die as one. Galeria was betrayed and killed before her plan was executed. But her son, Arrius, carried her vision forward."

Helena smiled. "I use this legend as an example of what *not* to do in a crisis," she said. "The queen acted from her heart, with little regard for logic. The decision was full of unknowns. What if the sickness spread to the healthy people? How would the city-domes sustain the increase in population? Queen Galeria made the wrong decision."

"Did she?" Agreios said. "I know your mother taught you the value of balance between logic and emotion. Surely you haven't forgotten? Not you…"

"I remember the lessons," Helena said. "But I believe you are making the same mistake as Galeria."

"Queen Galeria realized that *all* Antarans deserved a chance at life - together," Emperor Agreios said. "Like her, I am choosing to build a better future for everyone, not just those lucky enough to avoid the destruction caused by the war. No, my daughter, my decision is the correct one."

Helena analyzed her father's arguments and found her heart conflicted. She prepared to bombard him with her logic at allowing the war to continue in their skies. At least their race wouldn't face extinction. However, she appreciated the finality of the plan. Neither the Humans nor Proxans could bring a war to their doorstep again. If they succeeded.

Lowering her eyes, Helena said, "I apologize for doubting you, Father."

Agreios lifted Helena's head with his finger under her chin. Smiling, he said, "You remind me of your mother in many ways."

"Father… I…"

"I know," he said. "Your thoughts are unusually readable today. You wish things were different. So do I."

On the brink of losing her composure, Helena calmed her emotions and reined in her fear. Her mother warned her that fear was the doorway to oblivion. For the first time in her life, Helena understood those words. If she feared the outcome, she would fail.

"I'm sorry," Helena said. "I should exhibit more control over my emotions. Rest assured my sisters will not see my weakness."

Agreios squeezed her shoulder and said, "Perhaps they should."

Chapter 7

Helena emerged from the aircar to a row of praetorians extending into the landing strip and to the starship ramp. The media gathered behind the praetorians, attempting to snap the perfect picture of the Antaran Heir on her way to negotiate with the Human Confederation.

Claudia and Terentia accompanied Helena on the trip to the star port. The three sisters hugged each other.

"I'll miss you," Terentia said.

"Me too," Claudia said.

Claudia and Terentia, the two most emotional of Helena's sisters, wanted to be with their older sister until the last moment. Through the years, Helena marveled at Claudia's ability to synch herself with other people's emotions. Whenever Helena had a problem, she always consulted Claudia. Sometimes, Claudia could resolve things by simply revealing Helena's own fault of action. Unlike Valeria, Claudia didn't point her finger or twist an angle. Claudia, instead, was always concerned with the well-being of her sisters.

"I packed some dried kilva bread for you," Claudia said. "I've been saving it for a special occasion. So eat it when you are far from home and you're thinking of us."

Helena smiled and kissed Claudia on the cheek. "You are always concerned for others," Helena said. "Remember your training and think of your countrymen here on Antares when you fulfill your mission. We are all counting on you."

Claudia nodded. "I will be strong, my sister."

"And-" Helena paused, unsure how much emotion she could allow to show. She said, "And take care of father until I return. He will need you."

"I will look after him," Claudia said.

Helena's thoughts drifted to the ceremony at the palace earlier that morning. Her father appeared so strong in front of the Antaran people, yet Helena sensed his despair. He feared sending his heir so far away to an uncertain fate. She thought maybe he doubted her ability, but then she remembered his words. When she had children, she'd understand why he was laden with guilt.

"Me too," Terentia said as she embraced Helena. "And I'll study every hour until you return. I'll prove my worth and you will be proud of me."

Helena looked into Terentia's eyes and said, "I already am."

Before she exposed her feelings in her heart, Helena turned away from her sisters and walked between the columns of praetorians. Each guard stared through her as she advanced towards the looming Human starship.

What else waited for her on this journey? Could they really succeed with so much uncertainty? Helena gazed with her mind's eye at the precipice on which she stood. The fall was a long and dark one.

As she approached the Humans, she caught Captain Connor's eye. Her heart flared into life. She warned herself that she was experiencing an irrational crush and she pushed aside her excited feelings before they could gain any solid ground. Her mission was all that mattered.

"Good afternoon, Lady Helena," Captain Connor said.

"Good afternoon, Captain, Ambassador," Helena said, noticing the ambassador's amusement as he studied her Gima facial tattoos.

Ambassador Bergem faked a smile and said, "On behalf of the Human Government, we welcome you aboard the *Venture*."

Helena examined the massive vessel and said, "Indeed."

Larger than an Antaran sky-liner, Helena estimated the ship was meant for transporting cargo and passengers. She sensed between two and three hundred crew members before the ambassador interrupted her thoughts.

"Your guards are already on board, but we couldn't allow their weapons," Bergem said.

Helena again tried to pierce the ambassador's mind, but she found only surface thoughts. Was he trained in the mental disciplines? If so, Helena decided she must be careful.

"Very well," Helena said. "I understand."

"Well," Captain Connor said, simultaneously nervous and excited, "I have a ship to fly."

Ambassador Bergem motioned to the ramp and said, "Please, My Lady, let me show you to your quarters."

Helena's heart skipped and flopped as she ascended the ramp. The fear of never seeing her home again threatened to overtake her serenity. However, Helena pushed the fear aside and quashed her swirling emotions. Now wasn't the time to forget her training.

Humans scurried through the wide corridors and interior rooms of the starship. A few of them stopped and gawked at the tattooed alien on their ship, but most kept their poise. Helena extended her thoughts throughout the ship and sensed her guards at the far end of the starboard corridor. She forced another small pocket of fear from her mind as they were so far away.

"Have you ever been aboard a *real* starship, Lady Helena?" Ambassador Bergem said, mocking the Antaran's lack of faster-than-light ships.

Helena shook her head, "Nothing that can travel the stars at these speeds."

Bergem led her though a series of smaller corridors to a wider passage. "Well, the battleships travel the fastest,"

Bergem said. "Much faster than this freighter. However, we cannot risk such a resource on a trivial mission."

Shocked at his rudeness, Helena decided to confront him. His closed mind frustrated her.

"You think the Antarans trivial?" Helena asked.

He shrugged. "I spend my time negotiating alliances and peace with other factions who have the technology to travel faster than light. Of course, they don't have battleships, but they are at least politically relevant. No offense, but the Antarans are not."

"If you judge a race of people based solely on their ability to travel the stars," Helena said, "then I take no offense from your shortsightedness."

Bergem grunted. "Your quarters."

Helena opened the door and her praetorians formed rank.

The ambassador continued, "Use the intercom if you feel you must leave. However, everything you need is in there. Please do not bother the captain or crew. They are quite busy."

"We are confined?" Helena asked.

"Yes."

"This is no way to treat diplomatic guests," Helena said.

Bergem sneered. "You may have beaten the captain, but you have little to offer. The Antarans are not as important as you think, little girl. The universe is a big place."

Helena leaned closer to him and he seemed surprised by her advance. "No, Ambassador, you listen to me. How you treat people reflects how you will be treated. Remember this, as I have no patience for insignificant men who think themselves better than they are."

"Do you even know who you are talking to?" Bergem said. "I can throw you off this ship right now."

Helena scanned his thoughts and found his bluff. He didn't have the authority. Only the captain or Bergem's superiors on Terra could make that decision.

"Then do it, if you're so important."

"Don't force my hand." Anger boiled in Bergem's mind and he said, "Stay in your quarters and we won't have a problem."

After he stalked away, the praetorian captain, Duronius, said, "Is everything well, My Lady?"

Helena nodded and entered. She recognized Duronius as one of her father's most trusted guard commanders. Yet another sign of how much the emperor valued his heir. "Yes, the ambassador and I are not watching the same sun at the moment," Helena said.

"We'll keep an eye on him when he's around," Duronius said.

"Thank you, Centurion," Helena said.

"We prepared a private room for you near the back," Duronius said. "The only entrance and exit from that room leads to our main area here so nobody can get to you without first dealing with us."

"Very good."

"All your provisions are there as well, My Lady," Duronius said. "They confiscated our weapons. However I picked this group because of their proficiency at hand-to-hand combat. You are well-protected, My Lady."

Helena broke protocol and used the guard's name. "Centurion Duronius, you have done well. Thank you for your protection."

Duronius bowed and said, "It is an honor to serve, My Lady. Do you require anything else at the moment?"

"No, thank you Centurion."

Helena nodded her approval when she entered her private room. Her overnight bag was on the bed, within easy reach. The other luggage rested near the corner in an open crate. The praetorians hung fabric over her area to give her the semblance of privacy, but she could hear them as they moved around in the next room.

After a quick change into more functional robes, Helena examined the rest of their passenger quarters. Though simple, the accommodations served their purpose. Unlike Marcella, Helena was accustomed to "roughing it" from time to time. After finding the communication intercom, Helena pressed the button and waited. A female voice crackled through the speaker.

"Hello?" the voice said.

"Hello? This is Lady Helena. With whom am I speaking?"

"Uhh, uhh... Lieutenant Sandra Rhom. I, uhh... hold on one sec."

The intercom fell silent and Helena turned to Duronius. "Apparently, they aren't too organized."

Duronius shook his head. "Not from what I've seen."

The intercom buzzed to life. "Lady Helena, this is Captain Connor. How can I be of service?"

"Captain Connor," Helena said. "Ambassador Bergem implied that we are confined to these spartan quarters. Is that correct?"

"I'm- No, check the repulsors first, then flood those lines," Captain Connor said, though Helena realized he was speaking to his crew. "Sorry, I need to take care of a few things here on the bridge. May I visit you in an hour?"

"Will you make some changes to our situation?" Helena asked, not ready to let him go without a plan of action.

"Yes, you have my word."

Helena sensed truth in the tone of his voice and said, "That is fine, Captain."

After a few hours, and the launch into space, the captain arrived at her quarters. Duronius eyed the Human, but Helena didn't fear him. They shared a moment during their chess match and Helena was curious to explore what that moment meant. He was clearly attracted to her and his thoughts confirmed her outward observations.

"I'm sorry," Captain Connor said, "but my orders were clear until we reached space. Now, I have a little more leeway."

"So, are we still confined to these quarters?" Helena said.

"No," Captain Connor said as he glanced at Duronius. "You and your guards are allowed access throughout the starboard corridor, including the lounge. Nobody, including the ambassador, should give you any trouble."

"That is more acceptable. Thank you, Captain."

Captain Connor nodded. "Please accept my apology this time. This ship was the closest to your planet, but it's not really rigged for diplomatic transport."

"The conditions do not bother me," Helena said.

"Oh, I thought-"

"Listen, Captain," Helena said, "diplomacy cannot blossom without trust. Your *Ambassador* seems to care as much for us as he does the bottom of his shoes. I hope all Humans are not like him or these negotiations will be fruitless. The Antarans have treated you and your wounded crew with nothing but the utmost respect, even though you were responsible for many deaths. All we ask is you treat us in kind."

"To be fair," Captain Connor said, "*we* were confined while we recovered in your hospital."

"Consider the circumstances, Captain," Helena said. "Your ship had just crashed and the peace talks had not been initiated. You must see now that things have changed?"

"I understand and I'm sorry. You see, Lady Helena, I'm not usually in command on these sorts of missions," Captain Connor said. "However, I do appreciate all the Antarans have done for us."

"A life is a life, Captain, no matter how alien or familiar. We Antarans respect *all* life, even the lives of our enemies," Helena said.

"Are we enemies?"

Helena evened the tone of her voice to deliver her lie with clarity and credibility. "I certainly hope to change the state of affairs," Helena said. "My people do not wish to be enemies with the Human Confederation."

Captain Connor eyed Helena, a crime punishable by lifelong imprisonment on Antares. Did he detect the subterfuge in her voice? Helena couldn't afford to underestimate these Humans.

"There's something I've been meaning to ask you," Captain Connor said, glancing at the praetorians.

Helena seized the chance to further obscure her intentions by changing scenery. "If you wish to speak in private," Helena said, "you may request my company in the lounge."

Captain Connor smiled. "Okay. Lady Helena, will you accompany me to the lounge?"

Helena nodded and said, "It would be my pleasure, Captain."

She scolded herself for allowing the off-worlder to talk so casually with her. Captain Connor seemed pleased to have her company, but she reminded herself about the truth of her mission. The Humans were her enemy.

Duronius followed them to the lounge and Helena suppressed a gasp as the entire front wall was transparent revealing a breathtaking view of her planet.

"Welcome to the forward lounge," Captain Connor said. "I'm not too familiar with this ship, but I see the view is as impressive as I've been told."

The off-duty crew members turned and stared at the alien in their lounge. Helena smiled as she accepted greetings from some of the Humans. The captain led her to a table near the forward window. Duronius, dressed in the grey-blue uniform of a praetorian, took a position at the door.

"What would you like to eat?" Captain Connor said. "They'll make pretty much anything."

Helena said, "Can they make a cheeseburger? I read about them in my studies and I'd like to sample this Human staple food."

Chuckling, Captain Connor said, "I wouldn't call it a 'staple' food, but I guess I can see why you'd think that."

After ordering her meal Helena said, "You wanted to ask me something?"

Captain Connor's mind was alive with activity. He also seemed genuinely interested in spending time with her. Yet his thoughts focused on Marcella from time to time and his intentions weren't pure.

"When it comes to politics, I'm not very involved," Captain Connor said. "Which is probably why I haven't been given a battleship command. But that's not relevant. I don't care if the entire Antaran people are chess experts and you lied to the Human Council. That's fine. I just need to know how you beat me."

"I already told you how I defeated you," Helena said. "We Antarans are masters of math and logic. Your game is a simple one."

"Well, I don't know if I agree with you there."

"You played well," Helena said. "A few of your moves showed intelligence."

Captain Connor smiled. "You're too kind."

Helena nodded, though she realized the Human was using sarcasm. She considered playing along but she needed to maintain her credibility. As much as she enjoyed the captain's company, she wasn't there for herself. Her people needed their future empress to focus entirely on her deception with the Human Confederation. Helena realized this mission would require the full spectrum of her talent and energy.

"Anyway," Captain Connor said, "I was impressed. If you're not too busy after we land on Terra, I have a few academy buddies I'd like to introduce you to. Watching them lose a chess match would pretty much make my decade."

Helena allowed a smile to cross her lips. "I think I'll be quite busy on your homeworld," she said. "In all seriousness, Captain, thank you for fixing things for me and my guards. It would have been a long trip if we were forced to remain in the same room."

"I'm happy to help."

Helena sensed the ambassador's presence before he entered the lounge. Angry, and on the verge of violence, Bergem stalked towards their table. Helena tensed and noticed Duronius do the same.

"Captain! You were under orders," Bergem said.

"Ambassador, pull up a chair," Captain Connor said, attempting to avoid a scene. "How good of you to join us."

Smiling tersely at the watching crew, Bergem sat and lowered his voice. "The Antaran party is confined to quarters until we reach Terra. Have you completely lost your senses?"

"Of all people," Captain Connor said, "I thought an ambassador would know how to treat distinguished guests."

"Distinguished?" Bergem scowled at the captain. "Why don't you pilot the ship and leave the diplomatic duties to me. Does that sound good to you?"

Captain Connor leveled his blue eyes at the ambassador. "We're in space. My rules now."

"You can't just disregard an order from the Council!" Bergem said.

"Captain's discretion," he said. "That order would have put my crew in danger."

"What danger?"

Captain Connor smiled at Helena, studied her blue face tattoos for a moment, and said, "I usually do everything in my power to avoid the wrath of alien princesses."

Chapter 8

After her fourth trip to the lady's room, Helena decided the cheeseburger experiment was a poor decision.

"Are you well, My Lady?" Duronius asked from the main room.

Hopeful the last of the Human food was purged from her system. "Yes, Centurion, I am going to get some sleep now."

Before laying her head on her pillow, Helena tore open the kilva bread and silently thanked her sister. Alone in her dark room, far from home, she allowed some fear to creep into her heart. Every now and then, she felt safe in her uncertainty. Why shouldn't she fear? The Humans could discover their ruse and she may never see home again. She contemplated the serenity chant, but she decided to sleep with another blanket of unknowns.

For the next six days, Helena avoided Human food and remained in her quarters in meditation. The captain asked to see her on several occasions, but Helena denied the requests. She was concerned her judgment was clouded by her physical attraction to the off-worlder, so she chose to keep him at a distance.

Helena awoke with a jolt on the seventh night and scanned the ship with her mind. They were in battle.

The vessel shook from an impact and Duronius dashed into Helena's room. "Are you hurt, My Lady?"

"No, but we are under attack," Helena said, pulling a silk robe over her exposed shoulders. The centurion shouldn't have seen her exposed skin, but Duronius's quick reactions may yet prove more useful than Antaran tradition on the mission.

"Get me to the forward lounge," Helena said.

Duronius nodded and the praetorians escorted Helena to the lounge. On the way, a crew member stopped them and said, "You should return to your quarters!"

Helena touched the man on the arm and said, "We will be fine."

Yielding under the presence of the alien visitor, the crew member resumed his duties. Helena's group reached the deserted lounge and she scanned the open space in front of her. Reaching with her thoughts, she sensed the nearby asteroids which were a concern for the helmsman. She also sensed a ship in distress in those asteroids. Someone important to the Humans was on board that ship. Then, she sensed a trap. Proxan ships were hiding in the asteroids, waiting for a chance to strike. Something seemed strange about the Proxans and their minds but Helena didn't dwell on the oddity. Instead, she rushed to the intercom and signaled the bridge.

A female voice crackled through the speaker. Helena sensed it was Lieutenant Sandra Rhom, whom she spoke with before. "Who's there? The lounges are under lockdown!"

"Lieutenant, this is Lady Helena. I need to speak with Captain Connor."

"Lady Helena?" Lieutenant Rhom said. "Get to your quarters. We are under attack!"

"I have information about the Proxans for the captain," Helena said. "Please, let me speak with him."

A moment later, Captain Connor's voice carried through the speaker. "Lady Helena, you should return-"

"Captain," Helena said, "you are moving into a trap. Proxan ships wait to ambush you."

"How could you know that?"

"Just trust me-" Helena's voice trailed off as she sensed something awful about to happen – something about the ambassador. He was near.

"I can't-" Captain Connor said, but Helena interrupted him.

"No time!" Helena said. She turned to her guards and said, "Follow me!"

Helena tracked the ambassador's thoughts and found him in the adjoining cargo bay. His mind was full of violence as he rigged a bomb near some fuel canisters. This was a planned attack and the ambassador was stealing something important. Helena probed but couldn't discover his true intentions.

Ambassador Bergem drew a pistol from under his cloak and leveled it at Helena. "What are *you* doing here?" he asked.

A praetorian moved in front of Helena, waiting for her command.

"I was about to ask you the same question, Ambassador," Helena said as she finally broke through his mental blocks. He was no ambassador. "However, I think I know the truth about you now."

"Do you?" Bergem raised his pistol and the praetorian in front of Helena charged forward.

Several puffs of compressed air escaped the muzzle of the weapon and the praetorian's body convulsed from the violent impacts. He fell to the ground and Bergem pointed the weapon at Helena.

"Now," the false ambassador said, "your guard bleeds like we do. Let's see the color of *your* blood."

Helena tensed as she quickly calculated trajectories in her mind.

Then, Duronius appeared in the shadows behind Bergem and tackled him. The centurion slammed Bergem's face into the metal floor and it was over. Absorbed in the moment, Helena didn't notice Duronius's stealthy advance. And neither did Bergem.

Her senses clearing after the rush of the encounter, Helena blinked. "Is anyone else injured?" she asked as she knelt beside the fallen praetorian.

"No, My Lady," Duronius said.

Helena examined the wounds and turned to one of the other guards. "Go get my medical bag. It should be in the crate in my room."

The guard rushed from the cargo bay and Duronius watched the corridor. Helena applied pressure to the worst wound and smiled when the praetorian looked at her.

"My apologies-"

"No talking," Helena said. "Reserve your strength."

Moments later, the guard returned with the medical bag. Helena spent three years in the emergency ward at Tiberius Hospital, so trauma patients weren't a new sight for the Antaran heir. Following in her mother's legacy, Helena was an accomplished doctor and famous surgeon.

Working at a rapid pace, Helena injected a relaxer and then applied trauma patches to the wounds. Satisfied the bleeding was under control, Helena rose and wiped her bloodied hands on her nightgown.

Addressing her remaining three guards, Helena said, "Praetorians, I will return as soon as I am able. If the Humans move him to their medical bay, that is fine. But he is *my* patient. Don't let them practice their barbaric medicine."

The three praetorians acknowledged the orders and secured the room. However, Helena sensed fear and uncertainty in their minds. Though their training was extensive, they had probably never been in mortal danger this far from home. Neither had Helena, but she couldn't afford the price of doubt.

Deciding she could risk a moment for her guards, Helena said, "Listen, I know you are well-trained for your duty. However experience is a harsh teacher as you are presented with the test before the lesson. I am honored to have you all with me on this journey and you have performed admirably. Now, focus your thoughts and abandon your fear. Do not doubt for a moment that I value your lives as much as my own. If we watch over each other as we watch over our wounded brother, we will succeed."

"My Lady," one of the praetorians said as he put his fist to his chest. The others mimicked the action.

Helena sensed a new resolve form in their hearts. These men were now dangerous in a way that suited their goal.

"Duronius, you are with me," Helena said as she left the wounded praetorian and proceeded down the corridor.

The ship shook from another impact and Helena closed her eyes to concentrate on the nearby asteroid field. They were close, but the Proxans remained hidden. She still had time.

Duronius pressed the button for the lift and turned to Helena. "You meant what you said back there," he said. "I think they appreciate your honesty."

"Some of that was *confidence*," Helena said. "But, I do believe we should put our trust in each other since we are so far from home."

"And you have blood on your hands already," Duronius said. "Quite the ominous start, don't you agree?"

The door to the lift slid open and the two Antarans entered the cylindrical shaft.

"I'm sure you weren't expecting this when you were assigned to me," Helena said as she attempted to decipher the control panel.

Duronius pushed a button and said, "I volunteered, My Lady."

The lift ascended three levels and the doors opened to the bridge. Humans studied their screens and barked orders to each other. Smoke clung in the air and greeted the two Antarans. Lights flashed on panels and a hologram depicted their tactical situation. Captain Connor studied the hologram but Helena didn't get a chance to attract his attention.

"Halt!" A Human marine with a rifle stepped in front of Helena and Duronius. "Sir, I have a situation here!"

Helena raised her hands and said, "I must speak with Captain Connor."

Another marine joined the first and said, "Who are you?"

"I am Lady Helena, your diplomatic passenger. One of my guards was shot by Ambassador Bergem and you are about to fly into a Proxan trap. Please allow me to speak with the captain!"

"Who was shot?"

"We haven't much time," Helena said. Unfortunately, Captain Connor wasn't facing the lift, so Helena couldn't catch his eye. "You must allow me to pass."

"Not happening," the marine said. "You're not allowed up here, especially not *now*."

Helena decided to risk surprising the marine. She raised her voice loud enough for the captain to hear. "Captain! The Proxans have you trapped!"

All eyes turned to the lift.

"Helena?" Captain Connor said. "Let her through!"

The marines escorted Helena to the captain.

"Are you hurt?" Captain Connor asked, studying her bloodied robe with concern. "What are you doing here?"

"You don't have much time," Helena said as she examined the holographic display. "The Proxans wait in these asteroids. This is a trap!"

Another Human man stepped forward and said, "Who the hell do you think you are?"

The man was a good deal older than Captain Connor, and also larger around the midsection. Helena noticed his ranking insignia was similar to Captain Connor's. A brief scan of the man's mind revealed jealousy. This man was the captain of this ship until Captain Connor stepped aboard. Something about Human protocol relegated him to a second-in-command status. This didn't sit well with him.

"Captain Knowles," Captain Connor said. "This is the royal Lady Helena of Antares. Show some respect."

"In the middle of a battle?"

"You must move here, now," Helena said, pointing to a spot on the holographic map.

Captain Connor pulled Helena to the side and said, "Captain Knowles, take over for a minute. Concentrate the forward batteries on the raider."

"Aye, sir."

Though they were still in earshot of everyone nearby, Captain Connor lowered his voice and said, "I know you're eager to prove your value to us, but now's not the time. We are in battle."

Helena nodded to the hologram. "Move to where I indicated and we can deal with the ambushers on better terms."

"What ambushers?" Captain Connor said. "Our scanners show a raider and two scouts – not much of a match for this vessel. We are rescuing one of our ships from a Proxan attack. I assure you, there are no more enemy ships. Our scanners are quite sophisticated."

Helena added weight to her voice as she whispered in his ear. "You asked me how I beat you, but I was only partially truthful."

Captain Connor raised his eyebrows and waited on her words.

"My people have developed a mental discipline," Helena said. "I was reading your thoughts, as I now do the Proxan ambushers. You have less than thirty seconds before they strike."

"That's... that's not possible."

Helena concentrated to penetrate the depths of Captain Connor's memory. After a moment, she said, "Your parents are Olivia and Pascal. They were accused of Proxan sympathy and you saved them… but you were captured and forced into the military… you have two dogs, and you miss them. They were on your ship with you when it crashed. You named your first dog after a historical person of significance. Your first name is Nathan… how interesting. You are unmarried and you lust after my sister, Marcella… and-"

Captain Connor opened his palms towards Helena and said, "Enough! You convinced me."

The ship rattled from a nearby explosion and Captain Connor led Helena to the tactical hologram. "Helm, listen to Lady Helena," Captain Connor said. "Here, use this to mark your locations." Captain Connor handed a small electronic pointer to Helena.

"Move to this position," Helena said. She pressed the button on the pointer while she held it at a spot in the hologram. "That will give me time to assess this vessel's capabilities. I need a technical readout on this monitor – maneuverability and weapon emplacements for now. Skip the non-combat systems."

"Delay that order, helm" Captain Knowles said. "Have you lost your mind, Nathan?"

"Helm, you have your orders!" Nathan said, glaring at Knowles.

Helena suppressed a smile when she heard his name. Nathan. His name and everything about him was full of possibilities. Unfortunately, she couldn't give those possibilities the attention they deserved at that moment.

"I'm reassuming command," Knowles said. "You are relieved, Captain."

"You must move, now!" Helena said, jabbing the pointer at the hologram.

The hum of the ship systems filled the bridge as everyone waited. Helena glanced at the helmsman and focused on his mind. The Human was conflicted between the two orders. He had never been in a battle and he feared for his life.

"Too late," Helena said as she sensed the excitement from the Proxan ships. They sprung their trap.

"Sir!" Lieutenant Sandra Rhom said from her station. "Two new bogeys incoming. Mark seven-alpha and twelve-niner. Proxan frigates, sir."

Helena examined the vessels approach and pointed to a new spot on the hologram. "Accelerate and fly between these two asteroids. We will take damage on the aft starboard, but it will allow for a brief escape."

Captain Connor said, "You have your coordinates, helm!"

The helmsman looked to Knowles and said, "Sir?"

"Delay that order," Knowles said, scowling at Helena and Nathan.

"Dammit!" Nathan said. "We're outgunned. Listen to her!"

"We can't abandon that ship," Knowles said.

"They are firing, sir," Lieutenant Sandra Rhom said. "Eight torpedoes in the water. We're hot."

Helena reviewed the new data on the holographic projection and changed her mark. "Accelerate at two-point-five and squeeze through here."

The helmsman said, "That'll burn out engine four."

"You have three seconds," Helena said, studying the technical readout of the ship's propulsion system. It was going to be close.

Nathan pushed the helmsman from his chair and took control of the vessel. "Coming to bravo-seventeen," he said.

"Marines!" Knowles said. "Relieve the captain and put the *lady* in the brig."

"Sir?"

"Now!"

Helena turned to the closest marine, grasped a handrail, and said, "You might want to brace yourself."

The ship shook from the minor impact with the asteroid in their path. Then, the viewport flared as the torpedoes impacted with the massive chunk of rock.

"No direct hits!" Lieutenant Sandra Rhom said, elation and surprise in her voice.

Helena returned her attention to the hologram and pointed to three spots. "Helm, follow the waypoints to here. Maximum burn."

"We're down engine four," Nathan said from the helm. "We'll lose two more engines if we do that."

"Now!"

Back on their feet, the marines advanced towards Helena. Duronius stepped in their path. Nathan fired the engines and the marines tumbled to the ground again. Helena gripped the handrail and focused on the technical readout of the vessel's moderate armament.

"Do we have intelligence on those frigates?" Helena said.

The monitor to Helena's side blinked to life and Lieutenant Sandra Rhom winked at her.

Nathan righted the ship and the marines held on to the nearest rail, not willing to be tossed around the bridge any longer. Captain Knowles, however, was determined to regain control of his ship. He pulled a pistol from his belt and said, "That's enough! Step away from the tactical station!"

Duronius tensed, but Helena placed a hand on his shoulder. "No more blood today," she said.

With her eyes on the frigate readout, Helena stepped away from the hologram. The Proxan ships were more than a match for the Human freighter. However, Helena felt she could use the asteroids to her advantage.

The marines leveled their weapons at Helena as well, and the senior marine said, "My Lady, if you'll come with us."

"If she uses that pointer on the hologram," Knowles said, "shoot her."

Helena sensed the marines would follow any order from Knowles. She was trapped.

"Yes sir," the marine said as he grabbed Helena by the wrist.

"Captain Knowles?" Helena said. "What is your next move?" She handed the pointer to him.

"I- Get her to the brig!"

With a marine on each side of her, Helena was escorted to the lift.

"No good, sir," the marine said. "Lift's out."

Helena sensed some subterfuge from Nathan and Lieutenant Rhom. They rigged something.

As the helmsman resumed his station, he said, "Your orders, sir?"

"Mark fifteen-tango," Knowles said, "That'll buy us the distance we need to make the jump."

"You're running?" Nathan asked, shocked at the other captain's cowardice.

"We can't fight them," Knowles said.

"We can't abandon the admiral!"

Helena sensed the admiral now – recently retired from service but still respected in the Human Council. His ship was under attack, yet it was a trap. Everything revolved around the ambassador, but Helena didn't have the time to focus on the mystery.

"You can win," Helena said.

"Take her below decks!" Knowles said. "Use the maintenance lift! Just get her off my bridge!"

Helena said, "Lieutenant Rhom, scan those asteroids for their density and crystalline structure. I'm sure Captain Connor will be surprised with what you discover."

Chapter 9

The marines escorted Helena and Duronius to the maintenance lift and into the brig. While waiting in her cell, Helena sensed the tension on the bridge as Captain Nathan Connor attempted to sway the crew. She hoped he was intelligent enough to realize the mining lasers on their freighter could break apart the asteroids – violently. That would be enough to disable the frigates and secure the rescue of the admiral's ship.

"I'm sorry, My Lady," Duronius said from the adjoining cell.

"It was not your fault," Helena said. "However, now that we have a moment alone, perhaps you can enlighten me on something."

"Anything, My Lady."

"Why did you volunteer for this mission?"

Duronius waited for the ship to settle after the most recent impact and said, "I was on my way out of the praetorian guard to make way for younger, more capable soldiers. Then, the emperor came to me and asked for my advice."

Helena raised one of her eyebrows. "He did?"

Duronius nodded. "He asked me for my best man, someone to protect his daughter on her journey to Terra."

"And you volunteered…?"

"I have a daughter. She's grown now, but I cannot imagine any harm befalling her," Duronius said. "I sensed your father feels the same way about you. Your family has been good to me, so I saw my opportunity to show the emperor my gratitude and respect."

"My father holds his praetorians in the highest regard," Helena said. "And, now I see why. I am glad you volunteered, Duronius."

The ship rattled again, this time from the impact from many small particles. Helena sensed Nathan's victory on the bridge. They were using the mining lasers.

"Well," Helena said, "I hope the remainder of my mission is uneventful. I'd very much like to return you to your daughter."

Duronius studied her for a moment from the corner of his eye. "You'll make a formidable Empress, My Lady," he said. "Know that *all* praetorians respect you as if you already held that station."

"Thank you, Centurion," she said. "Your words mean much to me."

After a few moments of silence between them, he said, "May I ask *you* a question, My Lady?"

"Of course. Always feel free to speak candidly with me when we are alone, Centurion Duronius."

"You spoke at my daughter's graduation seven years ago, at Cyclades."

Helena nodded, though she didn't immediately recall any details about that particular event. She gave speeches at dozens of graduations each year.

"You said that Antares needed to remain apart from the galactic neighborhood," he said. "You said the dilution of our people would result in a loss of everything we were, and everything we are. That to nurture our past and cultivate our future, we must first build from within. Then, once Antares was strong again, we would look upon this new neighborhood around us and decide our part."

"I remember."

"Have we come so far in seven years? Is that what this mission is about?"

Helena shook her head. "We are generations away from completing the foundation I spoke of," she said. "This mission is one of necessity. The Humans and Proxans wage war in our skies. This must stop. Sometimes, *need* outweighs *wisdom*."

"I suspected as much, but I wasn't sure," he said. "Do you still believe in your words from seven years ago?"

"I do. With all my heart, I do. This is not how I wanted things to begin with Antares. This isn't on our terms."

Helena scanned the ship and found the battle to be over. Though nobody was actively listening to the quiet conversation in the cells, that didn't mean they wouldn't play back a recording at some later time.

She didn't wish to keep Duronius in the dark about their plot, but the safety of the mission's secret demanded she remain discreet. Nobody outside of her family could know of the true nature of their diplomacy. Treachery waited on the edge of a fang, ready to strike the heart of both the Humans and Proxans. Helena's goal was to sharpen that edge into a deadly instrument.

"They're coming," Duronius said.

Helena nodded and watched as the door to the brig slid open and two Humans entered.

"That was pretty amazing!" Nathan said as he approached her cell. "Though I'm still unsure how you were able to sense that trap or the asteroids." He motioned to his companion and said, "This is Admiral Stugardt…"

Before the admiral could speak, Helena said, "Did you tend to my guard?"

"Yes," Nathan said. "We have the ambassador in custody and your guard is in our medical bay."

"I need to treat him," Helena said. "Your doctors do not know our physiology and they could harm him. You must release me from this cell."

"He is stable," Nathan said.

Helena locked eyes with him and said, "I value my guards the same as you do your crew. You must allow me to see him."

"Very well," he said. "Right after I make a proper introduction."

Admiral Stugardt stepped towards Helena's cell and said, "I hear I have *you* to thank for my daring rescue?"

Calm, brown eyes behind silver spectacles returned Helena's gaze. Though bald, the admiral's white goatee betrayed his years. This man, like Nathan, had seen his share of battles.

"If you are offering your gratitude," Helena said, "I accept."

After studying her for a few moments, Stugardt said over his shoulder, "Marines, you are dismissed."

Helena sensed Stugardt's curiosity and Nathan's surprise. As the marines filtered through the door, Helena said, "Captain, why do you stare?"

"You-" Nathan said. "I'm sorry. It's just… this is the first time I've seen you without your tattoos."

Helena put her hand to her face and suppressed a gasp. An off-worlder shouldn't see her bare face. What would her father say? Valeria?

With the marines gone, Stugardt returned his attention to Helena. "Ok, Nathan," he said, "*now* can you tell me?"

Helena sensed Nathan's excitement.

"Of course," Nathan said. "I just don't know what to do with this information yet. So, I think it's best only a few of us know for now."

"Of course," Stugardt said.

Nathan turned to Helena with a wide smile and said, "Tell him what you can do. Well, just show him. Tell him things about his past, or something."

Helena shook her head. "I'm not here for anyone's entertainment. You've seen what I can do."

"She can read minds," Nathan said. "That's how she beat me in chess and that's how she rescued you."

The admiral's eyes widened. "Is that so?"

"Yes," Nathan said, "and she's on a mission to form an alliance with us. We may just get the upper hand against the Proxans for once."

"I think you're getting a little ahead of yourself, Captain," Helena said.

"I know," Nathan said. "It's just been an exciting few hours here. There's no way we should have won that fight."

"Maybe now you see how I defeated you at chess?" Helena said.

"What?"

"Yes, I was reading your thoughts, however, I also played to your weaknesses."

"How do you mean?" Nathan asked.

"Well," Helena said, "as the game unfolded, you planned your next moves and were somewhat limited by your own tactical plan. Sometimes you must improvise."

Nathan grumbled. "I know how to improvise."

Stugardt smiled and said, "After what I just witnessed, I think she knows how to improvise on a whole different level."

"Indeed," Nathan said. "Well, let's get you out of this cell. I'll escort you to the medical bay."

♦

Helena applied a salve to the praetorian's wounds, removed the projectiles, cleaned the surgery site, and sedated him for the night. Though Helena offered her services, the ship's medical staff preferred to tend their own injured Human crewmen.

After a few hours of sleep, Helena joined Nathan in the forward lounge. The void of space dominated the viewport and she suppressed a shiver.

"I'm truly sorry about your guard," he said.

"He should be fine now," Helena said.

Nathan sipped his coffee and looked into her eyes. "I promise I'll get to the bottom of Bergem's motivations. If that's even his real name."

"He was trying to steal something," Helena said, intrigued and intimidated by the full cup of the Human 'coffee' drink before her. The aroma was stronger than most Antaran drinks and after the cheeseburger, she was wary.

"Really? We didn't find anything in his clothing or in his quarters."

"I'm certain of it. The Proxans, the admiral, the trap – it's all connected."

He leaned closer and whispered. "Can you read his mind?"

Helena lowered her voice and said, "Maybe. However, he is well-trained. It may be difficult. Especially if he suspected my abilities."

Nathan reclined in his chair and scratched his chin. "Hmmm… I'd get a nasty reprimand if I allowed you to speak with the prisoner. However, if you happened to pass him in the hall while we moved him, that's different. I mean, there's no way my marines could predict you'd be in the starboard corridor in twenty minutes."

Helena smiled. "That would be quite the coincidence."

"Well," Nathan said, "I should return to the bridge."

As Nathan exited, Admiral Stugardt entered.

"Aha," Stugardt said, "May I take the captain's seat?"

Helena motioned to the empty chair and eyed her coffee. Was she brave enough to try another Human food?

"I hope you got some sleep after last night's excitement?" he said.

"Thank you for your concern, Admiral. I am well."

He nodded and said, "Good. So, tell me of your world. I've never been to Antares."

Checking her internal clock, Helena calculated the time she would need to reach the starboard corridor for her encounter with Bergem. She still had a few minutes.

"Antares has come a long way from our start in the domes," Helena said. "We have tamed our star and terraformed the surface of our planet. We are close to the vision of our homeworld portrayed in our history books – rivers, mountains, lakes, waterfalls. Our scientists predict we will reach our goal in the next several generations."

"Impressive," Stugardt said. "Tell me, if you don't mind, when did your people first discover their mental discipline?"

"Several generations after the first settlers. The radiation from our star was a blessing and a curse. Widespread birth defects and new diseases almost killed the early Gima before they could flourish. Even today, a successful birth is cause for an entire town to celebrate. We are not as prolific as the Humans or Proxans."

He raised one of his thin eyebrows. "Is that so? I hear you have six sisters."

Helena allowed a smile to trespass on her painted face as she thought of her sisters. "Indeed. My bloodline is special."

"And the titanium on the dark side your planet? How has that resource remained untapped for so long?"

"We have little use for the rigid metal," Helena said. "Since our population does not expand, we have no need to travel the stars."

"No explorer spirits amongst the Antarans?"

"A few, from time to time," Helena said. "However, as a homogenous culture, our people recognize the value of family and the homestead. Wanderlust is an unhealthy endeavor when one considers their own responsibilities to family and state."

Stugardt placed his elbows on the table and rested his chin in his hands. "I don't know," he said, "a little wanderlust is good for a civilization. Exploration opens new horizons, new possibilities. You can only grow so much with inward reflection."

"Without a perfect sense of self, external experiences cannot be fully integrated with a psyche. How can you know the truth of a thing without knowing the truth of yourself?"

"Self truth," Stugardt said. "Now that's something I've been meaning to get around to now that I'm retired."

"I apologize," Helena said. "I know our cultures are different and I should not project my beliefs upon you." She scanned his emotions and found his mind alive with activity, but he held back. Something made him uncomfortable. "My ways must seem simple to someone who has travelled the stars and fought battles."

Stugardt met her gaze and said, "I don't think there's anything simple about you, My Lady. In fact, you terrify me."

Helena read the admiral's thoughts easy enough. He recognized the threat she posed - not only to his privacy, but to his way of life. Humans valued their independence and individuality. Someone who could read their minds threatens to take away some of that independence. Helena hadn't considered that angle before, but now she held it in her mind and analyzed the trajectories. Could this endanger the mission? Would the Humans trust someone with her abilities?

Stugardt laughed. "Well, maybe *terrify* is too strong a word. I'm just glad you're on your way to speak with my government instead of the Proxans. I, for one, wholeheartedly support your claim that your people can provide valuable assistance to our fleet. Before we met, I was looking forward to enjoying my retirement. Now, I may just stick around to see this war to its conclusion."

Helena nodded and said, "A warrior's first and last home is always on the battlefield."

Stugardt sighed and Helena sensed his thoughts return to his family. He cherished them, much as Helena cherished her sisters.

"Indeed," he said.

"Admiral, I really must be going," Helena said. "But I should learn more about the Proxans without further delay. Could you arrange some material for me?"

Stugardt nodded and said, "I'll make sure you are provided all the material we have onboard. Also, if you like, I'm free tonight. I'll tell you everything I know."

Helena rose and the admiral mirrored her motions. "That would be acceptable," Helena said. "If you'll excuse me."

"Yes, of course. Good day, My Lady."

Helena smiled and picked her way through the chairs and tables of the forward lounge to the exit where Duronious waited.

"We don't have much time," Helena whispered to her guard. "Let's move."

Duronious followed Helena through the dim passageways. Then, she saw Bergem. Several marines led Bergem from a lift and in her direction. Helena and Duronious passed the group and Helena sensed Bergem's recognition.

"You... You witch!" Bergem said, struggling against his constraints.

Helena focused on his mind with all of her strength and ability. This was her one chance.

"Don't trust her!" Bergem said, but one of the marines raised his hand as if to strike and Bergem recoiled.

His mind was not as poised as before and Helena slipped inside like a thief in the darkness. She battered through the orderly partitions and through the streams of his memory. Something was wrong. Things were *too* perfect. As she extracted the information she required, Helena realized the shocking truth – this man was a machine!

Chapter 10

"A machine?" Nathan said, his eyebrows raised in doubt.

Helena nodded.

Admiral Stugardt leaned towards the captain and said, "It's not too far-fetched, Nathan. We knew the Proxans were developing this science."

The admiral, captain, and alien princess sat in Nathan's office. The hum of the freighter's engines permeated the room, as did the aroma of untouched coffee. A small window offered no light but an amazing view. The vastness of space and the distance of the stars churned Helena's heart in directions she hadn't thought possible. She found it full of possibility and mystery. Perhaps her heart reserved some wanderlust, after all.

Nathan rose and stood at the window. "You said you discovered his secrets?"

Helena nodded. "Yes. He is a thinking machine, constructed to imitate and replace his target. The real ambassador Bergem is dead, killed by this duplicate."

Nathan shook his head. "The possibilities are frightening."

"You found nothing on his person or possessions because the data he stole is stored in his cybergenic mind."

Stugardt's eyes widened and he asked, "What did he steal?"

"The location of the second tellium star you found."

Nathan and Stugardt exchanged glances.

"Do not fear," Helena said, "Bergem has not notified the Proxans of the location yet. He was on his way to do that when he was ordered to make a stop on Antares."

Stugardt leaned forward, "Very few people know about that star. If word were to be leaked-"

Helena raised her hand to stop him and said, "Remember that I am on a mission to forge peace with your people. This secret will remain with me. You have my word as heir to my empire."

Helena kept control over her face and voice as she delivered her latest lie. Though the Humans couldn't read minds, Helena dared not risk sloppiness now. Their natural insight could expose her if she wasn't careful.

Nathan turned towards Stugardt and said, "We're going to have to keep Helena's involvement between us."

Stugardt nodded. "The Council need not know how we came about this information."

"Alright," Nathan said, "As long as you keep your word, Helena, we should be able to keep you far from this mess."

"One last point," Helena said. "You must destroy Bergem."

"What? Why?" Stugardt asked.

"He has a long-range transmitter inside his skull," Helena said. "If a Proxan ship were to enter the same system, the range could be enough to transfer the data he stole."

"Damn," Stugardt said. "I was hoping to get him back *alive* to our scientists."

Helena said, "The decision is not mine, but I know what course of action I would take if our roles were reversed."

"You have proven resourceful yet again, My Lady," Stugardt said. "I think we'll throw him into the incinerator. It's the only way to be sure."

Helena nodded and rose.

"One more thing," Nathan said as he intercepted Helena.

"Of course, Captain."

"How were you able to read his mind? He's a machine, right?"

Helena scanned Nathan's eyes for suspicion and found him conflicted. He was a loyal man of honor. Lying to his government didn't sit well with his conscious. He also wanted to trust her, but his military training taught him to only trust his own countrymen.

Helena stepped towards him on put her hand on his cheek. Stubble pricked her flesh. Given the difficulty of her task, Helena decided to make a move earlier than she expected. Marcella taught her this little trick.

"Close your eyes," Helena said, adding a seductive thickness to her voice. "I want to share with you."

Uneasy at first, Nathan closed his eyes. Helena sensed Stugardt's embarrassment as he witnessed what appeared to be an intimate exchange of words between lovers.

Nathan said, "I'm not-"

"Shhh, no more words. Do you feel me in your mind?"

"Yes."

"I will show you his thoughts, and you will see," Helena said as she wrapped her other arm around his neck. "Do not resist."

Sensing Nathan's arousal and fear, Helena eased into his thoughts and shared her vision of Bergem's cybergenic mind. Grown from engineered Proxan cells, most of Bergem was organic. Cybernetic components were added for control, transmission and ability. Specific data on Bergem's target was fed to the brain over the course of many years, to simulate the gradual learning process shared by Proxans and Humans alike. Bergem was schooled in the art of deception and sent upon his mission.

Helena eased away from Nathan before she shared too much. After a few moments, he swallowed and opened his eyes.

"Wow," he said.

Helena parted after meeting his eyes and flashing him a coy look. She realized she needed to derail his doubts by clouding his judgment. Marcella was better at this device, but Helena was as fine a student as she was teacher. Admittedly, feigning interest in Nathan wasn't too far a leap for her. She felt *something* for him, but she couldn't afford to wonder about the newness of it.

He should be easier to manipulate after her stunt. A section of Helena's heart railed against her chest over her deceitfulness. How could she do such a thing to a man who has shown her respect and trust? Helena forced her thoughts on that matter to the background. She couldn't afford to empathize with her enemy, no matter how much that dark place in her heart hoped she sensed something more in his feelings as well.

"You see, now?" Helena said.

Nathan nodded.

She opened the door and eyed Stugardt. "Our meeting for tonight is still on schedule, Admiral?" Helena said.

Stugardt blinked and said, "Oh, yes. I wouldn't miss it."

Helena strolled through the corridors free from marine escort and arrived in her quarters with Duronius. She needed to sort some things out, so she used her guard as a sounding board.

"This changes things?" Duronious asked after Helena whispered, in a secret Antaran tongue, the news of a second tellium star.

Still talking in code, Helena said, "Yes. Everything. I've re-run the scenario and things are no longer in our favor. I must speak with my father."

"We're almost to Terra," Duronious said. "It could be some time before that is possible."

"I must give my father time to account for this new information," Helena said as she searched for alternatives, but she had already calculated the best course of action.

"I don't see how we can do that now."

"There is a way," Helena said, "But it is risky."

Duronious crossed his arms and waited.

"I could send a message back with Vespill, the injured praetorian," Helena said. "But, that act could raise suspicion. The Humans won't be able to crack the code, as I will make it unique for my sister, Prisca."

"Vespill is almost fully recovered," Duronious said. "They will suspect something."

"I know. It's not perfect."

"My Lady," one of the other praetorians said from behind Helena's curtain.

"Yes, Praetorian?"

"Lieutenant Rhom is on the intercom, she has news for you."

"Thank you, Praetorian," Helena said. "Well, Duronious, think on it. I would like alternatives before my hand is forced."

Duronious nodded and Helena approached the intercom. She pressed the button and said, "This is Lady Helena."

Sandra Rhom's voice crackled through the speaker. "Aha, Lady Helena. The captain wanted me to inform you that we have dropped out of high warp and we will be landing on Terra early tomorrow."

"Thank you, Lieutenant."

Reverting to their coded language, Duronious said, "We're a day ahead of schedule."

Helena shook her head. "No, they deliberately misinformed us. Apparently, we have not won their trust quite yet."

Duronius narrowed his eyes. "The feeling is shared, I assure you."

♦

True to her word, Helena arrived in the forward lounge to meet Admiral Stugardt. Noticing her enter, he stood. The room was aglow from the blue planet which dominated the forward viewport of the lounge.

"You are radiant, as always, My Lady," he said.

Helena smiled enough to accept the compliment without showing pride. "Thank you, Admiral. May I join you?"

Stugardt pulled a chair from the table to give her room to sit. "Please."

"Again, my gratitude," Helena said.

"I hope it's okay," he said, "But I ordered us tropical salads."

"That will be fine, Admiral."

The crewmembers in the lounge watched from the corners of their eyes and made detours to walk close to the table with the alien and the admiral. Helena sensed a great deal of curiosity amongst the Humans.

"Your planet is beautiful," Helena said.

Stugardt turned in his chair to admire his homeworld. "Yes, it is. Though, it has been quite some time since I have been here. Too long."

After a few moments of silence, Stugardt cleared his throat and said, "So, the Proxans... let us start at the beginning. Our histories state that we were both part of the same refugee fleet eons ago. Something happened to our home system, and we were forced to evacuate."

Helena leaned towards him and said, "Our histories tell the same story."

He nodded as a server placed the two salads on the table. Helena admired the dish which was full of leaves, bright fruit slices and fronds.

"We believe all the peoples we have encountered are from the same home planet," he said. "It would explain our common language, likeness and breeding compatibility."

"Our anthropologists believe the same," Helena said.

"Well, the Proxans didn't settle on Terra. They continued on to another system. For several millennia, we didn't have contact with them. Then, out of nowhere, we were attacked by a race of cyborgs. Later, we discovered the aggressors were the Proxans. They had embraced technology that meshes flesh and computer."

Helena nodded. That must be why she felt strange during the Proxan ambush. Their minds were part machine. However, Bergem's mind was mostly natural, which would explain why he was so difficult to read. Yet he appeared authentic. The facts of the past few weeks were coming together for the first time.

"We fought for decades until we discovered the tellium star," he said. "The Proxans found it first, and their prototype battleship was already close to completion. Those were some dark years. We lost planets and too many civilians and soldiers. Things were quite bleak until we finished our first battleship. Then, we were able to even the odds a bit."

"My people have heard stories of your battleships," Helena said. "Are they really as large as a comet?"

"Oh yes. They house an entire fleet and they travel at tremendous speed. The battleship is the pinnacle of weapons technology. None of the other scattered civilizations can match this advantage."

"Forgive my bluntness, Admiral, but these battleships have taken the war to my homeworld and my people have died as a direct result of your war," Helena said. "Please excuse me if my admiration of your technology is tempered."

"We have many battlefields," he said. "The ore on the dark side of your planet is not exactly abundant. So, yes, we do quarrel over it from time to time. I would apologize, but I'm uncertain my High Command would approve of that act. Let me just say that it saddens me to know that some of my orders and actions have caused suffering to your people."

"I am not expecting an apology," Helena said. "I was just speaking on the behalf of my people who have died needlessly and can no longer raise their own voice."

"Of course," he said.

"Please, continue," Helena said as she completed her mental assessment of the admiral.

Honorable and dutiful, he was a career military man. For many years, he had commanded a large portion the Human fleet. He married his high school sweetheart and their family was foremost in his thoughts these days. Though he wished to return to them, he viewed Helena as a possible key to victory. His heart was conflicted between returning home and helping to end the war.

"We once fought bloody battles at the tellium star over the rights to mine it," he said. "Then, when we were both at our weakest, a coalition of rival civilizations almost wrested control of the star from both Terra and Proxis. Since we both have our own enemies as well, there now exists an uneasy neutral zone around the star. We don't fight there, as any battle would escalate to such a level as to leave both Terra and Proxis quite depleted. Though we are at war, we cannot afford an end-conflict of that magnitude."

"I understand other civilizations have asked for mining rights to that star?" Helena said.

"Yes, but so far the offers have been less than balanced."

"Well, my people wish for nothing more than to be left alone in your conflict," Helena said. "I think our offer is a fair one."

"Indeed," he said, lowering his voice. "With your abilities, I think we can bring this war to a quick and decisive end. That should satisfy both parties, yes?"

Without wavering, Helena served another half-truth. "We would consider our alliance a success if the war was ended before more Antaran deaths."

Stugardt raised his glass and said, "I'll drink to that."

After a few moments of silence and eating, Stugardt clasped his hands behind his bald head and said, "From what Nathan tells me, you're not easily flustered. However, I think I should warn you about the Chamber of Truth."

Helena contained her surprise and asked, "Chamber of Truth?"

"All Human negotiations are handled there," he said. "There's something about the harmonics in the room. A liar is exposed when they speak. Amazing that the room is natural. The Human embassy was built around the room – well, more like a cave. I'm sure if Bergem was the real ambassador, he would have informed you. It could be quite a shock to off-worlders."

Chamber of Truth. The Antarans had no intelligence on this structure or its abilities. Helena finished her salad and excused herself as quickly as she could without raising suspicion. She hurried to her room and meditated in silence. How was she going to defeat the Chamber of Truth? She reflected inwards and sought wisdom from her mother that might help. Sleep came after several hours. Answers eluded her.

Chapter 11

"We've done some terraforming of our own," Admiral Stugardt said as the ship maneuvered for its landing.

Helena gazed upon the city and surrounding countryside from the forward viewport in the lounge.

"Breathtaking," she said.

Gentle green hills stretched from the city to whitecapped mountains in the distance. Wispy white clouds floated in the perfect blue sky. The scene could have been taken straight from an Antaran history book. Terra resembled their shared homeworld much more closely than Antares.

"It wasn't always this way," Stugardt said. "Steaming jungles covered the many islands of this archipelago world. We have since lowered the water level and tamed all but the harshest of regions."

They landed in the midday sun and Helena chose an airy white gown for her first meeting with Human diplomats. Before the ramp opened, Nathan rounded the corner and smiled when he saw her. Helena scolded herself for the elation that busted from her heart. Why was she so delighted to see him? She decided she must distance herself from this unwelcome temptation.

"Lady Helena," he said. "I'm glad I caught you."

"Captain."

"I'd like to thank you again for all your help on our little trip," he said. "We owe you much."

Helena tilted her head towards him and said, "Of course." She sensed trepidation in his emotions. What was he so nervous about?

"I have orders I must see to," he said as he wrung his hands behind his back.

"Very well, it was a pleasure to meet you, Captain," she said simultaneously relieved and crushed at the thought of not seeing him again.

He stepped to her side and said, "But I have some off-duty time tonight."

Realizing his angle, Helena interrupted him. "You deserve some time alone to rest and recover," she said.

Frowning, he said, "I was hoping to see you one last time. There're some great restaurants near the embassy. Would you join me for dinner?"

"Are you asking me on a date, Captain?" she asked, surprised at how easily she slipped into her repressed infatuation with the Human. Silly girl, she thought to herself, you should know better.

Nathan straightened his back and eyed her guards. "I… well, not exactly. I just wanted to get to know you."

Helena placed her arm on his bicep and caught her breath as she felt electricity between them. He stiffened in response and she sensed his excitement. "I will, of course, join you for dinner," she said, unwilling to surrender to the warnings from her logical mind. After all, what harm could come from a simple meal with a him?

"Great," he said as his eyes darted to her guards. "I'll swing by the embassy at seven o'clock."

"Seven o'clock," she said as the ramp opened.

An impressive contingent of guards and dignitaries met Helena's small party on the landing platform. The Humans wore simple tan uniforms and hats to keep the sun at bay.

"Welcome to Terra, Lady Helena of Antares," a male Human dignitary said. "I am Ambassador Jarvis." Helena noted the surprise over her facial markings and the man's young age. Certainly he wasn't wise enough to hold a diplomatic post, was he? Helena cautioned herself to not underestimate the man. These Humans were goal-orientated and driven. He could be quite skilled in negotiation and deception.

Helena looked through Jarvis and said, "Thank you for your hospitality, Ambassador."

"You must be exhausted from your journey," Jarvis said. "I apologize for your accommodations and unfortunate events surrounding Ambassador Bergem. The *Venture* was the only ship near your world. Please, let me show you to your rooms while you stay on Terra. You will find them more comfortable."

"Again, you have my gratitude," Helena said as Jarvis led them into a large stone building with silver spires.

Their footsteps and voices echoed along the blue-green marble floors. Small pockets of Humans dressed in simple working or business clothing huddled and spoke as the aliens passed them. Helena scanned each person and noted some surprise, but mostly frantic minds with too many tasks at the forefront.

"This entire structure was carved from a single piece of stone and marble. It now serves as our foreign embassy," Jarvis said as he made a sweeping motion with his hand. Helena noticed the man only had four fingers on that hand, however she didn't risk delving deeper into his memories. Now was not the time for idle curiosity.

"I hear your guests are subjected to a place called *The Chamber of Truth*?" Helena said, hoping to probe for enough information while remaining aloof.

Jarvis turned to study Helena for a moment, but Helena was more than a match for the young Human. If he could read her face, the man deserved any information he gleaned.

"Your information is correct," Jarvis said, "Though few off-worlders know of the chamber. We have been deceived to the point of great suffering in the past. Now, all important negotiations, even amongst our own planetary governors, are held in the Chamber."

Helena leveled her stare at the ambassador and said, "My people have a saying: 'To go through life without trust is to imprison oneself in the most lonely of cells.'"

Jarvis smiled and appeared unfazed. "We believe trust must be *earned*," he said. "Your quarters, My Lady."

He opened the door to a luxurious room adorned with silver furniture and the orange, purple, and black Human flag as accent draperies and upholstery. Helena immediately recognized a painting of her homeworld Antares above the spacious bed. Water trickled from a natural looking waterfall on one side of the room.

"This room is reserved for leaders of other civilizations," Jarvis said. "We hope you find it adequate."

Helena nodded, "This is quite lovely, thank you Ambassador."

"Your guards can take residence in the adjoining rooms to either side with as much or as little surveillance as you wish. Desiree will be your housekeeper," Jarvis said as he motioned to a young Human woman in his entourage. "She will get you anything you need and explain the workings of the suite."

Desiree stepped forward and bowed her head.

"Now, I'll let you get settled," Jarvis said. "I have duties to attend, but tomorrow we will meet and conduct our preliminary talks. There is much I wish to learn about your world and people."

"Until tomorrow, Ambassador," Helena said.

The Human contingent moved away, leaving only Desiree.

"Would you mind waiting in the hallway for a moment, my dear?" Helena said to the Human girl.

Desiree smiled and said, "Of course not. I will be waiting here."

Helena and the praetorians entered the suite. Within seconds, her guards were sweeping the room while appearing casual and curious. Helena sat in the center of the space and closed her eyes. Claudia taught her an empathic trick a few years ago and Helena hoped she could duplicate her success in the past.

Tuning out the movements of the praetorians, Helena focused on the falling water. Each drop was filtered through her ears and she absorbed the room. Her guards were nervous, but Helena needed to dig deeper, to before her arrival. What went on here? What did the Humans plant for listening devices? Helena tried to sense strong lingering emotions of the past, but her efforts were fruitless. If anything was dangerous about this room, Helena's skill was not enough to detect it.

Returning to her present mind, Helena opened her eyes.

"My Lady," Duronious said. "There is surveillance equipment, but it appears to be tied with the adjoining room so we could keep watch. I don't know who else would be watching if we activated it, however."

"That is fine," Helena said. "Just keep your senses on alert. You should be able to detect surprise, fear or pain from your room. Standard watch rotation with hourly checks should be adequate."

"Anything else for now, My Lady? The sun is still high." Duronious said, speaking in Antaran military code. He was concerned about the Chamber of Truth and the Human girl, Desiree.

Responding in code, Helena said, "The sun is high, yes, however I believe the night will be uneventful. I wish to listen to some songs on my datapad. Ask the girl about refreshments and fall into whatever rooms you feel are best to protect me." Though the last part wasn't code, Helena relayed her need to know more about the Chamber. Her datapad carried all the accumulated wisdom of her people. Perhaps a study in harmonics would lead her in the right direction.

Duronious saluted the 'danger' salute indicating he wouldn't rest until he was comfortable with the Antaran heir's safety. The praetorians filtered from the room and Helena stopped Vespill with a gesture. The praetorian approached, gave the same salute as Duronious, and waited.

"Praetorian, how are your wounds?"

Vespill said, "I feel strong, My Lady. Your healing skills have brought me from the brink of darkness."

More worship. If her people survived this gambit, Helena decided she needed to speak with her father over the religion he created. She wasn't divine.

"It pleases me to see you back on duty," Helena said. "Dismissed."

"My Lady."

Alone once more, Helena sat on her bed with her datapad. She keyed in her security code and adjusted the display to only be visible for her eyes. Harmonics was a massive topic. Though she employed harmonic principles to control her voice and sometimes read another's voice, Helena was unfamiliar with much of the science. The day was shaping to be a long one.

Chapter 12

"I heard from Admiral Stugardt that you liked the salad," Nathan said, "so I thought this might be a good place to try."

Everyone at the small, dark restaurant gaped when Helena first entered. These Humans, though close to the embassy, weren't accustomed to alien visitors.

"No more greasy food for you, I think," Nathan said.

Helena invisibly winced at the memory of the cheeseburger. "No, indeed," she said, remaining aloof despite her burning interest in this particular Human.

"So," Nathan said, his mind buzzing with questions, "ever think you'd be on Terra?"

Helena shook her head. "Most definitely not."

He studied her face as she spoke and watched her hands and she manipulated her fork. A quick scan of his mind told her that the interest was mutual. That would only make things more difficult.

"What's your favorite color?" he blurted.

Helena blinked. "What?"

"I don't know," he said. "I'm just trying to make conversation. It's been pretty one-sided so far."

Helena placed her fork on the table and met his warm, brown eyes. "I apologize," she said. "My mind is focused on my mission." She omitted the fact that she required all of her strength to *not* ask him the many questions she wanted to ask.

"That's understandable," he said, though Helena was only half listening. "You're far from home with people who have caused you great pain. I'm sure you miss your sisters..."

Her mind bounced between her desire at intimacy with the captain and her immediate duties on Terra. She couldn't decipher the logical reason for her internal conflict and that only frustrated her further.

"Blue!" Helena said. Her thoughts were in complete disarray when she was with him.

Nathan paused. "What?"

"My favorite color is blue."

"Oh," Nathan said as a smile stole across his face. "So is mine. Midnight blue, to be exact. The color of the night sky over the ocean is something I miss terribly."

"In my culture," she said, "blue represents peace, harmony, confidence, fidelity and strength. Though I must admit, I was drawn to the color even before I knew these things."

"On Terra, blue represents honesty and royalty," he said.

Helena reined her emotions tight before they could be exposed. Honesty. Would she ever know the word again? Her weave of lies had just begun and she was already sickened by it.

Desperate to distance herself from the word *honesty*, Helena said, "You live near an ocean?"

"Yes."

"I have seen pictures of oceans in our history books," she said.

"You mean, you don't have oceans on Antares?"

"No, we do not," she said. "Yet we believe our terraforming efforts will be able to produce large bodies of water within the next several generations."

"Wow," he said, "I didn't know."

"As a child, I remember asking my mother about these oceans," Helena said. "She told me that the power of the tides is one of the most primal and amazing forces in the universe. How she knew this, I am uncertain as she never left Antares either."

"Well, maybe we'll get the chance to show you the oceans here on Terra," he said.

She smiled. "I would like that."

After an awkward pause, Nathan said, "What else? What about your sisters? Are you all close?"

Helena sensed his arousal when his mind wandered to Marcella. She couldn't fault him. Her sister was radiant beyond poems or pictures.

"I am close to my sisters," she said as she suppressed her longing to see them again. "Especially Terentia, the youngest. When our mother died, I was left to raise her from an infant. She is very special to me."

"I'm sorry," he said, uncomfortable with the topic.

"Thank you, Captain," she said, "but that was a long time ago. My mother's memory is one filled with joy and warmth. There is no need for mourning any longer."

He nodded and Helena marveled at how quickly he was able to disseminate information and adapt to new circumstances. His mind was more impressive than she first gave credit for.

"Of course," she said, resuming the previous topic, "our family is not without its troubles. You witnessed Valeria's wrath first hand on Antares."

Nathan nodded. "I remember. She was a little angry at dinner that night, but I understand why."

"It goes deeper than that," she said, unsure why she was so loose with her tongue. "I sensed the same feelings from Captain Knowles onboard the *Venture*. He was jealous of your command position, yes?"

Nathan frowned. "Yeah, something like that."

"Valeria suffers from that same pride. If she is not in command, then you must watch your every step for she will expose your faults. It is a constant struggle. One that should remain behind our palace walls. I do not know why I feel comfortable talking to you about such things."

Nathan grinned. "Sounds like normal *Human* problems…"

Helena tapped his hand and felt Goosebumps erupt across her skin in response to the touch. "Please don't insult us," she said playfully. "We are not susceptible to Human weaknesses."

Before he moved, Helena sensed his desire to grasp her hand. Though she could have pulled away, she allowed his advance. He caught her hand and turned it over as his eyes followed the blue Gima tattoos which wrapped around her fingers and palm.

"What do these mean?" he asked.

Helena considered telling him about the meaning and discipline behind the markings. However, she decided she needed to maintain her upper hand in her dealings with not only the captain, but the Humans as well. This was one secret he would have to wonder about.

"I am sorry," she said, "but I cannot tell you."

Nathan leaned towards her and her breath caught in her throat. "Why not?" he asked. "And why don't they smudge?" He ran his finger over the back of her palm.

Too close, she cautioned herself. She pulled her hand from his and said, "You are not Antaran."

"There's no other way for me to know?" he said, his mind aware of her deception. He knew she was holding back. Was she *that* readable?

Instead of correcting her mistake, she revealed the truth of the secret. "There is only one alternative. We would have to be wed to one another."

Nathan leaned backwards and said, "Well, I guess you leave me no alternative-"

Falling into his trap willingly, she said, "And what is that?"

"I must now make my own assumptions as to their meaning," he said.

Damn, he was good. He sensed one of Helena's weaknesses – her need to portray herself exactly as she desired. Her unwillingness to convey the meaning behind her markings would only be in jeopardy if she was misunderstood, and he just told her that he was left to his own whims of misinterpretation. Enough play, she scolded herself. This Human was too dangerous. She was too readable and too vulnerable when she was with him.

"Okay," she said. "You win this round, so now we're even?"

He raised his eyebrows. "Even?"

"Well," she said, "I beat you in chess and now you defeated me in this. I will tell you what these markings mean."

"No victory against you is a small one," he said. "I'm sweating here." He wiped his brow and the back of his neck with his napkin.

"Indeed, you should be proud of yourself," she said.

"Believe me, I am!"

"Very well then. The markings on my hand represent discipline. If they move out of place while I am working towards my task, another Antaran would recognize my fault and correct me. At all times, my hands must remain steady on their course. They must not waver."

"Why only you and your family?" he said. "I noticed other Antarans weren't wearing the tattoos."

"Very perceptive, Captain," she said. "The royal family is in service to the Antaran people. We wear these marks so our people can scrutinize our actions. If we allow ourselves to be driven from our course, then the people will recognize the fluctuations on our faces and with our hands. They will recognize, and they will call for accountability. We must always be in control, always on the best path for our people. It has been our way since we settled Antares. And we have upheld this tradition."

"Amazing," he said. "So, the royal family is not above the people? I always thought monarchy was absolute rule, no room for democracy."

"Do not misunderstand, Captain," she said. "The people have the power to watch and observe us, but any change must come from *us*. If I am told by a citizen that my actions are not in the best interest of my people, then I feel a great responsibility to change. My duty is to my people and they know this. They will trust that I will change and that is how our system works."

Nathan digested the information and said, "What about a despot? What if one of you weren't able to change? How would your people react to that?"

"I'm sorry, Captain, but that is not possible."

"Humor me," he said, "and please, call me *Nathan*."

Her heart felt as if it was struck by a jolt of electricity. She sensed he wanted to be closer to her and that was a very tempting flame.

"Okay, Nathan," she said. "A leader acting for him or herself would be removed." Helena considered telling him the story of Queen Valeria, but she decided she had already spoken too much.

"Removed by who?"

Helena waved her hand. "Does all of this really interest you?"

Nathan smiled. "Can't you just read my mind to know that it does?"

She sensed he was more fascinated in *her* than Antaran politics. "I sense interest," she said.

A device on Nathan's belt beeped and he examined the screen. Annoyed, he said, "I have to go... I am very sorry."

As they rose from their table, Helena caught his arm and said, "Next time, we talk about *you*."

"Is that a request or an order?" he asked.

Helena smiled and cursed herself for her transparent emotions. "Do not mistake any of my orders for requests, Nathan Connor. Of course it is an order."

"So," he said, enjoying the exchange, "there will be a *next time*?"

"Have I said *no* to you yet?"

Nathan frowned. "I'm sure it's coming one of these days."

Chapter 13

"Everything was lost?" Ambassador Jarvis asked between mouthfuls of his omelet.

"Well, most everything," Helena said, taking only small bites of the Human food. Though the salads agreed with her stomach, the heavier Human fare violently didn't.

The balcony overlooked a wide plaza with many docks where space faring vessels came and went throughout much of the breakfast. Light shimmered from the calm lake to the south. Birds soared in the sky and Helena marveled at how far the Humans had brought their terraforming technology.

The Human Ambassador seemed less rushed than he was yesterday. Helena scanned his recent memories enough to learn that this was his first major assignment. That suited her. Let them send a rookie as that made Helena's job easier.

"When the first ship landed on Antares, our people did not think it would be the only ship. The remaining settlement ships hit a storm in the atmosphere and were destroyed."

"How many people settled the first colony?"

"According to our records, only about six hundred," Helena said as she sipped her green tea. At least this drink was similar to the one from her homeworld. "We pieced together our past from the scant histories left to us – mostly religious and government texts from an ancient empire. We have strived to imitate that model."

"Yes, yes," Jarvis had donned his spectacles and he reviewed some paperwork. "My information tells me your government is a Dynastic Aristocracy."

"True," Helena said. "My father, the emperor, rules as the final voice. However, the everyday decisions of state are left to the aristocrats who are trained for governing and policymaking."

"Very interesting."

"I understand the Human government is a democracy," Helena said.

"Indeed," Jarvis said. "The people rule here."

"With so many planets, you don't find this type of government cumbersome?"

"The Human people value *freedom* above all else," Jarvis said. "The ability to elect whomever they wish to govern them is one of our most basic freedoms."

"Would you hire a poet to fix your computer systems?" Helena asked.

"What?"

"It is a simple question, Ambassador. I just wish to learn more about your democracy."

"Um," Jarvis said, "no, of course I wouldn't hire a poet for that job."

"Then, tell me, why hire someone untrained in rulership to govern you?"

"I think *untrained* is a tad strong," Jarvis said. "Our candidates rise from the ranks of our most intelligent and influential groups – scientists, lawyers, regional governors-"

"Entertainers?" Helena asked, pleased her trap sprung so easily.

Jarvis frowned. "True, anyone with enough money can run for office and win. But-"

Helena considered offering him a smile, but she restrained. Offering only her words, she said, "Forgive me, I was just having a little fun at your expense. Examining a population's accepted form of government provides great insight into their culture. I'm merely learning, as well."

Jarvis chuckled and his nervousness from the day before returned. That suited Helena. This man was easier to throw off balance than *her* Captain Connor. She was disturbed to find she was the one in disarray when he was near her. That risk had to be corrected.

"Did you receive the materials on our legal system this morning?" Jarvis asked. Helena sensed the ambassador was desperate to change the subject. He felt outclassed.

"Yes, thank you," Helena said. "Though, I must admit – there's quite a bit of material there."

"I understand," Jarvis said. "So I took the liberty to bookmark some important sections on interspecies law and universal accords. I recommend you review them thoroughly before your audience with the Human Council tomorrow."

Helena nodded. "I will do so."

♦

After her breakfast with the ambassador, Helena returned to her suite to review the material. Over the course of the next day, she studied Human law and found it complex and brutal towards outsiders.

The morning of her audience with the Human Council arrived too soon for her liking. She preferred to over-prepare for anything this important. Unfortunately, the Humans worked faster than she had anticipated.

"Do you think you're ready?" Duronius asked in their coded language.

Helena flicked a speck of lint from her midnight blue dress and said, "The natural harmonics of the Chamber will be my biggest obstacle. If things turn sour, I suspect the worst they will do is brand me a liar and send me home. Well, that's my best interpretation from what I read in their interstellar law."

"Something else you read last night bothered you, didn't it?" Duronious said.

Helena reprimanded herself again. Was she *that* readable? Or, was Duronious more skilled than she had first thought? Why was she forgetting her years of study and discipline when it mattered the most?

She eyed the praetorian and said, "Yes, I discovered that the penalty for treason against the Human government is death. In our case, my father would bear the punishment and our people would be subjugated."

Duronious said, "I believe the emperor knows the risk."

Her speech still masked in code, Helena said, "I'm not sure he knows about the ultimate price to his own person for failure."

The light above Helena's door blinked and a soft chime signaled a visitor.

"They are here," she said.

The gathered praetorians jerked to attention and Helena inspected their ceremonial blue and black attire. Though a small group, Helena felt closer to her countrymen than she ever had before. Perhaps the feeling came from being so deep in the enemy's den.

Helena inhaled and opened her door.

"Greetings, Lady Helena," Ambassador Jarvis said. "I am here to escort you to the council. Are you prepared to depart?"

Jarvis wore a white suit adorned with a black sash and the purple and orange symbol of Terra. He appeared slightly recovered from their exchange of political views at breakfast a few mornings prior, but he was still awed by her. A fact that kept him sleepless.

Helena adjusted one of her white, elbow length gloves and leveled her painted face at the Human. Without any emotion, she said, "The Antaran Heir is ready to speak with your council."

Jarvis led them down a wide staircase, past statues and enormous paintings. Activity at the embassy seemed lighter than the past few days, but Helena focused entirely on her task. She must convince them to allow the daughters of Emperor Agreios onto their battleships.

As they descended, the rock became more uneven and natural. Their collected footsteps echoed in a patterned way. The Chamber of Truth was close.

After waiting in a small but lavish room, Jarvis reappeared and motioned Helena through a door. Alone. As Helena entered the Chamber of Truth, she recited the serenity chant in her mind.

Blue-green marble encased the room, though the numerous lights couldn't break the darkness above. Uneven formations served as natural columns and Helena recognized a pattern. This wasn't a natural cave. Someone or some*thing* manufactured this room eons ago, probably before the Humans settled here. She understood why the Humans thought it natural, but this room served one purpose – to detect fluctuations in sound with unerring accuracy.

A holographic image appeared near the center of the room and Jarvis said, "Please stand right here. I'll wait for you on the other side of that door."

After Jarvis retreated to the waiting room, Helena turned to the faces in the hologram. Three Human males and one Human female stared back.

One of the males spoke. "The Human Council welcomes you to Terra, Lady Helena of Antares. I am Councilor Durgess. In order to your right are Councilors Zedem, Oartil and Wethersund."

Helena nodded, but didn't speak.

"We understand your trip to Terra was marred by the Proxans?" Durgess said. "Please accept our apologies on that matter."

"Thank you, Councilor," Helena said, noting how her voice echoed in the room.

"We just have a few preliminary questions for you," the female councilor, Wethersund, said.

"Very well," Helena said, realizing they were attempting to establish her harmonic baseline.

"You are the heir to the Antaran throne, correct?" Wethersund asked, her eyes probing Helena.

With a stonewall face and even voice, Helena said, "Yes, I am heir to the throne."

"And you are here to open diplomatic negotiations with the Human Confederation?" Wethersund asked.

Varying her voice slightly to give her room for error later, Helena said, "Correct. My people wish to open diplomatic talks."

Councilor Oartil asked the next question. "And who was the Human captain you met on your homeworld?"

"Captain Nathan Connor," Helena said, changing her voice a tad in the other direction. "To prove my peoples' worth, I also bested the captain in a match of chess."

This time, councilor Durgess spoke again. "A game you have never played before?"

Helena returned to her first harmonic tone and said, "That is correct."

A few moments passed and Helena kept her emotions deep within herself. Now was not the time to second-guess her tactic. She required some vocal elbow room for when she needed to lay her groundwork of deceit. Helena hoped whoever built this cave could be beaten.

After another minute, councilor Wethersund said, "Very well, Lady Helena, we can proceed."

Durgess said, "We have the Antaran proposal in front of us and we wish some clarification before going into detail."

"Very well," Helena said.

"Your claim of telepathy is unlike any we've ever heard," Durgess said. "So, please excuse our skepticism."

"Do you not also have Admiral Stugardt's report?" Helena asked.

"Yes," Durgess said, "we have read the report in detail. However, we require a good faith demonstration, if you will."

Helena paused and waited.

"You cannot show us your powers?" Wethersund asked with skepticism heavy on her words and face.

"That is not the problem," Helena said. "I find your lack of faith in your own people... disappointing."

"We trust the admiral, and Captain Connor," Durgess said. "We just want to know the full extent of your capabilities."

Helena sensed both deceit and fear from the councilors. They mostly trusted the admiral's report. However, their faith was based on *seeing*, so Helena decided to give them a show. Perhaps she didn't need to defeat the Chamber of Truth, if that was even possible. She closed her eyes to concentrate and block visual distraction.

After a few moments, Helena opened her eyes and stared at the councilors. "You all sit in a room beyond the far wall. If I pass the tests of the Chamber, we will meet in person. Though you trust the admiral, you do not trust his report. Maybe he was delirious or perhaps he's losing his faculties at his age. Regardless, Councilor Oartil is constantly checking a report from a scientist. This scientist, Hines, is nearby also. He's monitoring the harmonics in the room and in my voice to detect variations and striations."

The holographic image of the councilors faded for a minute and then returned.

"Ambassador Jarvis could have told you all of that," Durgess said. "I wrote down three numbers on a sheet of paper in front of me. Please-"

"Seventeen, thirty-eight, two-thousand four hundred and five," Helena said. Now that she was in the councilor's mind, predicting his every move and scanning his surface thoughts was child's play.

Surprise spread over each councilor's face.

"Now, for the second test. You are going to ask me how many Human military ships maintain a high orbit?" Helena said, probing the councilor's line of thought. "And how many crewmembers in total?"

"I... um-" Durgess fumbled with his words.

Helena sighed and closed her eyes. "Try not to talk to me," she said.

Blocking all external stimuli, Helena focused outward and into space. She sensed pockets of emotion and activity. After singling out what she believed to be the starships, she kept her eyes shut and said, "Four starships."

Wethersund gasped and Helena furrowed her brow in concentration. This was no small task. The math flowed through her mind as she briefly touched each mind. Some were awake, some were asleep. Counting each one at such a speed was taxing, but Helena's ability to sense the presence of life was her strongest trait.

Then, exhaling, Helena said, "Two-thousand and ninety-two crewmembers total," Helena said. "Wait. Count three less. A shuttle just departed from the frigate called *Comet*."

Silence filled the empty spaces in the cavern. The councilors were shocked.

Helena opened her eyes and took some heavy breaths. "Councilor Oartil, look at your readout. Mr. Hines doesn't know what to make of it. The Chamber tells him I'm lying but we both know my numbers are accurate."

Oartil's face disappeared for a moment.

Helena used the time to compose herself. Then, she said, "Is there anything else you wish to be demonstrated? I would very much like to meet you in person and talk about the Antaran proposal."

Chapter 14

"Sounds like things went in our favor," Duronious said.

Helena entered the banquet hall flanked by her guards. Their footsteps fell in perfect unison, and more than one Human stopped to stare.

They no longer risked talking in code after Duronious found a hidden listening device in one of the antechambers. Time was scarce over the past few days as the Humans kept Helena on a frantic schedule. So she resorted to sharing information between official functions.

"After the dinner tonight, I am to meet with their commanding admiral to discuss where my abilities can be best utilized against the Proxans," Helena said as she returned her tattoo brush to its case. Though the tattoos didn't normally smudge through the course of a day, the rigorous movement from place to place in the embassy left them slightly altered – not that any Human would have noticed the minor corrections she made.

"And after that?" Duronious asked.

Helena smiled, looked at each of her praetorians and said, "After that, we return home."

Though she sensed relief from the men, they didn't show it on their faces. Each of them watched the shadows and Human onlookers. Her father's guards were ever vigilant.

The banquet hall opened from a triangular doorway into a room of crystal and rock which slanted upwards from the floor to a point three stories high. Chandeliers reflected light off the walls, throwing sparkles and prismatic colors in every direction. Already, the hum of the gathered Humans carried outwards from the hall's interior.

Ambassador Jarvis waited at the entry and bowed when Helena approached. "Lady Helena, you are radiant as always."

Helena sensed a feeling of utter awe from the ambassador. His first assignment was turning out to be an important one and he had gone to great lengths over the past few days to accommodate Helena's every wish. Like a potter molding the vase, Helena kept these Humans in the lines she needed between her hands. The only exception was Captain Nathan Connor.

"Ambassador, thank you for your kind words," Helena said as she handed her shawl to Duronious.

"We have arranged a table for your guards," Jarvis said. "If that is okay with you."

Helena glanced at Duronious and said, "That is fine."

"Your table is this way, My Lady" Jarvis said, crooking his arm.

"I thought I made it clear," a voice called from the crowd. Admiral Stugardt weaved between guests. "That *I* was to escort the lady to her table tonight."

Helena tilted her head and said, "Admiral, I am glad to see you again."

Jarvis hesitated and then allowed his arm to drop.

"Come with me, Lady Helena," Stugardt said. "I have some people I'd like you to meet."

The admiral offered his arm and Helena accepted. Admiral Stugardt's dress garb reminded Helena of the handsome Captain Nathan Connor. Why was he constantly in her thoughts?

As if he was reading her mind this time, Stugardt said, "Nathan couldn't be here tonight, unfortunately. He's quite busy lately with his new command."

"New command?" Helena asked, annoyed at the elation she let slip in her voice over the subject of the captain.

"Yes, I recommended him as my replacement," Stugardt said. "Sure, there were others in line to be Captain of *The Jupiter*, but I feel some younger blood should take the reigns in these troubled times."

The Jupiter! In her father's plan, the duty to destroy that battleship was Helena's responsibility. For the first time since the Human ship crashed on Antares, Helena allowed fear to creep into her mind. Could she really kill these people she's come to know and possibly admire? Could she destroy Nathan when the time came? Were her doubts founded?

No. Now wasn't the time to falter. Helena cleared her mind and scanned the crowd of Humans, her enemies. These people could never be her friends.

"Here we are," Stugardt said as he stopped and swept his other arm towards a table of seated guests. "My wife, Nadine, the famous reporter and universal traveler."

Helena smiled and said, "I am pleased to meet you, Nadine."

Tall, gaunt and gray, Nadine rose and shook Helena's hand. Though the gesture was shocking when she first arrived on Terra, Helena had accepted the Human custom as second nature.

"Oh hell," Nadine said as she pulled Helena into an embrace. Though her voice was weak from her years, strength resounded from within the woman's soul. "Thank you for saving my Gregory out there in space. All these years worrying, and he comes closest to danger *after* he retires."

Why did these Humans push physical contact so much? Did they respect no boundaries?

Helena waited for Nadine to release her grip. Then, she straightened her gown and said, "The admiral has been most kind to me on my journey."

Another Human male stood and extended his hand. "Lady Helena, I'm Josh. The admiral's son."

Helena took the hand but braced herself for another hug. Luckily, Josh wasn't interested.

"This is my wife, Chloe, and my kids – Adam and Hillary," Josh said.

Helena greeted everyone at the table and she was about to leave when the girl, Hillary, approached.

"Yes, my dear?" Helena said.

"Why is your face like that," the girl said.

Chloe choked on her water and said, "Hillary, come back here!" Turning to Helena, the embarrassed mother said, "I'm sorry-"

Helena kneeled and said, "No need to apologize. Children ask the most amazing questions. How old are you, Hillary?"

"I'm five," Hillary said as she splayed her hand out for everyone to see.

"Five solars old," Helena said. "Do you know, Hillary, why I am here?"

Hillary shook her head.

"Well," Helena said, "I'm here because my planet wants to be friends with your planet. I've answered many questions over the past few days, but you are only the second Human to ask about my markings." Helena turned to the table. "Isn't that amazing, the mind of a child? Sometimes, the most important information can be gained from the simplest of questions."

Helena knew the meaning of her words was lost on the Humans. They had no way of knowing that the early Antaran people used the markings to perfect their mental discipline. When the lines no longer moved, then complete control was obtained. Someone could tell Helena that the planet was about to explode, and her training would keep every line on her face in perfect alignment. This was but one step in a long regimen of mental discipline. Nathan had asked about the markings, so he knew. But the Council was too disinterested. Fools.

"Well, my dear," Helena said, "the lines represent my royal heritage. They mean I am a... What's your word? Oh yes, *princess*."

Hillary's eyes widened. "A princess?"

Helena tapped the girl on the nose and said, "That is correct."

Stugardt offered his arm to Helena again and said, "If we take this long at every table, we'll miss dinner. My Lady?"

Helena stood and wrapped her arm around the admiral's. Everyone expressed their pleasure at meeting Helena and she sensed their sincerity. She had duped them all, so far.

As Stugardt led her to another table, Helena said, "Nice that your family is allowed to be here. I sense much joy in your heart when you are with them."

"It was the least the navy could do," Stugardt said. "After they begged me to return to duty as an advisor."

"Advisor?"

"Though everyone still calls me by my old title," Stugardt said, "I can never again join active service. However, because I believe so strongly that you can bring a swift end to the Proxan conflict, I agreed to come along as a tactical advisor."

Helena sensed the conflict in the man. He wanted to return home, but his duty to Terra still held him tight. Perhaps they weren't so different, after all.

Stugardt introduced Helena to Humans from all manner of life – military, scientific, education and political. Helena stored each name, face and duty in her mental catalog. Then, she was left alone at the head table.

"I'll be right over there if you need me," Stugardt said, pointing to his table.

Helena sat and sipped her water as she scanned the room. The Humans carried on their conversations, looking at Helena from time to time. Some of them were bored or hungry. Nobody seemed too interested, except one individual.

This Human had just arrived on Terra. He stared at Helena and she was careful not to catch his eye. People called him 'Rowe'. She didn't have a chance to probe further, however, as Councilor Durgess began to speak.

"Distinguished guests," the councilor said, "we welcome you here today to announce the alliance between Terra and Antares."

♦

The night dragged into the early morning hours and most of the guests had departed. Helena accepted a dance with Admiral Stugardt and noticed that Rowe was still watching her.

As she danced she found an opening into Rowe's thoughts. He was an assassin. Though his mind was slippery, Helena learned that his orders were to shadow her and kill her if she exposed Human secrets.

Of course. The math came together in Helena's mind and formulae without known variables suddenly clicked together. The Antarans enjoyed open lives. Reading a mind was just as acceptable as noticing another person's hair color. To the Antarans, there was no invasion of privacy.

As a contrast, the Humans lead private lives. They would do things and then regret them. They kept secrets from their neighbors. Helena's mere presence in the room exposed the Humans, as all their secrets lay unshielded from the alien mind reader. Scientific, military and political knowledge was there for the taking.

The math settled into one conclusion as her eyes wandered to the marines stationed at each exit – the Humans would never allow her to return home. That would be an awful risk for the Humans to take now that they allowed Helena into their midst. And they realized this fact.

Chapter 15

As Helena exited the banquet room, she sensed Rowe behind her. The Human assassin was aware of her abilities and he seemed amused that his current task was so simple – remain in plain sight and kill the Antaran Heir if she attempted to contact anyone.

Rejoined with her guards, Helena weaved through the abandoned chairs and tables of the banquet hall and ushered the praetorians into her room. Her heart pounded in her chest. An assassin? For her?

Speaking in code Helena said, "We are certainly being watched. I don't think they intend to allow us to leave as we could compromise all their secrets. I can't believe I overlooked this possibility."

The praetorians waited, but Helena hadn't calculated her solution yet. How could she have been so naïve? The sudden and unexpected realization of a seemingly self-evident truth was always bitter.

Should she tell Admiral Stugardt? Captain Connor? Were they strong enough allies to secure her passage home so she could speak with her family? Her mind abuzz with activity, Helena shook her head. A Human gesture Valeria would no doubt chide her for using.

"Okay," Helena said, dropping out of code. "I just need a few moments to meditate."

"Of course, My Lady," Duronious said. "We'll keep an eye on you from the other room."

"Thank you, Centurion."

Helena sat in the center of her room with her feet together. She attempted to clear her mind, but the clutter from the past few days refused to be swept away from her consciousness. Two days ago, when she was face to face with the Human Council, her lies were easy to build. She pledged, on behalf of her people, that the Antarans would offer their tactical services to the Human military in the war effort against the Proxans. After the Council, Helena was whisked from one place to another to meet with top scientists and political dignitaries. Then, the banquet served as a formal announcement of alliance. The press was there, but they weren't allowed to question her. Admiral Stugardt's family showed her such warmth – a hospitality that she planned to repay with blood. Captain Connor awakened emotions deep within her heart. Emotions that weren't allowed. The assassin Rowe lurked beyond her door, in the hall. Would she ever see her home again? Why couldn't she calm her mind?

Reciting the serenity chant always soothed her nerves, but she had never before been faced with challenges of this magnitude. This time, the serenity chant failed. And so did her meditation. The mind cannot function if the body is deprived, she told herself. So, she decided to take a short rest. Unfortunately, with her thoughts buzzing, rest didn't come easy. She tossed around for what seemed like a few hours.

"Lady Helena?" Duronious whispered from his door.

Pushing aside the frustrating hazy cotton of her non-sleep Helena said, "What is it, Centurion?"

"I'm just reminding the lady that you are due at Human Central Command in a little under an hour."

"What?" Helena shot upright in her bed. When did she get here? Moments ago, she was on the floor, attempting to sleep-meditate. Helena looked to the mirror on the wall and saw her Gima tattoos were as smeared and unkempt as her hair. What happened last night?

"I'll tell the men you'll be ready in fifteen minutes," Duronious said as he closed the door to his adjoining room. Helena sensed a memory fresh on the surface of Duronious's mind. He was the one who scooped her off the floor and placed her on the bed. He feared waking her, so he didn't clean her face.

With no time to dwell on the events of the past night, Helena transformed into a dervish of activity in the washroom. She accomplished a quick shower, a spray of perfume, a jump into a simple dress and a hasty Gima painting in under ten minutes. When she was finished, she gathered herself together again on the floor and attempted to meditate.

This time, she was able to calm her swirling emotions and subdue her fear. Yes, Rowe still waited for her if she attempted to betray Terra, but a peaceful mind was needed for the day's tasks. Everything else would have to wait.

Helena and her guards were sped by aircar to another impressive building, this one in the shape of a pyramid.

"The Human Central Command," Jarvis said from the cockpit area.

Pure white granite rose from the ground at perfect angles to form the massive shape. The building stood in stark contrast to the lush green of the surrounding area.

As Helena and her guards entered, Helena sensed Rowe in the vicinity. He followed in his own aircar and kept Helena in his sights. Her heart skipped when she sensed Rowe move closer so he could get a clearer shot at her head, if necessary.

Jarvis led Helena's group inside and passed them off to a Human female named Commander Bethany Socian. After a few more waiting rooms, the Commander appeared through a side door and said, "Lady Helena, the admiral will see you now. Unfortunately, your guards must remain here."

"I understand," Helena said.

She followed the commander down a long hallway and through a set of secure doors. The room behind the doors was round with a low ceiling. A holographic image moved in the center of the room, throwing a blue glow across the faces of the assembled military men and women. Everyone was laden with medals and insignia.

"Thank you, Commander," a Human man said as he stepped forward and offered his hand. "I'm Admiral Leighton. It is an honor to finally meet you, Lady Helena. Admiral Stugardt sent along his personal regards. He speaks very highly of you."

"Thank you, Admiral," Helena said.

After meeting the other admirals, vice-admirals, captains and commanders in the room, Helena sat with Admiral Leighton at the main console.

"Before we begin," Leighton said, "I'd just like to remind you that everything you see here is *classified* information. You cannot speak of it to anyone else."

Helena's face remained still as a morning lake while she avoided committal and said, "Yes, I understand."

"Good," Leighton said. "I'm going to call-up a display of our current tactical situation. You can access data on all of our assets with the console to your left. I'll give you a few minutes to familiarize yourself with the controls."

"No need," Helena said as she tapped into the collective knowledge in the room to give herself an understanding of the Human interface devices. In moments, she manipulated the scrolling information on several consoles and holographic panes. Supply lines, tactical orders, new constructions, technical readouts, and recent skirmishes blinked into view and yielded their data to her.

"I see," Leighton said.

"I'm going to need a few more hours, at least," Helena said. "Can someone please ensure my guards are tended to?"

"Of course," Leighton said.

♦

After studying reams of military data, Helena pushed away from the console and rubbed her eyes. She covered the material in acceptable time, she thought. After chipping away at the numbers, she realized one truth.

"You are at a stalemate," she said. It wasn't a question.

"Yes," Leighton said. "We have been for many months now."

"I'm surprised," Helena said. "We thought your interstellar communication had a longer range. With all the systems under your control, we just assumed it so."

"We knock out their relay stations and they knock out ours," Leighton said. "Without long-range communication, it's difficult to coordinate massive invasions or respond quickly to attacks. We have both used this to our advantage."

Helena turned back to her console and then to Leighton. "How do you detect each other's communication relays?" she asked.

"Trans-light signals carry a certain wavelength," Leighton said. "They are very 'loud' in the vacuum of space. Very easy to find and destroy."

"I see," Helena said, returning her attention to the screens of information.

"If you have an alternative, I'm listening," Leighton said.

"No alternatives," she said, "just a shift of priorities."

"How do you mean?"

Helena stood and stretched her arms. "Well, if we cannot communicate, then how can we hope to defeat our enemy? You are blind and it is costing you."

Leighton folded his arms across his chest and said, "We cannot protect *every* relay station. That would spread us too thin."

"What will end this war?" Helena asked.

Leighton blinked. "Nothing short of putting a few battleships in orbit around Proxus."

"Very well. You have eight battleships," Helena said. "I have six sisters. I hope you are listening, because I'm about to tell you how to win this war."

Everyone in the room stopped their tasks and looked at the admiral. This man wasn't accustomed to viable competition. He was considered the most brilliant military mind on Terra. The only mark on his record was a chess match against Captain Nathan Connor. Helena risked probing his memory as her curiosity won over caution.

Through the admiral's memory haze, Helena saw that Nathan was on the verge of victory when both of them served on the *Mars*, the oldest battleship. Then, an alert sounded and everyone rushed to their battle stations. The officers on the *Mars* spread the story of Leighton's near defeat and, in response, Leighton almost ruined Nathan's career. To save his reputation, the admiral assigned Nathan to a dead end command while publically questioning his ability to lead.

Helena decided to tread carefully.

"You have our attention," Leighton said, his arms still locked over his chest.

"Okay," Helena said as she expanded the holographic display to show star charts. "Your strategy to keep communication alive is a good one. So with that in mind, and considering your goal to end this conflict, here is what I propose. Rebuild the relay stations starting *now*. However, leave them dormant until you start your offensive."

"Offensive?" Leighton asked.

"Yes," Helena said as she marked the map with a laser pointer. "Rebuild the stations so you can fall back and defend as needed. Then, of course, drop new stations as you advance into Proxan space. Activate all stations once you begin your attack. If one goes out, you know where to send defense forces. Once the location is defended, rebuild or repair the relay and your communication web stays intact all the way to the front lines."

"All of that sounds wonderful," Leighton said, full of loathing. "But how do you propose to take the fight to their doorstep when they have nine battleships and we have eight? It is suicide."

"Do you have the report from Admiral Stugardt?" Helena asked. "The one concerning the Proxan ambush?"

Commander Socian punched some keys on her console and said, "I pushed it through to you, Lady Helena."

"Thank you, Commander," Helena said as she pulled the report up for everyone to see. "You must know my abilities by now. I sensed both the trap and the asteroids. With my guidance, Captain Connor was able to defeat two Proxan frigates with the meager armaments of a freighter. Tell me, Admiral, is there any scenario where a freighter as lightly armed as the *Venture* could defeat one frigate? Two, even?"

"You improvised quite well given your surroundings," Leighton said. "But, if that was open space, you would not be here today."

"What if I could sense your enemy's movements, firing solutions and strategy before they happened?" Helena asked. "Do you think that would even the odds at all?"

Leighton paused. "You can do that?"

"As easily as you can distinguish colors in a painting, Admiral."

Leighton relaxed his arms and said, "Prove it."

He moved to a console and called a tactical display on the screen. "This is a replay of a recent battle-"

Helena shook her head. "I need to be able to sense the Proxan's minds. Plus, I'd have to be a whole lot closer to be able to act with the kind of speed necessary to counter the enemy."

Leighton backed away from the console and studied Helena. "I'm not going to put you and your sisters on my battleships. You aren't Human."

"Is it not your responsibility to win this war?" Helena asked.

"It's too risky. And you can't even prove your claim."

"Did the Council not tell you to utilize me and my abilities to assist with your task?" Helena said.

Leighton grumbled. "Politicians cannot tell me how to do my job."

"Nobody is telling you how to perform your duties," Helena said. "I'm just telling you how I can help. If you are unwilling to utilize my abilities, then this trip was a waste of my time. Yes, you are in a stalemate. No, you will never be free from it unless one side decides to push forward. Can Terra push forward? No. Not unless you start listening to me."

"The plan is sound," one of the vice-admirals said as he studied Helena's solution. "If she can really read their minds and predict their actions, then we certainly gain a big upper hand."

"I'm just not convinced," Leighton said.

Why did the Humans need to *see* everything to believe in it? Did they not trust each other?

Helena sighed. Yet another Human quirk she had developed during her stay. "Admiral, you were about to tell me to leave for a few minutes so you could discuss things with your senior staff. Commander Socian is contemplating going out on a blind date tonight. Vice-Admiral Toby is wondering if his anniversary gift will be enough to please his wife of three years. Admiral Vincen is considering a bathroom break in the next few minutes. Commander Grier is agonizing over what he's going to have for lunch, as the freeze-dried meal he brought with him today is not sounding good anymore. And Admiral Hert's ex-wife is using his credit line at a jewelry store as we speak."

After a moment of silence, the room erupted in laughter. With the tension broken, Helena said, "I know I didn't cover everyone, but how's that for predicting their next actions and reading what's on their minds? How did I do, Admiral? Are we finished with these wasteful tests? Can we talk about how we are going to defeat the Proxans?"

The assembled Humans clapped, smiled and pointed at each other. Helena didn't want to resort to parlor tricks, but stooping to their base level of understanding was strangely effective. Humans were so simple.

"Alright," Leighton said, smiling for the first time. "If you can do something like that on the battlefield, this might work. Let's take a look at this solution of yours and study the details."

♦

Admiral Leighton walked Helena outside after their day long strategy session. In the end, Helena accomplished her goal. The daughters of Emperor Agreios would be allowed onto the bridges of the Human battleships.

Helena sensed tension from her guards and surprise from Leighton as the late evening breeze washed over her body. Too late, she realized what was going on. With her attention fixated on her other tasks, she neglected to keep aware of her surroundings. Human soldiers surrounded the building. An armored aircar and Ambassador Jarvis awaited her. This was what she feared. The Humans couldn't let her roam free anymore, she was too dangerous.

"I'm very sorry, My Lady, but you are being moved to another residence for the time being," Jarvis said as he fidgeted with one of his rings.

Admiral Leighton furrowed his brow and said, "What's going on here?"

"The Council has decided that the Antarans prove too large a risk to national security," Jarvis said. "She's not under arrest, but she is to be watched."

"Don't you mean *detained*?" Helena said.

Jarvis nodded. "Unfortunately, you are not permitted to leave Terra at this time."

Chapter 16

"This is total garbage," Admiral Stugardt said over the holo-communicator.

Though Helena was permitted to receive the call, Rowe watched over her shoulder. Duronius eyed the Human and kept his ready violence below the surface. If Rowe made a move, Helena and Duronius would sense it.

"I have been quite agreeable throughout this process," Helena said. "The false ambassador, The Chamber of Truth, and now this? What more must I do to prove my intentions?"

Clearly upset, Stugardt said, "I'll see what I can do you get you a hearing or something. They're not being reasonable."

"Thank you, Admiral," she said. "Oh, and did my gift arrive?"

Stugardt smiled and said, "Yes, Hillary has been beaming from ear to ear since it arrived. You didn't have to do that for my granddaughter."

"As my note stated, that is a royal fan fit for a princess," Helena said. "It is very old and I was saving it as a gift for someone special on Terra. Make sure she knows how highly I regard her sweetness."

"Again, thank you," Stugardt said. "I'm heading to the Embassy right now."

Helena nodded as the holo-image faded. She turned to Rowe and stared into his eyes. "You can leave now," she said.

Rowe smiled as he removed the transmitter chip from the communication station. "I'll just be needing this," he said. "Council orders. No unauthorized communications."

After Rowe exited the small living quarters, Duronius sat next to Helena and put his hand on her shoulder.

"Don't let him rattle you," the Centurion said. "He's just a thug, nothing more."

"I know," Helena said, "which is why I'm so frustrated with myself. I should have seen all of this coming."

"We'll get through it," Duronius said, "one way or another."

"How are the men doing?" Helena asked, though she sensed their anxiousness and fear.

"I'll talk to them," Duronius said. "But I think they're fine."

Helena exhaled the breath she had carried around for the past few hours. "Thank you, Centurion. You have a calming way about you."

Duronius nodded and resumed his watch near the door.

Closing her eyes and clasping her mother's prayer beads, Helena allowed the maelstrom of thoughts to swirl in her mind for a few moments. She *needed* to talk with her father and sisters. So many things had changed. The existence of a second tellium star modified everything, as did Helena's new knowledge of Human ways and Proxan anatomy. Should she try to sneak away? If she had a ship, the task would be a simple one. No, that would put them right back where they started – powerless and on the outside of a war they didn't want in their skies.

Helena swam through the strands of time to the days when her mother was her teacher. How warm and safe those memories remained. An image materialized into view. Young Helena brushed her mother's silver hair and asked question after question. Her mother was about to start a long trip around the cities of Antares to gain support for the emperor's new religion which saw the deification of her family. Though the idea was set in motion by Helena's grandfather, this act represented a major shift in Antaran religion. Then, Helena's mother spoke to her. The quote rang in her mind as clear as a mountain echo.

"Win the people and you win the Empire," her mother had said.

Helena opened her eyes. Of course! The solution was as simple as it was brilliant. Win the people. All she needed was someone with enough media clout to get some exposure. For that, Admiral Stugardt might still be of use.

"Duronious," Helena said. "Can you fetch Rowe for me, please?"

The praetorian nodded and opened the door.

"The lady wishes a word with you."

Rowe entered the room again, flipping the transmitter chip between his fingers. He stopped two paces away, raised both his eyebrows and waited.

Helena sensed a moral flexibility in Rowe that frightened her. He considered life as trivial as a piece of food caught between his teeth. There would be no reasoning with this man.

"Rowe, I wish to make another call to the admiral," Helena said.

"Which one?"

"Stugardt," Helena said. "I wish to catch him before he reaches the Embassy. There was something I forgot to tell him."

Duronious caught her signal and moved closer to the door to block Rowe's escape.

Rowe eyed the chip and then turned to Helena. "Sorry, only one call per day."

"You can't be serious," Helena said. "I was *just* speaking to him."

Rowe turned to leave, but Helena was faster. She snatched the chip at the moment where Rowe was most off balance. He reached for his pistol, but Helena anticipated that action. She chopped at his elbow, disabling the joint and delivered a swift kick to his throat. Rowe fell to the ground, unable to speak and clutching his neck with his one good hand. Duronious locked the door and propped the Human on a chair as one of the other praetorians removed Rowe's pistol and dagger.

The fake ambassador Bergem taught Helena one important lesson. Don't hesitate.

"Now you listen to me," Helena said. "I'm going to make my call and you are going to watch. Blink once if you understand."

Rowe blinked.

"Good. Now, sit there and don't even think of trying to attack me. I can anticipate your actions before your brain can send the signal to your muscles. Further, it seems I'm better trained in hand-to-hand combat. I'd hate to break any of your bones, but I will if I must."

Helena jammed the chip into the communicator and dialed Stugardt's mobile device. Seconds later, the admiral's face appeared on the holo-screen. He was traveling in an aircar.

"Lady Helena," he said. "What can I do for you? I'm on my way to the Embassy."

"First," Helena said as she panned the camera to Rowe, "here rests the Human assassin sent to keep tabs on me. He wouldn't let me make another call, so I was forced to subdue him."

"Are you sure that was a good idea?" Stugardt said.

"To be frank, Admiral, I am just treating my captors as they have treated me. Open disregard and little respect," Helena said. "And my time is too valuable to be wasted here."

"I see," Stugardt said. "This may make things more difficult with the Council."

"Forget the Council," Helena said. "I'm done with them. I'd really like to meet with you and your lovely wife, however. Perhaps for a late breakfast? I forget what you Humans call that meal…"

"Brunch?" Stugardt said. "Nadine would be thrilled. I'll come and pick you up. Give me an hour?"

"Sounds perfect," Helena said.

"Will you be alright until then?"

Helena turned to Rowe and said, "Oh yes. I think we have an understanding between us now."

"Okay."

"Oh, one more thing," Helena said. "Please have Nadine prepare an interview for me on live broadcast, if possible."

"Really?" Stugardt said. "She's retired you know."

"Does she still have connections to the media?" Helena asked.

"Sure, of course."

"Perfect, have her give the interview to someone she knows then," Helena said. "And tell them to announce it as soon as possible."

"Okay," Stugardt said, unsure why Helena was asking for this. "This may take longer to coordinate."

"That's fine," Helena said. "We can have our brunch first, then interview afterwards. It's very important that the interview is announced now, however. I want as many people watching as possible."

"They may try to quash you," Stugardt said. "The Council isn't releasing many details about our alliance, though rumors have already been spreading."

"I understand that we do not want to reveal our tactical advantage yet," Helena said. "I will not speak of my mental abilities. You have my word."

"That's good enough for me," Stugardt said. "I'll see you in an hour."

The holo-image faded away and Helena turned to Duronious. "Gag him."

As the Centurion gagged the Human, Helena said, "I'm sorry, but I just don't trust you for the next hour. After that, you are welcome to join us and we will give you your weapons back. You can try to arrest me, but I'm sure the press would be interested to know why an unnamed assassin raised his hand against a diplomatic guest. You would be ruined, unable to resume your duties in the shadows. What need does Terra have for assassins who cause such a visible ruckus? They'll just replace you, and I sense your work is the only thing you care for. I'm happy to see you back doing what you normally do after this is over. Just sit there and don't get in my way."

"We're ready," Duronius said as he applied the gag to Rowe.

Appearing as if nothing was amiss, Helena and her guards exited the suite and asked to be transported to brunch with Admiral Stugardt. Since Rowe usually slinked out of sight, the Humans didn't think anything was wrong. After they confirmed the appointment with the admiral, they carried Helena to what she hoped would be her freeing speech.

Stugardt hugged her when she arrived and was full of nervous energy. He was fearful Helena's actions against Rowe would worsen things. Nadine also worried for Helena and they exchanged few pleasantries while they hurried through their meal.

Then, with cameras broadcasting, Helena began her campaign to win the common people of Terra.

"And they gave you no reason for your detainment?" Nadine asked. Though retired, the former reporter arranged to be the interviewer for a rare alien exclusive. All the major networks carried the breaking news.

Helena shook her head and allowed false meekness to show on her painted face. "I met with the Human Council. We talked and arranged an alliance, as your broadcasts earlier in the week reported. Then, when it was time for me to return to my family – as Heir to my throne – I was detained by the soldiers you see behind me."

The camera panned to the Human military presence. As Nadine remarked about the size and strength of the force, Helena reached outwards with her mind to the Embassy. She sensed the Council members rushing to their holo-sets, in shock over the interview. Let them scramble.

Nadine returned her attention to her interviewee and said, "I hear you're making the best of your situation, though?"

Helena smiled for the camera. "Yes. I have already contacted the nearby hospitals. On my homeworld, I am an accomplished surgeon. Indeed, when the recent Human starship crashed into our capital city, I was in the emergency ward helping save Human lives. I believe you have video?"

Nadine nodded. "As you can see in the corner of your screen, this is footage from a hospital on Antares. You may recognize some of our navy men and women. There you are, Lady Helena. You can see the Heir of Antares, a royal princess, on the front lines in her hospital saving Human lives. Powerful images-"

"Yes," Helena said. "So, I'm heading to Mercy Hospital in about an hour to talk with their chief of medicine. I brought along some formulae and other medical knowledge that my people have developed. I hope it can help the Human people. My people are only interested in sharing our knowledge with the Human Confederation. I wish I knew why the Council chose to keep me here against my will."

Nadine frowned and faced the camera. "Talk to your local representatives. The Human Council's treatment of off-worlders has shown a poor track record in recent years. We should be embracing our neighbors and learning from their technology and cultures. Watch me again tonight, as I'll have footage of the Lady Helena at Mercy Hospital and beyond. She is an amazing woman and I hope to see her safely home sometime soon."

"We're off!" a representative from the network said. "Great story, Nadine."

Helena clasped Nadine's hand and said, "Thank you. I know this must have been difficult for you to arrange."

Nadine dismissed Helena's concern with a wave of her hand. "You saved my husband. Plus, I'm appalled at how you've been treated."

"I think your government believes they have the biggest stick, so they use it to push the little planets around," Helena said.

"Well, thanks for the footage from your homeworld," Nadine said. "That'll get the people all stirred up."

Admiral Stugardt emerged from the cluster of cameramen and technical specialists. Helena sensed urgency in his manner.

"The Council has already called me," Stugardt said. "And Admiral Leighton. They're pretty angry at you two."

Nadine smiled and closed her eyes. "Music to a reporter's ears."

"They ordered those soldiers to escort you back to the Embassy. By force, if necessary," Stugardt said.

Nadine opened her eyes. "Really?" She turned to her crew. "Keep those cameras online!"

By now, a throng of onlookers gathered in the public square where the interview had taken place. Helena chose the location, as she suspected the Council would make that order as a counter. She decided to take her time walking towards Nadine's aircar to give the people a chance to see what would happen.

"Well, I would like to keep my appointment at the hospital," Helena said. "Are you up for this, Nadine?"

Nadine furrowed her brow in a determined stare. "Are you kidding me? This is what I live for!"

"Honey-" Stugardt said. He was unsure open defiance was a good plan and Helena sensed his fear.

"They know you don't control me," Nadine said as she took Helena's arm. "Do what you want to do, Greg. You know this is wrong and so do I. I'm going to fight it with Helena."

Stugardt sighed. "Just be careful."

Nadine led Helena to her aircar with the press close behind. The gathered onlookers followed them and voiced their support. Then, the soldiers advanced.

In one smooth motion, Nadine turned to the camera and said, "Is this how our Council honors the freedom of the press? By arresting us for telling the truth?"

Helena projected her voice over the crowd. "Why would your soldiers assault me?" Helena said, touching each mind and implanting a subtle suggestion to peacefully resist the soldiers. Marcella was better at this than Helena, but she knew enough to be dangerous. "I have done nothing wrong."

Though she didn't want to use them as shields, she sensed the Council would back down to avoid a scene. Sure enough, a group of citizens broke from the crowd and sat in the path of the approaching army vehicle. The cameras rolled as the vehicle came to a stop. Soldiers dismounted and stepped over the civilians.

"And they still come for her," Nadine said to the camera. "I have sources telling me that I am to be placed under arrest as well. Where have our freedoms gone?"

A soldier from the truck called to the advancing force, "Stop! We have orders to cease."

The men hesitated and Helena sensed Rowe hidden in the truck. He was livid. New orders came directly from the Council. They were pressured by several influential lobbies and representatives to stay their hand for now. Of course, those other parties didn't know about Helena's abilities. That didn't matter. She had accomplished the first part of her plan. Now, the hearts of the Human people were open to her. Helena smiled when she thought of how easy those hearts would be to win.

Chapter 17

"On behalf of the Human Council, please accept our apologies and our wishes for a safe and swift journey home," Ambassador Jarvis said, more to the cameras than to Helena.

Helena nodded and said, "I accept your apology for this misunderstanding."

With the cameras finally off, Helena felt relief wash over her weary heart. Three days of constant public appearances, speeches, and technology sharing physically and mentally wore her down. Nadine was a trooper through everything and captured every moment for the growing crowds behind their holo-sets. On the fourth day, the Council caved and allowed her passage home. When they saw that Helena did not divulge her secret about the Antaran's mental discipline, the Council agreed she was acting in good faith. Admiral Leighton arranged for the *Jupiter*, the Human flagship, to carry her to Antares. To Helena's delight, Captain Nathan Connor greeted her when she disembarked from her shuttle.

"Good day, Captain," Helena said, ignoring the rest of the welcoming party.

Yes, it was reckless, but she felt her heart quicken at the sight of him. Her physical attraction to the Human was undeniable. Though Helena hoped it was *controllable*. She probed his thoughts and found the interest mutual. Their last meeting at the restaurant solidified his feelings. Helena had replayed that night in her mind more than once over the past few weeks.

"So here we are," Nathan said. "I'd like to officially welcome you aboard the *Jupiter*, where Admiral Leighton has assigned you as my senior tactical advisor. Helping you in your task will be Admiral Stugardt, but he will not be joining us until we depart Antares. My orders allow for one week on Antares, will that be enough time, My Lady?"

Helena smiled and said, "That is very generous. Thank you, Captain."

"We will transport your sisters back to Terra where they will be brought to their assignments," Captain Connor said. "Is everything as you expected?"

"Yes." Helena wanted to say more, but she held her words. She didn't want to seem too chatty with him.

"I also understand that a Human agent will also be aboard," Nathan said. "This man, Rowe, will be allowed frequent contact with Terra and he is to monitor your transmissions? Is that correct?"

Helena boiled, but she didn't allow the emotion to surface. "That is correct. The Council wishes to keep apprised of my activities."

"We'll make sure he doesn't get in the way of your duties," Nathan said, winking at her. She melted. Nobody had ever shown her this much attention. She was the heir to her empire. She was untouchable.

"Now," he said, "I believe you know Lieutenant Sandra Rhom?"

Helena blinked to clear the haze of her infatuation. Now was not the time to forget her training. "Yes, indeed. I am glad to see you again, Lieutenant."

Sandra smiled and said, "I'm happy to see you too!"

Then, like Nadine and countless other Humans, Sandra embraced Helena in that cozy Human hug. "I've missed you. Thanks again for saving our skins out there against those Proxan frigates."

"Certainly," Helena said.

"Lieutenant."

"Sorry sir," Sandra said. "My Lady, allow me to escort you and your guards to your quarters. You'll be right near the bridge."

"And after that, a tour?" Helena said, though she knew those were the Lieutenant's next words.

"If you're up to it of course," Sandra said.

"I have much to learn about this vessel," Helena said.

♦

Helena spent the next three days studying the *Jupiter*. Weapons, propulsion, defensive systems, support craft, sensors and communications – she examined and analyzed everything. Sleep came in small doses and Helena almost didn't notice Nathan watching her as she reviewed the latest data set in the war room. She had been alone for many hours.

"I'm sorry," Nathan said. "I didn't mean to disturb you."

Helena straightened herself and tidied her hair. She must look a mess!

"I could use a break," she said. She rubbed her eyes lightly, lest she disturb her Gima markings.

"I brought you coffee," Nathan said as he placed a cup under her nose and sat across the table.

Coffee. Stronger than her beloved tea, this Human drink kept her active long after her body waved the white flag. Helena sipped and closed her data display.

"Thank you, Captain."

His eyes travelled the length of her face and he said, "Nathan… remember? Please, call me Nathan."

She smiled. "Thank you, *Nathan*."

"Don't mention it. I'm just glad to get a few minutes alone with you."

"Is something on your mind?" she asked.

"Can't you read it?"

"I try not to *invade*, as you Humans call it," Helena said. "You value your privacy and I try to honor that."

"You try?"

Helena smiled. "Sometimes your emotions are so close to the surface, I can't help but notice."

"Ah… I see," he said.

Before he entered the room, Helena sensed Rowe.

"Here you are," Rowe said, stalking towards her. "There's a communication device in this room. You're not allowed in here without my supervision!"

"Calm yourself, Agent Rowe," Nathan said. "That's no way to speak to a superior officer."

Rowe spat. "Superior officer?"

"On my ship, my advisors are part of my senior staff, got it?"

"Whatever. I don't answer to you, Captain."

Nathan stood and glared at Rowe. "On my ship, sir, you do!"

"My orders come from the Council," Rowe said. "And she's not allowed near an unattended communicator!"

Helena closed her eyes and exhaled. She wanted to throttle him again, but that might cause trouble.

"Well?" Rowe asked.

Without opening her eyes, Helena said, "I had the communications officer, Lieutenant Rhom, disable the transmitter in this room before I came down here. Check the logs, check with the Lieutenant, check the device right now if you want… I don't care which."

Rowe moved to the communicator and fidgeted with the console for a minute. "Okay. I'm going to review the logs to make sure nothing was sent from this terminal. In the meantime, I assume you'll watch her, Captain?"

"Well," Captain Connor said as he returned to his chair, "that doesn't sound too bad."

Rowe stormed from the war room and Helena opened her eyes.

"I don't think I like him," she said.

Nathan laughed. "I'm not a mind reader and I already guessed that one."

"I don't think he likes me either," Helena said. "But that's probably because I kicked him in the throat."

"Kicked him? What?"

Helena smiled and rose from her seat. "I'm exhausted, Nathan. Perhaps I'll tell you the story another time."

He mirrored her movement, a gesture that was considered polite by the Humans. "I'd definitely like to hear that one."

After walking her to the corridor, his smile melted her again. His charm was undeniable.

"Listen," he said, "we have to make a quick detour. Something I promised an old friend."

"Detour?" Helena asked. "Now?"

"I gave my word," he said, "and that's something I take very seriously."

"How long of a detour?" she asked.

"Not long," he said as he leaned closer. "I'm only telling you because... well-"

"You want me to go with you," she said.

He looked into her eyes and said, "I thought you were trying *not* to constantly read our minds?"

"My apologies," she said.

He eyed her and waited.

"I really don't have any details from your mind," she said. "Please, continue."

"Well, I'll be taking a shuttle down to the surface and I was wondering if you wanted to accompany me."

"I do not think I can spare the time…"

"I know you have much to learn about the *Jupiter*," he said, interrupting her. "However, I have somewhat of a surprise planned for you. I think you'll like it."

"A surprise?" Helena refrained from scanning his thoughts. The idea of a surprise delighted her.

"Though," he said, "I suppose you already know what I have planned?"

Helena shook her head. "Absolutely not. I will respect your privacy."

"So…?"

"You are most gracious, Nathan. Of course I will accompany you."

"Great," he said. "Get some sleep. You are off-duty tomorrow."

"So soon?"

He shifted on his feet. "Sorry for the short notice. It took me a few days to build the nerve to ask you."

Helena touched his arm and felt his muscles tense. She knew she was foolish to accept his invitation. However she was only marginally under control in his presence. "You Humans are so silly sometimes," she said. "What do you have to fear from a simple invitation?"

Nathan chuckled and said, "Well, rejection."

"Have I said *no* to you yet?"

Chapter 18

Helena pulled on the yoke of the spacecraft and watched as the bow rose in the air. Though Nathan was a good teacher, Helena's nerves were close to the edge. She'd never piloted anything before!

"Good, very good," Nathan said. "Now, I'm lowering the landing gear."

Helena clenched her teeth as the captain's yacht careened towards the runway. Was it always this fast? She was accustomed to resting in the royal quarters while her Antaran aircraft whisked her from city to city on her homeworld.

The spacecraft lurched when the wheels touched the ground and Helena allowed a frightened yelp escape her lips.

"Now, apply the brakes slowly," Nathan said. "Here, let me show you."

Nathan covered her hand with his own and suddenly the landing wasn't the most exhilarating thing anymore. His touch replaced everything in her world. The feel of his Human flesh against her own was dangerous and provocative. She knew she couldn't allow it, yet she craved it.

Shrugging his hand aside, Helena said, "I can do it."

"Okay," he said. "Just apply it smoothly. When you feel resistance, don't go further… good. See? You're a natural!"

Helena pulled the yacht into a hangar bay and locked the wheels in place. "Well," she said, "I think you are a good teacher."

As Nathan unstrapped his safety belts, he said, "These days, they practically fly themselves." Recognizing her look of disdain, he said, "Not to take anything away from what you just did, though."

Helena smiled. "I've always been a fast learner."

"Ready for Caledonia?" he asked.

Nathan opened the hatch to the yacht and led her onto a busy street. Gray skyscrapers rose in the distance behind an orange cloud of smog. Squat, massive buildings filled the space between her and the city proper. Humans bustled along the street and in their aircars. Everything seemed so disorganized compared to a large Antaran city.

"I still don't understand," Helena said as she allowed Nathan to help her into the taxi.

Nathan followed her inside and handed a scrap of paper to the driver.

"As I told you," he said, "I'm here to help an old friend."

"But you are on duty. And Rowe will likely follow us. Certainly this is no time to-"

Nathan interrupted her. "It doesn't matter. I gave my word and I'll take a few extra hours to meet him in person. As for Rowe, well let's just say Lieutenant Rhom will be keeping him occupied. And not in a good way."

"But why bring me?" Helena sensed excitement and subterfuge in Nathan's mind, but no malice. She promised not to pry into his surprise and reason for bringing her, and more than once she almost broke that promise. Almost.

Well, she thought, at least she was in control on *some* matters. She suppressed a sigh.

"I told you. It's a surprise. Of course, for all I know you have already read my mind." Nathan grinned and held her eyes for a few moments.

"I could if I wanted to," she said.

Nathan leaned towards her and said, "Are there no surprises for you anymore?"

Helena mumbled softly, "I'm not accustomed to surprises."

Nathan smiled. "That's because they're too uncommon for you."

As the taxi sped through the air and streets of Caledonia, Helena examined her face in the window. What was she doing? Her mission and her duty to her people should be first in mind, yet she found electricity between her and Nathan. Her heart hummed on a different level when she saw him. And to be sitting so close to him! The proximity was explosive.

"There's the Gaffer Tower," he said, reaching his arm across her space to point through her window.

Nodding, Helena said, "Impressive."

He was wearing a simple gray jumpsuit and jacket. Helena had grown accustomed to seeing him in his uniform. His civilian clothing only fanned her interest as she found the man behind the uniform just as pleasing as the starship captain.

The taxi hovered near a platform on the docks of a dirty river. Nathan and Helena exited and were met by a small group of grimy Humans in workman's clothing. One of them stepped forward and shook Nathan's hand.

"It's been a long time, Captain," the Human said.

"Too long, Sean," Nathan said.

Sean eyed Helena and said, "I see you're not alone?"

Falling into her well-trained habits, Helena scanned Sean's mind for violence and found the man a hard working leader amongst his people at these docks. He oversaw a large community of immigrants struggling from the economic inequity on Caledonia. Several years ago, Nathan helped Sean and his people settle on Caledonia, yet their relationship formed before those events. Sean helped Nathan with something emotional and important. Nathan still felt he owed Sean a great debt.

"This is Helena, from Antares," Nathan said.

"Nice to meet you milady," Sean said.

Helena tilted her head towards Sean and said, "You as well."

"To tell you the truth," Sean said, "I wasn't sure you'd show."

"I gave you my word," Nathan said.

Sean shrugged. "These days, *words* don't seem to be enough. We've hit some rough times."

"Well, I'm here and I'll help however I can," Nathan said.

Sean fidgeted with his belt and avoided eye contact. "What we really need," he said, "well, it's almost too much to ask. But I don't have anyone else to turn to."

"You know I'll do what I can."

"Yeah," Sean said, squinting to meet Nathan's eye. "That's why I feel like crap for even asking you. You'd be dumb enough to actually say 'yes.' Well, here goes. We need medical supplies-"

"Done," Nathan said.

"For a hundred thousand people."

Nathan whistled and raised his eyebrows. "That'd clean me out. I'd get more than a mere reprimand."

"Caledonia still sees us as outsiders," Sean said. "We really have no way of caring for our injured, sick and our young."

"Your government does not care for its people?" Helena asked. "How is this possible?"

Nathan shook his head and said, "Only when a citizen cannot afford their own medical care. However, Sean's people are still considered immigrants here on Caledonia. They really have no recourse if they cannot afford it."

"So," Helena said, "in many ways, your culture expects its citizens to fend for themselves?"

"There's always a way," Nathan said. "Okay, Sean, give me a minute."

Nathan led Helena away from the group and contacted the *Jupiter* on his mobile communicator.

While waiting for a response Helena said, "You are going to hand over the *Jupiter's* supplies?"

Nathan nodded. "I gave him my word I would do anything in my power to help him if the need ever arose. I am keeping my word."

"How did he help you?" Helena said.

Nathan paused, but his communicator was still dark. Then he said, "When my parents were accused of Proxan sympathy, they were sent to a detainment camp. Sean helped me rescue them from a fate of hardship and isolation."

"I see," Helena said. "And that is cause for you to compromise the *Jupiter's* supplies? You would put your crew in danger to fulfill your oath?"

"Of course not," Nathan said as his communicator flashed into life and Lieutenant Sandra Rhom's face appeared on the device.

"Yes, Captain?" she said.

"Lieutenant," Nathan said, "I need you to do me a favor."

"Sure, Captain," she said.

"We need another full spread of medical supplies for *Jupiter's* medical bays," he said.

"Sir, we're already-"

"I know, Lieutenant," he said, "it's not for us. I want you to arrange a trade with one of the merchant houses here on Caledonia. We're carrying several tons of useless star cataloging equipment in hangar bay seven. By the time we get around to delivering that stuff to the science lab at Vega, the war will be over. I'm sure hangar bay seven will suffer battle damage between now and then. We may as well help some people out here with the value of that equipment before it's lost to a Proxan torpedo. Understood?"

Sandra smiled and said, "Aye, Captain. I'll get right on it."

"I'm sending you the address for delivery of the supplies," he said.

"Aye, Captain," she said. "I'll let you know when everything's arranged."

"Thanks, Lieutenant," he said as he cut the uplink.

"That's sneaky," Helena said, impressed with Nathan's ingenuity.

"Sometimes, you have to make your own equilibrium," he said. "Sean's people need those medical supplies more than the scientists at Vega need their lenses and lasers."

As they walked towards the waiting Humans, Helena said, "Besides, as you said, cargo bay seven may fall victim to the rigors of space battle. It would be a pity if all that equipment were destroyed."

"I'm actually saving it, if you think about it," he said with a playful smirk on his face. "Maybe it will make its way to Vega faster in the hands of a merchant house. After all, we're at war and it could be quite some time before we're in the Vega system."

Helena smiled as she enjoyed his fiesty gambit. "Excellent point."

"You're all set," Nathan said.

Sean cocked his head to the side and said, "What?"

"The supplies should be here within a few days," Nathan said. "Enough for everyone."

The Humans gasped and smiled at each other. Sean stepped forward and embraced Nathan in a manly hug.

"You're the man," Sean said. "I feel like a jerk for doubting you."

Nathan tightened his grip and whispered into his ear, "No, my friend, it is *you* who is still the better of us. You've sacrificed enough. I will always be here to help, however I can."

Helena eyed Nathan as they reentered the waiting taxi. He noticed her attention and said, "What is it?"

"You are a very interesting Human, Nathan Connor."

He smiled and said, "How do you mean, Helena…?" He paused, distressed.

"Your intuition is correct," she said as she sensed the reason for his alarm. "You have never heard my surname. And that is because I do not have one. Antaran females are not given their family's surname at birth like Humans. Instead, we either live our life without one or we inherit our husband's surname."

"Now *that's* interesting," he said. "Me? I'm not too interesting."

"I must disagree," she said. "Your actions with Sean speak to your strength of character. From what I have read about your culture, such acts of kindness are not commonplace."

"The media prefers stories of violence," he said. "I'm not surprised if all you've heard about Human life is our history of war, murder and greed."

Helena nodded. "From what I've studied, that sounds accurate. Of course, since I have arrived, my opinion has changed. Your ability to terraform your world into one of beauty is a marvelous achievement. People like Admiral Stugardt, Nadine and yourself have given me hope that your race is not a lost cause."

"Lost cause…" he said. "I hope we're not *that* bleak in your eyes."

Helena allowed the question to linger as they sped through the streets in their taxi. Buildings, other vehicles and pedestrians whipped by her window in a blur of brown and gray. The smog-filled sky cast a sickly pallor on everything and everyone. This planet wasn't as beautiful as Terra.

After a few minutes, she asked, "We are headed deeper into the city?"

Nathan nodded.

The taxi landed in a crowded market and Helena coughed when she inhaled the pollution. Humans pressed together in an amorphous mass. Hawkers yelled to attract customers. Pickpockets moved amongst the shoppers, searching for easy marks. The aroma of street-cooked food mingled with the smog to constitute a heavy air.

"You can buy anything here," Nathan said as he led her through the throng of people.

"I've... I've never seen anything quite like this," she said as she held her kerchief to her mouth.

"Aha! Here it is," Nathan said and he held her arm and they ducked under a low overhang.

Her eyes adjusted to the dim light. As if a curio store had erupted from the ground, oddities and trinkets surrounded them. Helena had never seen such a vast assortment of junk and unidentifiable items in her life. Shoppes on Antares had a purpose and usually a theme. This place had neither. Cabinets were filled on the inside, on top and underneath with treasures. Furniture and mounds of cloth partially blocked her view to the rest of the interior. Only narrow, meandering pathways gave the store a semblance of structure. A Human man with thinning grey hair smiled from behind a counter.

"Look around," Nathan said. "I love coming here."

Helena remained at his side and whispered, "Why?"

"I guess I like the uncertainty of this little store," he said. "I always find some fascinating things."

"More surprises," Helena said. "You Humans are odd indeed."

Nathan turned towards the counter and Helena sensed his misstep before he made it. His arm knocked over a tall, glass and gold smoking pipe. Before he could open his mouth to gasp, Helena darted forward and caught the pipe. She placed it on its table, with a dozen other oddities.

"Please try to be more careful," she said.

He smiled and continued to the counter. Helena strolled through the place, but there was just too much to look at. She felt that she could have passed by the same section of the store three times and still not see everything. Then something caught her eye. Three orange, glowing orbs held her captive for a few moments. No larger than one of her fingernails, the gas within swirled and danced to its own tune.

"Find anything interesting, Lady Helena?" Nathan asked.

She hadn't heard him approach but she controlled her surprise. "Yes," she said pointing at the tear-shaped globes. "These are exquisite."

Nathan peered through the glass of the curio cabinet to inspect her find. "Very nice," he said. "Let's ask Arthur where they're-"

"They are from a gas planet whose name is long forgotten," the shopkeeper said over Nathan's shoulder. Helena hadn't noticed Arthur either. Were the globes interfering with her perception?

"Fascinating. What powers them?" Nathan said.

Arthur opened the cabinet door and said, "Oh, they are self-sustaining." He lifted the three attached globes from their resting place and stepped towards Helena. "May I?"

Helena nodded.

Arthur clasped the globes to her hair over her ear and he examined the fit. "You are a masterpiece, my dear," he said. "Tell me, where are you from?"

"Antares," she said as she inspected her new adornment in a nearby mirror.

"Well, Helena of Antares, I do believe these were meant for you," Arthur said.

"I agree," Nathan said. "How much?"

"Seventeen thousand."

Helena allowed Nathan to pay for the jewelry. The gasses within the globes twisted and changed from a dark yellow to a vibrant red and back again. The motion was both calming and enchanting.

"Thank you," Helena said as they exited the shop. "I love them."

Nathan smiled and said, "My pleasure."

After catching another taxi, they sat in silence for much of the ride. Then, the buildings fell away from Helena's view. Endless water replaced the grimy Human structures. A sandy and rocky beach extended from the road out to the crashing blue waves. Helena's years of training and control melted away in an instant. She gasped and held her hands over her mouth.

Nathan smiled as he watched her. "I know you don't like surprises. But after you told me you've never seen an ocean, I thought about coming here with you."

As the waves rolled, Helena felt lost in Nathan's surprise. Nobody, besides her mother, had ever shown her so much thoughtfulness. Her eyes swelled with water and she attempted to conceal her unabashed joy by turning away and wiping her face.

Her heart was sinking to a place she dared not explore.

Chapter 19

"I... I-" Helena found her words reluctant. She was both awed and terrified at the sight of so much water.

"It's not as nice as the beaches on Terra," Nathan said, "but we were going to be here anyway. And we have a few hours to kill."

"Breathtaking," she said as her composure returned. "I want to get closer."

Nathan tapped the driver on his shoulder and tilted his head towards Helena. "That's the plan."

The taxi stopped in a paved lot next to the beach. Nathan led Helena to the ramp that descended to the sand. He began to remove his shoes.

"What are you doing?" Helena asked as she struggled to retain her balance while gazing upon the enormous ocean.

"Sand is quite uncomfortable when it gets in the shoes," he said as his eyes traveled the length of her body. "Are your feet also tattooed?"

"No," she said, uncertain about the whole beach experience. A few other Humans walked along the banks, but it wasn't crowded like the market.

"Don't worry," Nathan said with a wink, "I promise I won't look at you feet."

"That's not... I just-"

Laughing, he said, "I think this is the first time I've seen you at a loss for words, My Lady."

Helena straightened herself and said, "We are to walk barefoot on the sand, then?"

"It's pretty much mandatory for first-time visitors."

Helena frowned. "Very well," she said as she slipped her shoes into her hand. She knew he was making a joke, but her trepidation over the nearness of so much water left her humorless.

"Don't worry," Nathan said, "I won't let you fall."

"Fall?" she said. "I assure you, I am in no danger of falling on the sand."

"Why so hesitant then?"

Helena exhaled and said, "The sun has already set. Are you sure this is a good idea?"

"We still have a few hours of light," he said, his face unyielding.

"Fine. Let's go walk on this beach before I change my mind."

He smiled and extended his hand. "May I help you down the ramp?"

Leery of his touch, and the emotions it swirled within her heart, Helena coyly refused the offer and walked past him. "I am fine, thank you."

Distance. She needed to remain at a safe distance from this temptation. Well, too late for that, she thought. She should have stayed on the *Jupiter*.

As they walked along the sand, Helena noticed that Nathan was leading her closer to the water. She calculated the rhythm of the surf and decided upon a safe distance. When he tried to bring her closer, she stopped.

"What's wrong?" he asked.

"I'm not sure…" she said.

"The water isn't too cold," he said as he moved close enough for the surf to wash over his feet.

Foolish girl, Helena said to herself as she followed him into the cool water. Her nervousness quickly faded as she felt a childlike glee with each new wave. The roar of the surf, the salt in the air and the crisp breeze combined into a powerful experience.

"See," Nathan said, "I knew you'd like it."

A couple with entwined hands smiled at Nathan and Helena as they passed.

"Are they married?" Helena asked.

Nathan squinted at their backs and said, "I think so."

Helena paused and stood in the ankle-deep water. Puzzled, she said, "Is that common?"

"Is what common?"

She pointed at the couple and said, "Just... spending time with each other like that?"

"Of course," Nathan said. "Is that strange to you?"

Helena cocked her head to the side and said, "I guess for someone in my position, yes. I suppose I'm not very familiar with the everyday life of Antaran citizens, however."

Nathan scooped a smooth rock from the shore and skipped it along the rolling surface of the ocean. "Seems to me," he said as he snatched another rock, "that's an important piece of information for *any* ruler. Wouldn't you agree?"

Before Helena could contemplate his surprisingly insightful words, he stood beside her and said, "Close your eyes."

"Why?"

"Trust me," he said. "Face the ocean, plant your feet and close your eyes."

Though skeptical, Helena followed his instructions and waited. As the waves pulled away from the shore, her feet sunk into the wet sand. The power of the tide entered her soul and she felt quite insignificant in the presence of the mighty ocean. Another wave passed over her feet and the receding water pulled at her ankles again. Helena felt exposed yet relaxed in a way she had never known – not even in her deepest meditations. The ocean's violence and beauty threatened to overwhelm her. She opened her eyes and noticed Nathan's smile. He was studying her. His mind was alive with possibilities and eagerness. His heart was sinking into love as fast as his feet in the sand. To Helena's shock, her own heart mirrored the movement. Was the final destination *love*? No, it couldn't be.

She turned away from him and said, "Shouldn't we return to the *Jupiter*?"

He smiled. "I made a call. They're not expecting us until much later."

"Oh."

He moved closer to her. "Why the rush?"

Helena held her ground and said, "No rush. I'm just curious about our itinerary."

"I don't believe you," he said. "You're uncomfortable."

Thunder rumbled in the distance and the wind grew colder.

"Shouldn't we find shelter?" she asked.

"I don't think the rain is that close," he said softly.

"I mean, from the darkness. On my homeworld, the evening darkness is without warmth. We are not prepared for a sudden drop in temperature," she said.

Nathan shook his head. "Not here. It gets a little colder, but not enough to hide indoors."

Helena decided to lie. "I'm cold," she said, "and a little hungry."

"Okay then," he said as he wrapped his jacket over her shoulders. "Let's get going."

Helena almost melted in his jacket as it was heavy with his exotic Human scents. Her discipline kept her surface composed, but her stomach flipped with each step. He was so close, but to reach out and touch the object of her desire was an act of treason. He was the enemy and for the first time Helena realized the cost she would pay might be higher than she anticipated.

"Here we are," he said as they climbed the wooden ramp to the street.

Helena frowned. "The taxi is gone."

Chuckling, Nathan said, "I'm sure there's a nice, warm place to eat within walking distance."

They reached a small restaurant just before the rain began to fall. Helena sensed something amiss with the scent of the rainwater.

"Acid rain," Nathan said. "Good thing we made it inside."

"This planet has toxins in its atmosphere?"

"Sadly, yes," he said. "Though Caledonia was once a very beautiful place."

They were the only patrons in the restaurant, but this time the employees didn't balk at the alien in their midst. From what Helena saw in the marketplace, she guessed the Humans on Caledonia were exposed to visitors from faraway worlds quite often.

They shared a warm bowl of pasta and Helena avoided eye contact throughout the meal. Doubt and anxiousness swirled together at the base of her stomach. What was she doing here with this Human?

She watched him eat and everything about him enticed her to want for more. More time, more contact, more surprises. More.

"So, now it's my turn," Helena said after they finished their meals.

"Your turn?"

She steeped her fingers and held his gaze. "Last time, on Terra, we only talked about *me*."

"Ah, I see where you're going with this," he said. "Can't you just read my mind and save us some time?"

Helena frowned and said, "I'm sure there are things you don't wish me to know…"

"Like my lust for your sister?" He was referring to the last time she read his mind, on the bridge of the *Venture*.

"Among other things…"

He smiled and said, "Okay, what do you want to know?"

"Start from the beginning," she said. "Where were you born? Why did you choose the navy?"

"Well," he said, "I was actually born and raised here on Caledonia. Not far from here, in fact."

"Do you still live here?"

"No, I live on a planet called *New Detroit*," he said. "As far as the navy, well, that's a long story."

"Why the rush?" she asked playfully.

"Well, the *Jupiter* is expecting us. But I'm guessing the rain will keep us grounded tonight," he said as he checked his commlink datapad. "Yup, we're not going anywhere tonight. I'm sorry for the delay."

Appalled at her elation at the thought of spending the night alone with him, she wanted to cool the air between them. However, her analytical mind was napping.
Instead, she said, "We have time, then."

He raised his eyebrows and said, "Apparently."

"So-"

"Okay," he said. "I was in the Academy, following after my grandfather's great legacy, when my parents were accused of treason. At the time, the Proxan hatred was at a high point. Human sympathizers were sent to detention camps, lest they turn and aid the Proxans. My parents, merchants by trade, wouldn't have lasted long at one of those camps."

"That sounds terrible," Helena said as she grasped his hand. Claudia taught her an empathic mental trick to sooth another person's nerves and anxiety. Though she wasn't certain it would work on Humans, Helena sensed Nathan's pain and attempted to help him. He relaxed under her touch and continued.

"So, when I heard of their arrest, I stole a ship and helped them disappear underground to a remote planet," he said. "I'm not proud of my actions, but I couldn't stand aside while my own government committed these atrocities against innocent people."

"What happened to you?"

"I was caught," he said, "and sentenced to a remote labor camp."

"Did you go?"

"I did," he said. "For two years I saw neither sunlight nor hope. Then, one day, they set me free."

"They just pardoned you?"

"It is a custom, when a High Human Councilor resigns, that his or her final request be granted," Nathan said. "My grandfather was good friends with one such retiring councilman. It also took my grandfather's resignation, but I was pardoned and given a distant assignment where I couldn't cause any more trouble."

"And you've played nice?"

"No, not entirely," he said. "When the Proxan attacks renewed, I led a major evacuation and earned the commendation of one of the admirals at the time. He reassigned me to his battle squadron and that's how I came to crash into your city. Then he gave me command of his ship after his retirement and here we are enjoying dinner on Caledonia."

"Admiral Stugardt?"

"Yes. He has been like a father to me, in many ways."

"Are your parents still safely hidden?" she asked.

"Yes," he said, "though Human inquisitors assure me that they will not arrest them if I surrendered their location. I don't want to take that chance, however."

"And Sean helped you?"

Nathan nodded. "We were both cadets at the Academy. He helped me steal the ship."

Helena sensed his memories and said, "He was not pardoned."

"No," he said. "Sean labored at the work camp for seven years, to the end of his sentence. I still owe him everything..."

"I see," she said.

After a few moments of silence, he looked from her hand to her eyes and said, "How did you do that?"

She pulled her hand away from his and said, "Do what?"

"I'm not certain. I just feel so *right* when I'm talking to you. It's so easy."

"Thank you," she said, "that is a fine compliment."

"You were doing something," he said, suspicious of her touch. He was more observant than she gave him credit for.

"I was," she said. "You seemed disturbed by these memories, so I soothed you much like certain medicines dull physical pain."

"You can do that?"

Helena smiled, but she didn't respond.

Nathan cleared his throat and said, "We should find a place to stay for the night." He produced his datapad and moved his finger along the surface. "Here we go. I'll call a taxi."

Under the cover of umbrellas and the taxi roof, they traveled through the pelting rain to a tall tower. Nathan secured adjacent rooms and they parted for the night. Realizing her heart wasn't to be trusted, Helena kept her distance from him and voiced a hasty 'good night.'

With only her travel bag at her side, Helena removed the Gima markings and sunk into a warm bath. After relaxing, she retrieved fresh bedclothes from the closet and slipped into the silken sheets of the spacious bed. Part of her wanted to knock on Nathan's door and invite herself inside. However, she squashed that desire and focused on her mission. Now was not the time for weakness. At some point, she would have to kill the captain, the admiral and everyone onboard the *Jupiter*.

Chapter 20

Helena and Nathan shared a quick breakfast before heading into the morning sun. The acid rain had receded, but the upper atmosphere still made it unsafe for any ships to leave the planet until later in the day. Helena's resolve to keep her distance had been shattered late the previous evening when she had an inappropriate dream involving Nathan. After that, she determined that while she was on Caledonia, her actions couldn't possibly endanger her mission. Why not enjoy her time and explore Human sensibilities.

She justified her reasoning by telling herself she needed to study her enemy, though she knew her reasoning was thin. For once, she decided to ignore her logic and 'go with her gut,' as Humans often said.

They decided to spend some time on the beach, but Helena had only the dress she wore when she departed the *Jupiter*. After much coaxing, Nathan convinced her to enter a beach store to look for something called 'swimwear.'

"I don't know," she said as she examined a slinky bathing suit. "This hardly qualifies as *clothing*."

A Human teen with dyed hair and a name badge approached and said, "Can I help you with anything?"

Nathan smiled and said, "Can you help my friend find a suit? She's having some difficulty."

The teen, Tiffany, examined Helena's dress and then she noticed Helena's tattoos. "Nice ink," she said, "but that dress has *got* to go. You can't waste a rare sunny day all covered up like that."

"So, you'll help her?" Nathan said.

"Definitely," Tiffany said as she led Helena to a dressing room.

Moments later, the hooks on the inside of the room were full of bathing suits. Some of them were no more than several strings attaching microscopic patches of cloth. Helena decided to skip those garments.

"With your body," Tiffany said, "I'm thinking micro. How about…?"

"No," Helena said as she closed the door on the eager salesperson. "I'll try on some of these one-piece suits."

Tiffany peeked over the door and said, "Look at you, girl. I'm *telling* you, go for a bikini. Your man won't be able to keep his hands off you!"

Helena glared and said, "Some privacy, please?"

Free from the watchful eye of the store employee, Helena shed her remaining undergarments and analyzed the complex nature of the suits. They weren't simple contraptions. After settling on a black one-piece with a covering skirt, Helena emerged from the stall. Nathan, dressed in trunks and a tank top, eyed her with renewed vigor. He seemed surprised and pleased at her exposed body. How did Humans consider this type of clothing proper? However, as soon as the thought popped into her head, she felt her own arousal. Nathan's defined arms and legs caught her attention and breath. He was sculpted, much like the Antaran heroes in their history books.

The beach was packed with people, blankets and music. Humans frolicked in the water and on the sand. Children ran from the waves to blankets and back again. Couples walked together along the water and occasionally stopped to examine sea shells.

Though Helena's tattoos extended along her entire face, torso, and arms – she felt exposed. Sure, some of the women were wearing much less than she was, but this was new to her.

As they searched for a suitable patch of sand to lay their blanket, a ball careened towards Nathan's head. Helena deflected the ball at the last instant.

"Whoa," a shirtless Human man said. "Good reflexes."

Helena smiled and noticed the man was playing a game along with a group of other young Humans.

"What's that?" Helena asked.

"Volleyball," Nathan said. "They hit the ball over the net until someone misses."

"You guys should play," the shirtless Human said. "We just lost two players."

"I don't know-" Nathan said.

"We'll split you up," the young Human said. "It wouldn't be fair to have two older people on the same team. Come on!"

"Older?" Nathan said.

The young man chuckled. "Sorry, but so you know, most of us play on the school team. We're pretty good."

"I want to play," Helena said, aware that the last time she enjoyed true exercise was before she departed for Terra.

"Are you sure?" Nathan asked.

Helena eyed the game hungrily and said, "Yes."

"Alright," Nathan said as he reached for the glowing globes in her hair, "we'll just put these aside so they don't get ruined."

They joined the game, and Tyler – the one who invited them – instructed them to either side of the net.

"Looks like we're enemies," Nathan said.

Helena's heart paused when she heard his words. If he knew how close to the truth he was he probably wouldn't be so cordial with her.

For the first few minutes, Helena studied the game. It was simple enough. One team 'served' the ball and points were scored when someone missed a shot. To her delight, she discovered the game was one of angles and reflexes. She entered her opponent's minds and readied herself for action.

One of the opponent's 'spiked' the ball in her direction, but she anticipated the shot and bumped it into the air for her teammates who scored.

"Whoa, that was awesome!" one of the Human girls said with her hands in the air. She expected a hand-slap from Helena.

"Thank you," Helena said as she completed the Human gesture of victory.

Now, Helena was at the net, across from Nathan. He jumped to perform his spike and Helena calculated the angle. Unfortunately, she misjudged his power. The ball deflected off her hands and the other team scored the point. Helena fell to the sand with a *thud*.

"Are you okay?" Nathan asked as he dove under the net to help her to her feet.

Helena refused his help. How could she miss the shot? "I'm fine," she said through clenched teeth. She wasn't accustomed to this kind of defeat.

"Ooohh," one of the Humans said, "she don't like losin' to her man!"

Nathan returned to the other side of the net and accepted the hand-slaps of his teammates. He was pleased with his second victory after their chess match.

On the next volley, Helena jumped and sent a vicious shot towards Nathan, but he somehow blocked the ball and received a set for his own spike. This time, Helena was prepared for the force of his shot and she blocked it into a vacant patch of sand near the back of the court.

Nathan rose from the ground and brushed the sand from his chest. Smiling, he said, "Nice shot."

Helena nodded. She wasn't sure if she received her competitive streak from her mother or father, but one thing was certain – she gave no quarter to her opponents. The remainder of the match was exhilarating. She dove around the sand and blasted the ball at every opportunity. When it was over, and her team was victorious, she dropped to the beach blanket. Both she and Nathan were short of breath after the exertion.

"That water looks pretty inviting, doesn't it" he said. "You can swim, can't you?"

"Yes. We have *water* on Antares," she said, "just no oceans. Race you there?"

They ran along the sand, but Nathan's powerful legs were no match for Helena's lithe running style. She reached the shallow waves and dove beneath the surface. The cool water washed away the sweat of the volleyball match and also much of her Gima markings. She didn't care. Nathan joined her in the rolling waves.

"I must admit," Helena said as she dropped to the blanket again, "the beach is now one of my favorite places."

Nathan turned to her and squinted in the sunlight. "It has always been mine," he said.

After the sun re-warmed their bodies, Nathan's communicator buzzed to life. Grumbling, he examined the display and said, "Time's up. We're heading out."

"Lieutenant Rhom was able to get the medical supplies?" Helena said.

"Yup, we better get moving before my reprimand grows any larger," he said.

As they packed their little area, Helena wanted to embrace him and thank him for a wonderful experience. However, the time for play was over. Her people needed her and she felt guilty with her overindulgence.

They reached the captain's yacht in the late afternoon and Nathan again showed her the prelaunch routine. Helena stored the information in her mind for when she would need that knowledge to abandon the *Jupiter* after she sent it into the tellium star.

Chapter 21

"Don't you walk away from me, Captain!" Rowe said with flared nostrils. "You weren't authorized to take her to the surface!"

Helena stepped from the yacht into the middle of a verbal fight between Nathan and the assassin, Rowe.

"I am well aware of your orders, Agent Rowe," Nathan said. "She never left my sight and you have my word she wasn't allowed access to long-range communications."

A small crowd had gathered to welcome the captain aboard the *Jupiter*, but now they stared in shocked silence as he was challenged by an agent of the Human Council.

"Yeah," Rowe spat, "I'm sure you watched her *closely*."

Nathan stepped towards Rowe and said, "Careful. Be mindful of how you speak to me on my ship."

"This won't be your ship for long," Rowe said. "The Council will hear of your recklessness and impropriety."

"Of what impropriety do you speak?" Helena said. "The captain was acting upon *my* request. I wished to see more Human culture before I returned to my homeworld. I find my visits to your cities more enjoyable when I don't have an assassin's gun pointed at my back."

Several of the crewmembers gasped and turned to Rowe, their eyes filling with realization.

Rowe pointed at Helena and said, "You are a devious little witch! I'll expose you for the danger you are. The moment my orders change, I'm going to-"

Nathan took another step towards Rowe, clenched his fists and said, "Are you threatening a member of my senior staff?"

Rowe backed away from Nathan. "No, Captain," Rowe said as he composed himself. He realized he was outgunned. "I am out of line. But please, in the future, tell me *before* you leave with her as she is my responsibility. How can I fulfill my mission if I don't know where she is?"

Nathan relaxed and said, "That's not my problem, Agent Rowe. I don't have the time nor the patience to play the Council's game. Lady Helena is a valuable tactical asset and *I* decide what's best for her. Understood?"

Rowe and the crowd dispersed. Lieutenant Rhom briefed Nathan on the recent happenings onboard the *Jupiter* while he escorted Helena to her quarters.

Interrupting the Lieutenant while they waited for the lift Helena said, "So, I am merely a *tactical asset?*"

Nathan turned to her and said, "What?"

Helena lifted one of her eyebrows and said, "And *you* decide what's best for *me?*"

Lieutenant Sandra Rhom chuckled. "You did make her sound like a piece of equipment, sir," she said.

"I did?"

Helena nodded and turned to the Lieutenant. "I think he's still raw after losing in a game of beach volleyball."

"You lost, sir?" Lieutenant Rhom said.

"To my team," Helena said.

"You know that's not what I meant," Nathan said. He reached for Helena's hand, but he stopped when he realized Lieutenant Rhom was watching their every move. She was suspicious of what happened overnight in Caledonia.

"I know, Nathan," Helena said. "I was just having some fun at your expense."

Helena sensed he regretted telling her to use his first name. In front of the Lieutenant, it wasn't proper. The lift doors opened, closed, and they sped towards Helena's deck.

Correcting his mistake for him, Helena said, "So, Captain, how long until we reach Antares?"

"Two days," he said as the lift doors opened and Helena's praetorians snapped to attention in the hallway.

"Very well," Helena said. "In the meantime, do allow Agent Rowe unrestricted access to my movements and orders. I'd hate for another scene between you two."

"I think I can handle him," Nathan said.

Helena winked at Lieutenant Rhom and said, "I'm sure you can, Captain."

The doors slid shut and Duronious was at her side. "Are you well, My Lady?" he asked as he visually and mentally inspected her. Almost immediately, he spotted the one new detail. "That jewelry in your hair. Is it safe?"

"It is not a spying device," she said as she led her guards down the corridor.

"Things have been tense, My Lady," Duronious said. "That man, Rowe, is aligned against you. He requested, on several occasions, to search your quarters in your absence. We, of course, did not allow it."

"Thank you, Centurion," she said. "You have done well in my absence."

"We're almost home," he said, "but our vigilance is doubled. We will not fail you in these last few hours."

Before parting with her guards, she leaned towards Duronious and said, "Thank you. This voyage was not an easy one and you have been my rock in uncertain waters. I will speak these same words to my father and I hope to return you to your daughter very soon. May your twilight years be free from violence."

"I hope they are full of peace, My Lady."

"That is why we are here."

Duronious allowed the corner of his mouth to curl into a smile. "You know I'll defend you to the last breath, My Lady."

"I know, Centurion. But your battle will soon be over," she said. "You have served your term with honor. The Archives will honor you."

Without another word, Duronious disappeared into the adjoining room. Helena sensed his vigilance. He wouldn't sleep until they stepped on Antaran soil. His devotion came from his heart, not from his sense of duty or a god-struck awe of her royal family. He genuinely cared for her as he did his own daughter. Helena meditated on this problem. Was *emotion* stronger than *logic*? Before she met Captain Nathan Connor, Helena was convinced that logic was supreme and emotion full of weakness. Now, she wasn't certain.

She fingered the orange globes before retiring for the night. The gasses danced and appeared as if they wanted to tell her a story.

"What tale do you have to tell?" she asked them.

She snuggled under the warm blankets and reminisced of a simpler time when she dreamed with her sisters about grand adventures and forbidden romances. Why was it, after tasting parts of those nearly forgotten dreams, that she now feared them? Perhaps she now realized that only misery awaited her at the end of those dreams?

Chapter 22

"Heir Helena, you have done well," Emperor Agreios said. "To accomplish all you have with the obstacles you faced... your mother would be proud."

"Thank you, Emperor."

The remainder of the trip home was uneventful. Helena studied all the data she accumulated while on Terra and prepared for her arrival. Safely back in the palace, their time for action was at hand. Forgoing sleep and official functions, Helena immediately called the war council.

"Now," Agreios said, "I sense you wish to discuss the second tellium star?"

Helena nodded and activated the holo-table. "As you can see, the star is in a remote location. After many failed attempts to manufacture their own star, the Humans stumbled upon this smaller version. It must be destroyed."

Agreios scratched his chin and said, "Of course it must. Valeria will alter her plan to include the destruction of this star."

Valeria smiled and peered at everyone through her raven hair.

"A wise decision, Father," Helena said.

"I will not fail," Valeria said and Helena didn't doubt her sister's words. Valeria always shined when she faced a test. Unfortunately, Valeria viewed Helena's status as heir a personal challenge as well.

"I have everyone's assignments as well," Helena said as she pushed the small tellium star to the corner and called seven readouts to the forefront. "These are the seven battleships where we will be assigned."

She sensed her father's anger before he spoke. "Seven?" he said, shaking his head. "No. Terentia stays."

"I would not presume to argue with the emperor," Helena said. "Please allow me to offer my alternative, as the second tellium star changes my equations."

Agreios leaned backwards in his chair and waved his hand. Helena sensed her father knew the truth of their new success chances, but he was resolute in his wish to keep Terentia on Antares.

"Thank you, Emperor," Helena said. "As you can see, my assignment is to the flagship called *Jupiter*. It is the largest and most heavily armed, though all seven battleships carry weaponry of extraordinary magnitude and a full support fleet within their bellies. I have already won the complete trust and affection of the captain and a retired admiral. So, I have an advantage. The rest of you will have to work harder to win the trust of your captains and crew."

Valeria huffed and Helena sensed her sister in her mind. She was probing her feelings on Captain Nathan Connor. Raising her mental defenses, Helena glared at her sister before continuing.

"Valeria, your ship is the *Kraken*," Helena said. "I'm told their captain is a real xenophobe. Please do try to keep your insults to yourself."

"My sister disrespects me," Valeria said. "I know the gravity of our mission."

"My apologies," Helena said. Turning to Justina, Helena said, "You are assigned to the *Nova*. I'm told their captain is a man of faith, so you two would probably have much in common."

Justina bowed her head. "My sister has made a very wise choice," Justina said. "Though our faiths differ, I'm sure a study in Human religion will help us."

"Also," Helena said, "you'll have something to discuss from day one. Use that angle."

"I will heed my older sister's advice," Justina said.

"Very well," Helena said. "My dear Marcella, your vessel is called the *Waterloo*. I'm told the name is significant to Human history, but I have not had the chance to research the topic. From what I hear, the captain is an unmarried Human male of renowned comeliness. I hope you don't mind, but I calculated your skills the best to win him over."

Marcella smiled. "I will ply my skills to him with a fervor that would make our mother proud."

"I'm sure you will, dear sister," Helena said. Then, turning to Claudia, she said, "Tender Claudia, your ship is the *Minotaur*. This vessel has seen the most battles and their captain is a woman. You have a difficult task, as some of the devices the rest of us will use cannot be used on your captain. I trust you will find a way."

Claudia smiled and said, "Thank you, sister."

"Prisca, dear Prisca," Helena said. "Your vessel is the *Saturn*. The captain is a man of science. You two should have much to discuss."

Prisca tilted her head and said, "Thank you, sister."

Helena turned to her youngest sister and her heart changed its rhythm. Terentia looked so much like their mother! Helena shared her father's love of the youngest daughter, but their success depended upon all seven sisters. It was unfair for Helena to ask so much of her sister, but sometimes the most precious of jewels are forged in adversity. Her mother said those exact words to her once. Perhaps it was foresight.

"Young Terentia," Helena said. "I have watched you blossom from a quirky girl into a beautiful and poised young woman. If the emperor agrees to include you on this mission, do you feel you are ready?"

Terentia obeyed protocol and replied, "Yes, sister."

"Very well, then," Helena said. "Your ship is the *Mars*. This is the newest of all the battleships and the captain is still working through system glitches and malfunctions on a weekly basis. I felt, with the added confusion of this vessel, you would be well-placed to deceive and ultimately destroy the vessel."

"Thank you, sister."

Helena's heart thumped with pride. Though she sensed excitement in Terentia, her sister kept herself under control and within the bounds of protocol.

"Each of you now has a detailed report of both your vessel and Human customs. I will make my battle strategy against the Proxans available to you tomorrow," Helena said. "I suggest you study all materials over the next week before we all depart for Terra. My new calculations bring our success rate to over eighty-percent. We must not fail, my sisters. Our lives and our culture depend upon our actions over the next few months."

"I want you to meet with each of them privately," Agreios said. "Answer their questions and prepare them for their task."

"Yes, Emperor," Helena said.

"Now, my daughter, I sense a great deal of fatigue in you," Agreios said. "Please rest. You will all need your strength."

"Thank you, Father," Helena said.

Helena waited for her sisters to leave the room and she gently closed the door behind them. She needed to be alone with her father for this discussion.

"You wish to discuss Terentia," Agreios said. He was in her mind, searching for a way to keep Terentia safe.

"Yes Father."

Agreios sighed. "I know, and I will eventually agree with you. So, let's just skip to the part where I plead with you."

Taken aback, Helena said, "You do not plead-"

Interrupting her, he said, "Terentia is my last joy, the final connection I have to your mother. She looks so much like her. I cannot lose Terentia. Not her. Promise me you will keep her safe. I don't know how you will do this, but just promise me."

Helena calculated the risk in her mind and said, "Father, I cannot make such a promise."

"I know you can't. Please, just lie to me this one time."

Chapter 23

Helena decided to confront her most difficult task first – her meeting with Valeria. Though they were rivals, Helena respected her sister's ability to both invade and control another mind. Valeria required little guidance, but Helena had to follow her father's orders to conduct a private meeting with each sister.

Before she reached Valeria's dormitory, Duronius met with her in the halls of the palace.

"It's good to see you again, Praetorian," she said with a tilt of her head.

"You as well," he said. "I came to tell you that my retirement is final. The emperor has released me from my duties with honor."

"If I am able, I will attend the ceremony," she said. "And I won't forget your bravery during our mission to Terra. You have my personal thanks, Praetorian."

"Thank you, My Lady. That means much to me."

"Go with peace and wisdom," she said.

"You as well, My Lady."

She watched him head towards the armory to relinquish his arms, most likely. Men like Duronius would likely be needed if they failed. Though she didn't have the gift of foresight like her mother did, Helena reasoned Duronius might return to the armory before this whole gambit was concluded.

Helena sensed anger and heightened emotions from behind Valeria's door, so she rushed inside. She found her sister practicing with her sword.

"Oh," Helena said, "I-"

Valeria stopped mid-motion and glared at her sister, trying to gain entrance into her mind. "You are getting sloppy, Heir," Valeria said. "Your time with the Humans has made you weak. I can sense it."

As Valeria returned her sword to its resting place, Helena followed. "I'm sorry to have disappointed you, sister," Helena said.

Wiping her forehead and chest with a towel, Valeria said, "We're alone. No need to obey tradition. Father isn't watching."

Helena studied her sister for a moment. "Where does your anger for me dwell?" she asked.

"Right here," Valeria said as she balled her fist and placed it against her heart. "You really don't see it, do you?"

Helena shook her head.

"We were born minutes apart," Valeria said. "But, you gain all the favor. You are the Heir. Do you think it was easy for me to watch our mother favor you? Our father? You got everything you ever wanted and I was left with scraps."

"You know that's not true," Helena said. "You are loved."

"By you?" Valeria grinned. "No, I don't sense love for me. Disapproval and frustration hold a special place in your heart for me."

"What do you want from me?" Helena said. "Tradition dictates that the dynasty pass to the eldest child. Do you think I view the throne as a prize to be won?"

Valeria shook her head and tossed her towel over her shoulder. "You won the moment you were born before me," she said. "No amount of skill or dedication on my part can change that fact."

"Since we're disregarding tradition here," Helena said. "What dedication? You rail against your duties and openly defy our father every chance you can. Your decisions are rarely thought out and you act from your heart instead of your head. How is any of that *royal?*"

"Royalty? You speak of *royalty?* We are plotting to massacre two civilizations. Do you really think our father's actions are noble?"

"His plan will keep us safe-"

Valeria waved her hand. "You can do better than that. Don't spout his words as if you are a lapdog. You demean yourself."

Helena sighed. "I *do* believe in his plan," she said. "Perhaps my sister needs another lesson in probability?"

"Don't you dare," Valeria said. Her words were laced with venom. "Don't you talk down to me like I'm wet behind the ears. You and I both know my analytical skills surpass yours."

"Valeria, if we were calculating the effect of a multi-tier tax adjustment for the entire city of New Olympus, I'd gladly step aside for your superior computational powers," Helena said. "But we're not. We're talking about rulership. And, frankly, you're not ready. You may never be. Even if you were the eldest, father would still have named me Heir."

"Well," Valeria said, "aren't we a little high on ourselves after our big trip to Terra? I read your report and I'm not impressed. You told them too much. They know more than they should about our mental discipline."

"What are they going to do, mimic our powers? I divulged what I needed them to know so we could gain a position on their battleships. Everything is falling into place."

Valeria studied Helena for a moment and Helena felt her rummaging around in her recent memories. She was so very skilled!

"Maybe for you," Valeria said. "While you were gallivanting with your captain, we were studying and preparing.

Is this how you show your people that you are ready to be empress – by sharing meals with your Human lover?"

Helena's heart quickened at the intimate possibilities with Nathan, but she closed the lid on those thoughts as soon as they surfaced. Valeria could read them.

"We are not lovers," Helena said, sticking to simple mental images.

Valeria glanced at the iridescent orange globes affixed to Helena's hair and snorted. "Whatever. Your heart is conflicted and I will tell father of your weakness for these Humans."

Helena had no answer for her sister's accusations. They were accurate. She was weak when Nathan was near. Would her vulnerability endanger her mission? No, it couldn't.

"I will succeed in my task," Helena said. "My befriending of the Humans is nothing more than leverage."

"Don't lie to me, sister," Valeria said, "I can see right through you. Someday, everyone else will as well."

"And what do I look like through your eyes?"

As if she had the answer prepared, Valeria said, "You are a weak woman who has no business ruling Antares."

"Better weak than empty," Helena said. "You have nothing but your spite. And, for that, I do pity you. One day you will awaken alone and despised. When that day comes, I will not be there for you. Your prison will be of your own making and none of us will save you from it."

Valeria narrowed her eyes and said, "Careful, sister. Take care to keep your insults buried deep where they are safe."

"Insults? Since when is the truth an insult?" Helena said. "Unless you are ashamed of your past actions, then I can understand. Remorse is a path you can yet choose."

Valeria reached for her sword and Helena stepped to the dueling paired blade.

"Are you serious?" Helena said. "You wish to duel me? *Now?*"

"I wish to give you a nice scar to regret your insult to me," Valeria said.

Helena grasped the blade as Valeria attacked. She parried her sister's strikes and swept around to a better position. "I am not your enemy," Helena said.

After jumping over Helena's leg sweep, Valeria said, "You are wrong in that, my sister. We are enemies, just not *mortal* ones. Do not fear, the Humans have my ire for now. So long as we share that common enemy, I will not raise my hand against you."

Helena grunted as she blocked a vicious strike from her sister. "And what do you call this? You're not holding back!"

"Should I be?" Valeria said as she moved closer. "The Humans will give us no quarter. Why should I?"

Helena gritted her teeth and waited for her opening. She assaulted her sister's mind and sword with the contained fury of a tigress, as her mother had taught her. Her physical movements came automatically as Helena broke down Valeria's mental barriers. When Valeria was out of control like this, the task was far easier.

"You can't win," Helena said as she disarmed her sister and kicked her midsection.

Valeria fell to the floor and laughed. Her mood swings were as extreme as the vast desert.

"There's the violence I so love in you, my sister," Valeria said, extending her hand to Helena. "There's the tigress."

Helena helped her sister to the sofa and they both fell into the soft pillows. For a few minutes, they panted and calmed their running hearts.

"Do you remember when mother would call us that?" Valeria said.

Helena smiled and said, "She was a good teacher. The image of the tigress is always in my mind when I enter battle nowadays."

"Mine too."

Helena reached out and embraced her sister. This was the closest the two had ever been to each other since they shared the womb. Helena sensed her sister's surprise, but also a flicker of warmth. Perhaps there was hope for Valeria, after all.

Helena whispered, "Our people need us. Let us be tigresses."

Chapter 24

"Why are you so flushed?" Justina asked. "Here, sit and allow me to get you some tea."

Helena accepted the tea and said, "I just came from Valeria's. We fought… physically. But it's not as bad as it sounds. I think we found some common ground for once."

"Facing death has a way of covering old wounds," Justina said. "Though the wound is still there, we are oblivious to the pain it once caused. This too will pass."

"Speaking of old wounds," Helena said, "I'm here for two reasons. We need to discuss strategy. However, first I want to talk about what our family has done to Antaran religion."

"As you know, I am a woman of faith," Justina said, "I believe in the Gods and the Light. I do not worship the emperor, or myself, for that matter. Deification of our rulers will only end in a theocratic state. No good can come of it. Religion has no place in politics."

"Slow down," Helena said as she touched her sister's arm and smiled. "I agree with you."

Taken aback, Justina said, "You do? Then why didn't you support me years ago when I confronted our father about this?"

"I wasn't strong enough then," Helena said. "But I am now."

Justina shifted on her chair to face her sister. "What, exactly, are you telling me? You know my station as high priestess. You can't just casually talk about such things with me."

"I know," Helena said. "But I do not wish to upset our father. So, this must stay between us for now, okay?"

"Of course," Justina said.

"Once I am Empress, I plan to set things right with our religion," Helena said. "I will denounce my own divinity, and I'll need your help to do it."

Justina held her hand to her mouth. "Valeria will unseat you."

"That's why I need a plan. And a little help," Helena said.

"Why the sudden change of heart?" Justina asked as she attempted to sort through Helena's recent memories. "What happened to you out there?"

Helena looked into her cup of tea as if it held some answers. "I'm not sure," she said. "I suppose my eyes were opened for the first time. It's a vast universe out there and I think I'm finally starting to see my part in it."

"Self-purpose is one of the first steps in the path of Light," Justina said. "I've been hoping for this in you. Your soul may yet be saved."

Helena held a hand towards her sister. "I'm not ready for a spiritual revival or anything," she said. "I'm just beginning to see the larger picture and I don't think a theocracy is what our people need."

"We are in total agreement there," Justina said.

"Our father believes that religion gives solidarity to our governing – that we are somehow given an absolute identity with a divine past, present and future authority," Helena said. "What better place to find *meaning* than in our Gods?"

"*Individual* meaning for one's existence is the path of Light," Justina said. "Our father has warped that into a controlling force wielded against the masses. It's perverse."

Helena held her index finger towards the ceiling. "It's brilliant," she said. "Deified, we wield naked power and undeniable authority. Our logic and reason are inscrutable when it comes from the Gods."

Justina wrinkled her nose, sending her freckles in all directions across her cheeks. "You don't sound changed now. You talk as if you are resolute in our father's path to theocracy. I'm confused"

Helena smiled. "While I respect the power we now have through our theocracy, I do not believe it is the best way to rule our people. In the past, we educated our rulers and they were held accountable for their actions. We must return to that, lest we devolve into a mob of godking-worshipping followers, incapable of individual thought or knowledge of self-worth."

Justina eyed her and said, "This is quite a turnaround for you. I'm sensing the Humans had something to do with it."

Helena tilted her head towards her sister and said, "True, I won't deny my journey has left an impact on me."

"On your soul," Justina corrected.

"Very well," Helena said, "I can accept your terminology in this matter."

"Whether you believe in your own soul or not, you have changed. That change will affect everything you do from this point forward - much like a new layer of molten rock below our planet's crust pushes the layers above in new and dynamic directions."

Helena considered her sister's words and said, "Your insight is remarkable, as always."

"I thank our mother for my gift of insight," Justina said. "I wish she were here now to guide us in our darkest hour."

"Her delicate hand and wise eye would certainly be a boon," Helena said. "She'd also make a better diplomat than I. I've made some errors in judgment in all of this."

"Mistakes are but pebbles on the path to enlightenment," Justina said. "Study them, learn from them, grow stronger from them. Too often, we view our mistakes as failure. Instead, we should see them as a sign of growth or a step towards a greater understanding of our world and universe."

Helena put her hand on her sister's leg. "Sometimes when you speak you remind me so much of *her*."

Justina held Helena's eyes for a moment and said, "Thank you, my sister. Your words are too kind."

"It is true, you are so much like mother…" Helena said as she reached into her gown and handed their mother's prayer beads to Justina. "These helped me find my way on Terra when I thought all was lost. Now, I think they should return home."

Justina accepted the beads. Her eyes trembled as she said, "Sister, I… I have no words."

Chapter 25

Helena waited outside Marcella's door. Though she sensed heightened emotions from the room, Helena decided to probe deeper before bursting into the room. She was fortunate she took the moment, as Marcella was enjoying the company of one of the praetorians. After another fifteen minutes, they stopped their afternoon lovemaking and the praetorian emerged. He was embarrassed under the stare of the Antaran heir.

Marcella wrapped a silk robe around her perfect body and said, "Hello, my sister. Were you waiting long?"

Helena entered Marcella's suite and said, "Shouldn't you be studying your material?"

"Sex has a way of clearing my mind," Marcella said. "I've been waist-deep in the stuff all day and I just needed a little break."

"Waist-deep?" Helena said as she raised her eyebrow. "Well, I'm here to answer questions and brief you on your mission."

"No you're not," Marcella said. "You want to talk about that Human Captain."

Helena blinked. "What?"

"Don't worry, your secret is safe with me," Marcella said. "Try to hide your emotions a little better, though. I think Valeria noticed too."

"I'm not... I'm playing to the captain's weaknesses. He's attracted to me, so I took a chapter from one of *your* lesson books."

Marcella sat on her waterbed and eyed her sister. "Don't lie to me about love. I know how to read a heart. And yours is aglow, my sister."

Helena joined Marcella, hesitated and said, "Is it really that obvious?"

"Not too obvious," Marcella said. "I guess it won't matter though, as you won't have to deal with questions from Valeria or anyone else. You get him all to yourself once you are on that ship of his."

"Well, it's a big ship. I hope-"

Marcella nudged her sister and said, "I hope – for your sake – that it is, indeed, a *big* ship."

Helena blushed, surprised at her lack of control. "That's not what I meant. I just hope I can keep my distance and not lose focus like I did on Caledonia."

"That's no fun," Marcella said. "Enjoy yourself. Enjoy *him*. He's not going to throw you off his ship because you make love to him."

"Marcella!"

"What? He's not! Unless you are unskilled," Marcella's eyes flew open. "You are *skilled*, aren't you?"

Helena calmed her sprinting heart and said, "I haven't exactly had time for... Well, my duties have kept me-"

"You're a virgin?!" Marcella yelled.

"I don't think the Humans on the starship above our planet heard you. Be a little louder this time."

"Oops, sorry," Marcella said. "I mean, at your age-"

"I'm only thirty-four solars old," Helena said. "Plenty of people wait."

Marcella shook her head. "This is no good. You have *theory* and no *practice*."

"Well, I'm not going to just go out and-"

Marcella untied her robe and left it open at the middle, barely covering her naked body underneath

"What are you doing?" Helena asked.

Sighing, Marcella said, "You need a crash course. Let me show you how to please that man of yours."

"What? No!" Helena sprang from the bed. "This is not proper."

"You are my sister," Marcella said. "I would do anything for you, including teaching you how to love."

"But-"

Helena's protests went unheard as Marcella wrapped her arms around Helena's neck and lightly kissed her lips. "You start slow," Marcella said. "Even before physical contact, you meet with the eyes."

Marcella was already in her mind soothing her. Was there any harm in learning from her sister? Helena had taught Marcella how to focus her mind, why would this be so different? It was just another lesson to be mastered and Marcella was the most qualified teacher.

Helena wasn't certain her thoughts were her own. Marcella may have been manipulating her thoughts to calm her racing fear. What was she so afraid of? Marcella was warm and kind. If this helped Helena to win the favor of Captain Nathan Connor, then why shouldn't she allow Marcella to impart her wisdom upon her?

When did they return to the bed? Helena lost track of time for a few moments as Marcella traced kisses down her neck and rubbed her thigh with her hand. Her skin tingled in response to her sister's touch.

"Every inch of his body is new terrain open for your discovery," Marcella said. "And the same goes for you. He will want to explore and you should let him. Think of him now."

More kisses. The room spun. Before Helena lost control she pushed away and sat at the edge of the bed, panting and lusting for Nathan.

Marcella knelt behind her and rubbed her shoulders. "You are a very sensual woman, my sister. Do not keep your tigress caged. She must be allowed to roam. You will do just fine with your man."

Still panting, Helena clasped her sister's hand and said, "Thank you… For this lesson."

Helena felt Marcella's smile as her sister said, "My door is always open to you. Return anytime and I can teach you more. We've only touched the surface."

Chapter 26

Helena skipped the rest of her private meetings with her sisters after her lesson from Marcella. Strangely, she felt nothing perverse about her time with her sister. Instead of fearing closeness with Nathan, Helena now counted the seconds until she could be near him again. Marcella was right – why not enjoy his company to the fullest extent possible? Helena planned to be the tigress in more than one way upon her return to the *Jupiter*.

The next morning, she found Claudia in the royal gardens. Strands of fruits hung over the passageway leading to Claudia's favorite spot – the rose gazebo.

"I knew I'd find you here," Helena said.

"Helena!" Claudia pushed aside her datapad to embrace her sister. "I've been going over everything you sent us."

Helena joined her sister in the gazebo. "I have additional information for you this morning. Inside the data packet, you will find my attack strategy against the Proxans."

"Thank you, sister."

Helena studied her sister for a few moments. Then she said, "I sense a great deal of fear in your heart, Claudia."

Presenting a false bravado, Claudia smiled in her sweet way and said, "I'm managing the fear."

"If you want to talk about your fear, I'm here."

Tears formed in Claudia's eyes as her bravado melted. "I'm afraid of failing you," she said. "And failing father."

Helena held her sister to her chest and said, "Shhh. Quiet now."

"You and Valeria and Prisca are so skilled and so perfect," Claudia said. "I'm just the one who cooks the food and…? What else? I'm not a famous scientist or heir to the throne. I'm just clumsy, foolish Claudia."

Helena rocked with her sister in her arms for a few minutes.

"I'm sorry," Claudia said as she wiped the tears from her face. "I just needed a moment. I'll be fine."

Helena detected her sister's lie. "Listen, I do not think of you as a fool. You are my sister and I am very proud of you."

Slipping back into the familiar blanket of protocol, Claudia said, "Thank you, sister."

Her sister needed some courage and Helena knew just the remedy.

"Let me tell you of the tigresses in the cold, northern forests of our world," Helena said. "Mother used to tell this story to Valeria and me when we were little girls. I think it's time you heard it."

Claudia beamed. "Okay!"

Helena settled in a comfortable position and smiled. "When we first arrived on this world, it was a cold, harsh place. Our early people, the Gima, were forced to live in domes. But we knew of creatures who braved the wastelands. These beasts were somehow able to survive. One season, in Queen Galeria's dome, the hydroponics failed. Thousands died from starvation, as not enough relief was sent from the nearby domes. The queen herself led a hunting party out into the northern forests, where animals were rumored to roam free.

"The hunting party discovered vegetables growing in the soil and herd animals fit for taming. The expedition was a success, but the queen pushed onwards. She wanted to reveal more of the forest's secrets. That's when she discovered the tigress. White and black, the majestic animal was on her deathbed. She was an old tigress. However, Galeria wanted to bring the creature back with her to the dome, as a pet and companion. Surely, subduing such and ancient beast would be a small task for the queen. Galeria readied her net gun and spear in case the animal got too close. The tigress seemed docile, resigned in her defeat until Galeria fired the net. In an instant, the tigress avoided capture and pounced on the queen. After ripping open Galeria's shoulder with her claws, the tigress retreated into the deep forest.

"Galeria commanded her guards to remain at the camp and she pursued the tigress alone. The queen held so much respect for the tigress she felt the battle between them must be fought honorably.

"For six days, Galeria hunted the tigress. She sensed the tigress wished not to be tamed. They shared a mental bond as Galeria tracked the beast into the snowcapped pine forest. It was there, amongst the white flakes of winter that Galeria finally cornered the tigress. Fang and claw fought against spear and sword. Though age had slowed the reflexes and weakened the muscles of the tigress, her claws were still razor sharp. The tigress fought with a ferocity that surprised the queen. In the end, however, the queen was victorious and she returned to her camp with the white and black hide of her respected enemy.

"Queen Galeria instilled the same ferocity she found in the tigress into her people. They built sophisticated structures and transport systems to collect, purify, and prepare the roaming herdbeasts of the northern forest. Instead of relying on rationing and aid from the other domes, Queen Galeria's people found their own solution to the food shortage. She led everyone to help build the most massive cooperative construction endeavor since the early Gima built the domes.

"In many ways, our father is teaching the universe this story. The Humans and Proxans view us as the old tigress, weak and insignificant. They do not have the same respect for the tigress as Queen Galeria had.

"They think us weak, but we have strength hidden in our mental discipline. They think us slow because we have not harnessed the power of space travel, but our cunning has been honed after generations of outsmarting our harsh environment. They think us insignificant because we do not colonize the galaxy, but we are rich in our culture and national identity.

"They believe they can demand what they want from us, because we cannot resist, but our father's plan shows that our claws and fangs are sharp, ready for the quick strike.

"My sister," Helena said, "you must embrace the tigress inside of you. The time will come when we must strike, and you will be ready. Remember the story of Galeria and her tigress for it is now time for us to hunt."

♦

There was little time for rest after her meeting with Claudia. As usual, Helena found Prisca in the astrophysics lab at the palace. Helena recognized Prisca's expertise in their father's plan to destroy the tellium stars. Dependable Prisca.

After briefing her sister on all things Proxan, Helena watched and waited as Prisca processed the information.

"Amazing! So the Proxans have embraced technology that melds with their flesh?" Prisca said.

"Yes," Helena said. "Their minds work differently – signals get interrupted, enhanced, or modified. It's a tad strange the first time you go in there."

"Interesting. I'll keep that in mind."

"The first thing your Human captain will ask of you is to scan the entire ship for Proxans," Helena said. "We ran into one that looked Human, so they are quite paranoid right now. It is my guess that the duplicate I encountered was an early prototype, but they still had me scan the *Jupiter* nonetheless.

Have no fear. Detecting the differences in Human and Proxan brain activity should be quite simple, even if you've never encountered a Proxan before."

"Thank you, sister," Prisca said. "These Proxans interest me, scientifically of course. I would like to get my hands on a sample."

"The Humans share our belief that we are all from the same planet," Helena said. "So, Proxans probably have the same basic anatomy."

"That makes sense," Prisca said. "I'd still like to cut one open, though."

"Admiral Stugardt told me that the Proxans have enhanced organs which can resist the aging process far better than natural organs," Helena said. "So I guess I share your curiosity. I'd like to medically study those organs. Perhaps we can learn something of use."

"Okay," Prisca said with a smile, "You get the internal organs below the neck and I get to study the brain. Deal?"

"If we happen to be in the same room with the specimen, then we definitely have an accord," Helena said similing at her sister's mental vigor.

After a few moments of uneasy silence, Helena detected Prisca in her mind. Helena knew she would ask about her conflicted emotions. They were so closely connected, Helena often wondered where her own thoughts ended and Prisca's began.

"I sense a storm in your heart," Prisca said. "You must share it with me so we can calm it."

Helena nodded. They sat across from each other and clasped hands. In moments, Helena shared her entire experience – from the time she stepped aboard the *Venture* to the moment the *Jupiter* landed on Antares. This was Prisca, so Helena held nothing back. Her feelings for Nathan bared, she hoped her sister understood.

Prisca opened her eyes and exhaled. "Wow," she said, "we grossly miscalculated the *emotional* toll this mission would take on us."

"That's the conclusion I have come to as well," Helena said. "We are not impervious to the matters of the heart, as we so thought. These Humans are led by their hearts, and I must tell you, it's quite liberating."

Prisca studied her sister again and said, "I know your heart is true. When the time comes, you will not fail our people."

"Certainly, my duty to Antares is the strongest force in my heart," Helena said. "However, my feelings for this Human cause my compass to spin in all directions. I fear I may slip at the wrong time and be discovered. Marcella urges me to enjoy my time with him, but I am uncertain if that is the most prudent course of action."

Prisca exhaled again and said, "If you're looking for advice of the heart, I'm afraid Marcella is a wiser woman than I. Like you, my romantic life is but an echo in the background."

Helena suppressed a blush and said, "I've already spoken to Marcella. She insists I should follow my heart and indulge myself with Nathan. I guess I'm talking to you about this because I value your opinion above anyone else. Am I being a fool?"

Always the scientist, Prisca said, "I wish I had more data on the emotions you are feeling. Or, at least, a common frame of reference. Then perhaps I could analyze everything and give you a conclusion. As far as endangering the mission, I suspect your goal will be much easier if you have the captain under your complete control."

Helena frowned, frustration in her heart. "I agree," she said.

"However," Prisca said, "if your emotions cloud your judgment, then I suppose it is possible for even you to raise your chance at failure. One slip and the whole charade comes crashing down around all of us."

"I know," Helena said, "and I'll not endanger my sisters like that. I just feel... I don't know. *Alive?* I cannot describe the way my heart soars when I am with him. It's as if nobody on Antares was meant for me and my only chance at personal happiness rests with my enemy. Confounding, to say the least."

"You are not able to bury these emotions?"

"That's the frustrating part," Helena said. "This isn't some small or transient emotional lust flitting by. This is something much larger and more powerful. Like the swelling waves on Caledonia, I feel powerless to stop its advance or momentum. I fear I may be pulled under-"

Prisca smiled. "Do you remember when you first started to train me?"

"Yes. You were more interested in math and science. You didn't believe in the power that rested in your own mind."

"I was determined to undermine you," Prisca said. "I knew that my scientific studies were far more important and useful to our people than the 'mind games' I stood to learn from you. I was a silly girl."

"No," Helena said, "you were a *stubborn* girl, just like I was."

"My point is – though I resisted my duty to my family because my heart was elsewhere, I eventually came to my senses. I melded the two principles together and I believe I am both scientist and royal daughter of Antares. You are both surgeon and royal heir. Valeria is both raging bitch and, well, *raging bitch*. You see? If we allow our hearts and minds to grow, we have room for all that is in our lives. I know you will find room for this as well."

"I spoke with Valeria yesterday and our words turned into a swordfight. Raging bitch? Probably."

After they shared a laugh, Helena hugged her sister and said, "You are wise beyond your young years. My thanks. You have calmed the storm in my heart. I will think upon your words and incorporate my new emotions with my old ones. There must be space for everything until-"

"You cannot fear the future," Prisca said. "The future is unknown, even to us. It makes no logical sense to fear the unknown."

Helena's heart had returned to a more regular beat. "Dependable Prisca," she said. "I'm honored to go into battle with you."

"I'll not fail you like I did with that false ambassador," Prisca said.

"I was unsuccessful at detecting Bergem's motives as well, my sister. There is no need for apologies."

Prisca squeezed her sister's hand and said, "Listen, be careful out there. I don't know what my world would be like without you in it."

Helena blinked away her tears and said, "You too, my sister."

Chapter 27

"Really?"

"Try to control your emotions, sister," Helena said.

Terentia straightened herself and said, "Thank you for choosing me for this mission. I will succeed!"

Memories of raising her from an infant to a young woman threatened to consume Helena. The youngest of the Antaran daughters had a most open and caring heart – something their mother strived to place in all of them. Love and acceptance came easily to Terentia. Her heart knew no limits.

Keeping her feelings for her sister from overwhelming her consciousness, Helena glanced at the harp in the corner of the room and said, "Were you playing?"

"This morning, yes. It calms my mind," Terentia said. Then, she held her datapad aloft. "I've been studying though! Don't think me lax."

"Dear Terentia, you should have been able to sense that I knew you were not abandoning your duties. You need to remain vigilant and alert, especially while talking with the Humans," Helena said as she moved to the harp. "It is the only way you will succeed."

Terentia bit her lip and said, "I'm sorry, sister."

"Apology accepted," Helena said as she sat and strummed the strings. "There's no room for error while you are aboard your ship, surrounded by Humans. Remember that."

Terentia kneeled next to her sister and said, "I'll not forget your words."

As Helena tested the tune and resistance, she sensed her sister's troubles. "You are fearful of failure," Helena said. "That is something we all must reconcile before we depart for Terra."

"I know," Terentia said. "Everything's just been so serious around here lately."

"Of course it has," Helena said, suppressing the urge to hold her sister in her arms and tell her everything was going to be alright. Now wasn't the time to treat her like a child. She needed to become a woman.

Helena played a tune on the harp and allowed the math of the music to flow through her fingers. Though she preferred the smaller string instruments, the harp held a special place in her heart. Her mother trained her on the harp, and Helena had taught Terentia.

When the last of the notes faded into the walls, Terentia said, "You're still better than me at this... at everything. You are all so skilled and perfect. Am I really ready?"

"That is what I am here to test," Helena said. "But first, know this – you are greater than us all, Terentia. I sense tremendous potential within you. We all sense it. Mother gave you a gift before she passed on and you will learn to master it far beyond even Valeria's vaunted skill. Trust in yourself. The delicate time where you could afford doubt has passed you, my sister. Now is the time for strength and action – we will see if you are ready."

Helena sensed her sister's hesitation. Terentia had planned to finally ask a question which had haunted her since her birth. She struggled with the words in her mind for a few moments and Helena allowed her to work though her pain.

Finally, Terentia asked, "What was mother like?"

Since her birth, Terentia carried the guilt of her mother's death. The circumstances of her birth tormented her.

After all those years, she now found the strength to face her guilt with courage and dignity. Terentia had never before broached the subject of their mother.

Helena smiled and allowed Terentia to curl up against her side. "I'm more than happy to tell you about mother," she said. "Safe and warm when we were children, she was our world. She taught us what it meant to be an Antaran, but she did this through example rather than instruction. A day did not pass without mother engaging the people in some way - a speech, a visit to a place that needed hope, and many other selfless gifts of her time and energy. She was as much a force on this planet as the winds and plants."

"And she taught you how to harness our mental discipline?"

Helena nodded. "More than that, she showed us how to weave that ability into our unique personalities. Claudia is in tune with all things in nature. Valeria has gone as far as to be able to control the actions of others. Prisca has a deep understanding of the physical and stellar sciences. Justina is spiritual to a degree I cannot even begin to comprehend. Marcella can soothe a crowd. And you combine all of these elements into a dynamic balance. We're all proud of you and your potential."

"You mentioned a test?" Terentia said as her young eyes searched her sister for a clue. "How will I know if I'm ready?"

"We do not tell you about the test, because mother believed this is something that should *not* be studied for," Helena said. "You are either ready or you are not ready."

"What is the test?" Terentia asked.

Helena sat in front of her sister and locked their eyes together. "It is a test of mental discipline. Mother gave the test to me and now I give it to you. Clear your mind and prepare yourself, my sister. This will not be easy."

After invading Terentia's mind, Helena trapped her in a virtual landscape of bleak sand and a dark sky. She sped time so hours in the real world translated to years in Terentia's dream world. She stripped everything away from her sister and watched her struggle to find an end to the desolation.

For weeks in the dream, Terentia meditated. She slowed her body's metabolism to a near halt and attempted to find the spark of life by reaching her mind out across the wasteland. To Terentia, this world was her life. Helena supplanted Terentia's memories with a blank slate, leaving only her core personality and instinct.

Terentia found life miles to the east. Before she struck out, she mined the collective thoughts of nearby ant colonies to find sources of water.

Exhausted and near death, Terentia arrived at the desert settlement. The people there took her in and Terentia found work as a tailor. As she lived this pseudo-life, she realized the oppression of the sultan when he came and took all the young women as slaves, Terentia included.

This was the part of the dream where each sister had taken their own path. Helena had enlisted the aid of a rival nation when her mother gave her the test. Though she wasn't certain how Valeria reacted when their mother tested her, Helena assumes Valeria killed the sultan in cold blood and assumed ruler ship. Prisca became the sultan's vizier and made the dream world a better place for the inhabitants. Justina brought religion to them and established the first churches. Marcella seduced the sultan and he made her his bride. After that, a simple poisoning ensured she could govern free of the sultan's interference. Claudia dutifully assumed her role as harem concubine and appealed to the sultan's mother to dethrone the sultan. Then, Claudia served as the advisor to the new ruler of the dream world.

Now, it was Terentia's turn.

Helena watched as her sister suffered in the harem and eventually became the sultan's favorite. Through the years, Terentia discovered a softness in the sultan stemming from his troubled youth. She carefully helped the sultan realize that part of his personality and he became a beloved ruler.

Stunned at Terentia's approach, Helena allowed the dream to continue farther than she had in the past. She marveled at her sister's infinite compassion and ability to see the kindness in any heart.

Then, Helena slowly pulled the veil of the dream away and allowed her sister to sleep after the marathon test.

She had passed. Though her mother never revealed if there was a right and wrong way to conquer the dream, Helena believed that Terentia had "solved" it. Nobody was killed, the people's core values weren't changed, and everyone prospered internally and externally.

Terentia was the greatest of them all and Helena stroked her sister's hair until she awoke several hours later.

At first, the youngest sister was confused. She was expecting to awake in her bed at the sultan's palace an old woman. Instead, she looked into the strange face of her sister. The worlds slowly divided in her mind and Helena watched as her sister sorted things out in her mind. She had now lived two lives and that realization was taking hold in her heart.

"H-Helena…?"

Helena nodded. "I'm here, my sister."

"I… I-"

"Take some time," Helena said. "Most of us meditated for days afterwards. I can return when you call me."

"No," Terentia said. "I don't need time. I think I understand."

Helena watched Terentia reconcile everything from inside her mind. Though it would take time to incorporate everything into the Antaran Terentia, Helena sensed her sister would succeed.

Could she send Terentia into battle? Could she risk losing their future? Now Helena realized why her father resisted involving Terentia in the war. And now it was too late to change the plan and also ensure success.

Chapter 28

Helena returned to space before she felt like she had a chance to catch her breath. The seven daughters of Agreios were whisked to Terra where they were formally received by Human diplomats.

"This is absurd," Valeria said. "We should be preparing for war, not prancing around in our gowns at a ball."

Helena was once again in the crystalline Human Grand Banquet Hall. The battleships had been returning home since the Antaran princesses arrived on Terra. Now, to celebrate their new allies and repair their image, the Human Council decided to organize a ball to honor the aliens.

"Marcella is having a good time," Terentia said, pointing to the dance floor.

Indeed, Marcella was the center of attention as always. Her gown flowed magically as she twirled around the Human men. Helena noticed a few unsavory looks from shunned wives and girlfriends.

She also noticed Admiral Stugardt approach them with a wide smile on his face.

"We didn't put this together so you could stand to the side and watch," Stugardt said as he brought his wife forward. "This is my wife, Nadine."

Nadine smiled and said, "My, you are an impressive group of women."

"I am pleased to see you again, Nadine," Helena said as she bowed her head. "Allow me to present my sisters – Valeria, Justina, Claudia, Prisca, Terentia. And Marcella is dancing with, well, several men at the moment."

"It is a pleasure to meet you all," Nadine said.

"If you don't mind, my dear," Stugardt said, "I'd like to ask the Lady Helena for this next dance."

"Mind?" Nadine said. "Please, go. It'll give me a moment to get acquainted with these lovely women."

Stugardt led Helena to the dance floor and demonstrated the steps to the current dance.

"Oh, this is quite simple," Helena said.

"So, are you ready for tomorrow?"

"The war council?" Helena said. "Yes. I think the plan is a wise one."

"You know, I've never met anyone quite like you," he said.

"Why thank you, Admiral."

"That stunt you and Nadine pulled took some guts. I didn't think they'd back down."

"Well, they still haven't, not completely," Helena said. "Agent Rowe continues to shadow my movements on the *Jupiter* and here on Terra."

"Once things get in motion, I'm sure they'll reassign him," Stugardt said.

"Ahem," a voice said from behind Helena. Without turning, Helena knew the speaker was Captain Nathan Connor. Though she kept her distance from him while onboard the *Jupiter* for the return trip to Terra, Helena's heart soared with jubilation in response to his proximity.

"Admiral, you can't monopolize all the beautiful alien princesses," Nathan said.

"There's five more over there," Stugardt said.

"I saw this one first," Nathan said, interposing himself between Helena and Stugardt.

"Take good care of her," Stugardt said as he wandered back towards Helena's sisters.

"How is the evening finding you, My Lady?" Nathan said as he stepped in tune to the music and smoldered her heart with his beautiful, brown eyes.

"Quite well, thank you, Captain."

"Nathan," he said. "Remember? When we're not on the bridge of the *Jupiter*, call me Nathan."

"I'm sorry. Your rules of propriety still perplex me."

"May I call you, 'Helena'?"

Helena spun under his arm and returned to his dancing embrace. "No, you may not."

"What about 'Princess?'"

Helena allowed a smile to escape and she said, "Please, no!"

"*Lady Helena* it is, then," Nathan said.

After a few moments of uncomfortable silence she said, "Why do you stare at my face?"

"I'm just trying to remember that time I saw you without your facial markings," Nathan said. "That was a while ago."

"I guess," Helena said, sensing his desperation and need to reveal his feelings for her. However, he held back.

"I've been thinking about our time on Caledonia…" he said.

"Yes?" she said as she found strength in her sisters. His charm was easier to resist under their watchful eyes.

"I… I just had a great time with you, that's all," he said as he angled his head to the side. "I see you still wear the globes we found in that shop?"

Helene touched the glowing orbs with her fingertips and said, "I do love them. Thank you."

"My pleasure, Lady Helena."

The song ended and everyone on the dance floor clapped for the band. Councilor Durgess stood at the microphone and waited for the noise to subside.

"Honored guests, senators, distinguished friends, and my fellow councilors," Durgess said, "we are pleased to welcome the daughters of Emperor Agreios to Terra."

The room erupted into applause as everyone searched out the painted faces of the aliens. Helena sensed a great deal of excitement from the crowd. She also sensed a disapproving stare from Valeria.

"Tonight we raise our glasses in respect to our new allies from Antares. May our friendship stand the test of time and may our walls hold strong. To the daughters of Antares!"

"Here! Here!"

The Humans raised their glasses and drank to Helena and her sisters. Human customs were so strange. The music resumed and Nathan led the seven sisters to their table. Throughout the evening politicians, scientists, and military officers came to the table to greet and talk with the sisters.

Then, Admiral Stugardt appeared at Helena's side and said, "We have an emergency. The Proxans attacked one of our planets a few hours ago. We just received word."

As the news spread, the party dispersed. Helena and Stugardt were transported by aircar to the Human High Command. Inside the bowels of the secure building, admirals and officers scurried from screen to screen and into meeting rooms. Helena found the man in command of all Human forces in his command chair reviewing a datapad.

"Well, I guess we do this a day early," Admiral Leighton said as he pushed aside his work and examined Helena in her royal gown.

Helena studied the main holographic tactical display and the many monitors in the war room. The Proxans attacked, with great force, a Human planet that has served as a staging point for mining preparation of the second tellium star.

"I think they know," Helena said.

"Know what?" Leighton asked.

Stugardt interjected and said, "She was the one who captured the Proxan spy and she has kept the location of Beta a secret."

"Well, now everyone knows," Admiral Leighton said.

"This doesn't change things," Helena said. "Are the communication stations in place?"

Admiral Leighton nodded. "Yes. We have everything ready to go. We haven't activated them yet and so far the Proxans haven't discovered them."

"Good," Helena said as she activated the laser pointer. "We should move with haste. The *Jupiter* is ready to go. We should send her to deal with this immediate Proxan threat."

"There are reports of *two* Proxan battleships in that area," Admiral Leighton said. "We should send three of our battleships. I already gave the order to prep the *Jupiter*, the *Saturn*, and the *Nova*."

Helena pointed to a location in Proxan space. "No. The rest of the fleet should begin their assault here. Claim this system and setup a communication station. From there, strike out as we planned to disable communications along this line. They won't be prepared for this kind of assault. Not this quickly."

"With all due respect, the *Jupiter* is no match for two Proxan battle fleets," Leighton said.

Stugardt stepped forward and said, "Not to disagree with you, sir, but you are talking to the *Jupiter's* two tactical advisors. I've seen the lady in action and I'm more than happy to go to battle with her against most any odds. I think once the Proxans hear about the major advance into their space, they'll not stick around for long."

"Exactly," Helena said. "Once we're done there, we'll rejoin the fleet, activate all the communication stations and resume the attack plan."

Admiral Leighton studied the holo-display and said, "Very well. You two better get moving."

Stugardt looked at Helena's gown and said, "We could use a quick change, as well."

Helena changed into a plain Human jumpsuit, attached her "advisor" insignia and tied her hair into a high pony tail. As she painted her Gima tattoos across her face, she imagined her sisters performing the same motions before boarding their ships.

Now she was truly alone. Duronius was safe on Antares, back with his daughter and family. Helena's sisters were scattered to their various ships. Their people waited in their homes unaware of the emperor's plot.

Helena again wondered if they had made the right decision. Queen Galeria's gamble worked, so the Archives remember her has a hero. What if they failed? Would the Archives remember Helena and her sisters as villains? Would there be anyone left on Antares to remember the tale of the seven daughters of Agreios and their secret plot against the Humans and Proxans?

Lieutenant Sandra Rhom descended to the landing platform in the captain's yacht. The vessel's massive twin engines roared and then fell silent as the ship settled. Helena joined Rhom in the cockpit and they shot into space towards the Human flagship.

"Feels like we were just doing this, eh?" Rhom asked.

"After the first time, I thought I'd never become accustomed to flying up and down so much," Helena said as she indulged the Human's desire for idle chatter. "Now however, I don't mind it so much."

Rhom wanted to talk about something, but something held her back. Deciding not to pry, Helena waited.

After a few moments of uncomfortable silence, Rhom said, "I just want you to know that I don't agree with what some of the other crew members are saying."

Helena raised one of her eyebrows. "And what are they saying?"

"Can't you just scan their thoughts?"

"I prefer to respect your privacy, as you call it," Helena said.

"Well, some of the crew are resentful and suspicious," Rhom said. "They don't like the idea of an alien on the bridge."

Helena sensed it now as they approached the massive form of the Jupiter. The crew even knew that Rhom approached now with their alien advisor, aboard the captain's yacht. For reasons that bordered on petty jealousy, some of the crew and officers viewed Helena as a threat to them. She was an outsider given all the privileges they were denied. They also resented their new captain. Nathan wasn't necessarily next in line for that command, but Admiral Stugardt's clout was enough to secure Nathan's promotion.

Helena stored each variable for meditation once she was settled in her quarters. This task was far from trivial and she lowered the chance for success every time she encountered some new Human twist. Everything would have been easier if Humans weren't ruled by their emotions. Helena could conquer logic. Emotion gave her more trouble.

The Humans eyed her as she boarded the Jupiter again and Helena scanned their thoughts to ensure no violence was imminent.

"This way," Rhom said as she broke into a jog. "They're not wasting any time. We'll be in high velocity by the time we reach the bridge."

"They were just waiting for me?" Helena asked as she kept pace.

Rhom nodded. "Nobody's taken on two battleships before. I think we're going to need more of your magic from the asteroid field."

Helena kept her thoughts to herself. She was confident she could win against what the Humans call "impossible odds," but a part of her doubted. What if their insurrection ended before it began? Was she really skilled enough to coordinate such an attack?

Well, she thought, we will soon discover the limits of Heir Helena's mental abilities.

Chapter 29

The *Jupiter* rattled from the impact of the torpedoes.

Captain Nathan Connor turned to Helena and said, "Are you sure about this?"

Helena examined the holographic tactical display showing the *Jupiter's* position in relation to the two Proxan battleships and the myriad of support vessels. The battle was more impressive than their little skirmish back in the asteroids with the small Proxan frigates.

"The other ship has already powered-on their engines. They are returning to Proxan space to deal with our attack there," Helena said.

"I get no reading from that ship, sir," Lieutenant Sandra Rhom called from her station.

"Trust me, they're leaving," Helena said.

"Okay, helm," Nathan said. "Bear down on that second battleship. Use Lady Helena's mark."

"We're taking some serious hits," Admiral Stugardt said, his face plastered with concern.

"Just a tad further," Helena said. "Then we can take out our target's engines. By then, the other ship will be gone and we can destroy this one."

"Another salvo!" Lieutenant Rhom said.

"Come to gamma-one," Helena said, pointing with the laser. "Fire batteries S7 through S19 at forty-seven degrees in three seconds. Two seconds. One second. Fire!"

The batteries fired and everyone on the bridge waited. Flashing lights backlit smoke from released pressure. Monitors flickered and nobody moved.

"Sir, torpedoes destroyed!" Lieutenant Rhom said with a sigh of relief.

"They're sending everything at us," Stugardt said.

Helena sensed excitement as the other Proxan ship winked from the display. It was gone.

"Now!" Helena said, pointing to a new spot on the map. "Come to bravo-seventeen, full thrust."

"You're doing a number on my engines," Nathan said.

"They will hold," Helena said. "They're changing course to avoid us. Or, they will in a few seconds. New firing solution – bravo-sixteen, three seconds. Two second. One second. Fire torpedoes!"

"Torpedoes away," Nathan said as he reviewed his monitor.

Helena waited. Smaller ships danced and winked out of the display as they were destroyed, but her attention remained fixated on the retreating Proxan battleship.

"Direct hits!" Lieutenant Rhom called. "Their engines are disabled, sir."

"Continue the advance," Nathan said. "Engage full."

One of the weapon officers said, "Aye, sir."

Helena watched on the holographic map as the *Jupiter* moved forward for the kill. Though she loathed violence, Helena felt a rush of excitement as they battered their opponent into submission. Perhaps she was more the tigress than she admitted to herself.

"Move the frigates in and take out their batteries," Nathan said.

A communications officer relayed the order to the support craft and Helena watched as the small Human ships swarmed around the disabled battleship.

"Good work, people," Nathan said. "Lieutenant, inform hangar bay four to launch marines. I want to secure that vessel as quickly-"

"Wait!" Helena said. She sensed urgency and deceit from the Proxan battleship. Something wasn't right.

"What's wrong?"

"Just... I need a moment," Helena said as she closed her eyes and concentrated on the enemy.

"Should I give the order, Captain?"

"Hold a minute," Nathan said.

Then, Helena opened her eyes and said, "Get everyone out of there!"

"What?!"

"Get your frigates out of there and move us to alpha-twelve," Helena said. "The Proxan ship is overloading their power core. They are going to explode in under thirty seconds."

"A self-destruct device?" Stugardt said, punching in orders to some of the frigates.

"Helm, you have your coordinates," Nathan said.

Moments later, the Proxan battleship imploded. The shockwave washed over the *Jupiter*. Lights flickered. Everyone rushed to their consoles.

"No major damage," Lieutenant Rhom said.

"Well, that was interesting," Stugardt said.

"We've never been able to destroy one before," Nathan said. "Lesson learned." He faced Helena. "You just saved hundreds of men and women under my command. Thank you."

Helena grasped the rail for support. Keeping tabs on thousands of minds and scores of spacecraft proved to be a taxing exercise.

"Are you okay?" Stugardt asked.

Helena nodded. "Just a little woozy."

"We can mop this up," Nathan said. "Why don't you head to your quarters."

"Yes, I think that is a good idea," Helena said.

As she walked to the lift, the entire bridge crew stood and applauded. Apparently, she had just secured them their first major victory in the war.

Exhausted, Helena fell into her bunk and closed her eyes. However, she remained connected to the bridge in case they needed her. She focused on Nathan's mind and sensed him approach a few hours later.

"May I enter?" His voice crackled through the intercom.

"Of course."

The door slid into the wall with only a few minor groans. Excited and full of caffeine, Nathan crossed the threshold and beamed.

"Would you like to hear the response from Admiral Leighton?" he asked.

She propped her head on her elbow and said, "Certainly."

Though she valued her privacy, she couldn't deny the captain entrance into her quarters. Perhaps she might finally be able to allow him into her heart – a feat she couldn't accomplish on Caledonia. Or, was she maneuvering herself into a position where she could more easily destroy the *Jupiter* when the time came?

She remained in her cot while Nathan recited the content of the communication from the admiral.

"He reports that the rest of our fleet won their first battle with ease. Valeria's ship, the *Kraken* hunted the lone Proxan defending battleship and dealt serious damage to it. That ship won't be joining the fight anytime soon." Nathan tapped the screen of his datapad and continued. "The communication station is already in place and we obviously have full signal back to Terra. He reviewed the replay of the battle and he personally commends your skill as a tactician. He sends along his apologies for not trusting you at first and he wishes us swift speed to the front lines."

"How much damage did we suffer?" Helena asked.

Nathan sighed. "And here's the bad news. We took some heavy hurt chasing down that Proxan ship. We're going to need a few weeks before we can join the fight again."

"I'm sorry. I felt the destruction of that ship was worth-"

"Are you kidding me?" Nathan said. "It was well worth the damage we sustained. We just evened the odds today. That's huge."

Helena smiled. "I hope we proved more than that today," she said. "Is the rest of the fleet pressing the attack to disable Proxan communications?"

"Yes," he said. "It looks like Valeria is spearheading the assault in the *Kraken*. The *Waterloo* and *Minotaur* are also heading for their targets."

Valeria, Marcella, and Claudia. Helena hoped they could avoid harm.

"The rest of the fleet is securing our beachhead, if you will," Nathan said. "We should be with them in approximately fifty-two hours. Then, they can press forward to their targets. We will defend the communication station and points inward while making our repairs."

"That sounds like a wise plan," she said.

Nathan studied her for a moment and said, "Are you sure you're okay? Do you want me to send for a doctor?"

She smiled and hoped her feelings weren't painted on her face as clearly as her Gima tattoos. "I am a doctor."

"Oh yeah."

"I just need some sleep," she said. "Wake me if I'm needed on the bridge."

"Yes, milady."

As Nathan departed, Helena's heart scolded her sense of propriety. She wanted to ask him to stay. For some reason, the thrill of combat sent her emotions into a whirlwind. She craved more excitement and, for the first time, she admitted to herself that she was ready for more from Nathan as well.

Chapter 30

"How are you doing, really?" Helena asked her sister. Though she could see Terentia's face through the holo-link, Helena couldn't read her sister's emotions. They were close enough, but Terentia held her mind locked. Good girl.

Keeping her face even, Terentia said, "I am fine, thank you, my sister. The battle was intense, but the *Mars* was only providing support. Valeria and Prisca were in the most danger. I feared for them."

"You are doing well," Helena said. "I am very proud of you."

Terentia tilted her head and said, "Thank you, sister. I am still meditating on the lesson you taught me before we left Antares. Everyone went through that?"

"Yes," Helena said. "Mother gave the test to Valeria, Prisca and myself. Then, she taught me how to administer the test and I have been doing it since. At first it was very taxing for me. Now however, I think I have mastered that skill. Well, with my sisters at least. I have yet to attempt such a thing on an unwilling target."

Helena glanced over her shoulder at Rowe. The blue glow from the holographic projector gave him a sinister glow in the otherwise dim room. He seemed disinterested as he fidgeted with a small electronic device.

"I think I realize the truth behind the test," Terentia said. "Now I must analyze what that truth means to me."

Helena nodded. "It took me three years. Don't rush to your conclusions, sister. Allow your thoughts about the experience come naturally to you. *Organically*, as Claudia would say."

"I will. Thank you, sister."

Back to business, Helena said, "I understand you are leaving in a few hours for your target — a Proxan communication hub and refueling depot."

"Yes. The captain has already requested my presence on the bridge," Terentia said. "So, with a heavy heart, I must say farewell for now."

Helena smiled and touched the holographic image of her sister. Terentia mimicked the gesture.

"Be safe, my sister," Helena said.

"You as well, Heir Helena."

Terentia's face winked away and Helena repressed her tears. What were they doing out here in space playing warrior? Could they really succeed? Now that the plan was in motion, Helena realized the myriad of uncounted variables. Emotional variables. This was no small task. Helena sighed and turned to Rowe.

"Why are you still here?" Helena asked.

Rowe shrugged and removed his feet from her table as he rose to retrieve the transmitter chip. "My orders stand. So until the Council tells me differently, you're stuck with me."

Helena sensed the man was telling the truth. The Council was too far away for Helena to attempt to discover their motives. If there was anything more to the situation, she couldn't sense it.

Rowe scratched his black face stubble and said, "I guess they still don't trust you. And neither do I. On my planet, we would brand you a witch and hang you."

Helena gazed at the assassin and said, "How very enlightened of you."

"God didn't make you," Rowe said. "But I have an idea who did. When this is over, maybe I'll do some freelance work for the Church. I'm sure they'd love to know the truth about you and your sisters… of what you are capable."

Helena delved into Rowe's mind and he stepped backwards as his eyes widened. He sensed her presence. She discovered a religious fanaticism present in the man that could prove dangerous. Helena misread his moral flexibility before. Rowe wasn't without a conscious. Instead, his religion sanctioned even his most brutal of deeds. In the name of his god, he could do no wrong.

Helena leaned towards him and bore into his eyes. She said, "If you threaten me or my sisters again, I will kill you."

Rowe opened the door and paused. "Be careful with your threats," he said. "You never know who may be listening."

Helena detected an active recording device under his jacket. What did he hope to accomplish? His mind was alive with possibilities and ideas. He aimed to bring her down, but he wasn't sure *how*.

Nathan met her in the corridor and eyed Rowe as he disappeared around a corner.

"Is he still causing trouble?" Nathan said.

"No," Helena said as she turned her face away from him.

He put his hand on her shoulder and attempted to catch her eye. "What's wrong?" he asked.

"Nothing," she said.

His voice was tender, concerned. "You can tell me-"

She looked into his eyes and said, "I just miss my sisters. Talking with Terentia… I'm sorry. You shouldn't be burdened with my problems."

"Terentia is your youngest sister, right?"

Helena nodded. "She has the type of heart that forgives the moment it is slighted," she said. "It is the kind of perfection I have strived for ever since I recognized the quality of her character. She welcomes you without saying a word, and you want to stay forever. She is my father's greatest joy. And mine as well."

Without another word, Helena rushed to her quarters. She couldn't allow Nathan to see her weakness and the tragic truth – she would defy her emperor for her sisters. Why did she allow him to even see a portion of her vulnerability? Why was she making so many mistakes around him?

She realized she needed to distance herself from him again, so she spent the next few days in the *Jupiter's* medical ward tending wounded crew members. Some of the thrill of battle wore away when she saw the price many Humans paid for their victory. However, she couldn't allow pity into her heart. The Humans were her enemy.

After their victory and Helena's time tending wounded Humans, the crew warmed to her presence. The sideways glances transformed into warm smiles and appreciation. They realized how valuable she was.

After a few days apart, Helena encountered the captain in the officer's lounge. She knew he was there, but she rationalized that she needed to resume her duties on the bridge now that the *Jupiter* was close to full strength again.

The forward lounge on the *Jupiter* shared all the concepts from the lounge on the *Venture*, but added some luxury. For starters, it was larger. Instead of bolted titanium, the walls were paneled with a dark wood. Soft lighting illuminated the important areas and left some booths shrouded in intimate darkness. Music drifted from the corners of the room at an acceptable volume and the serving staff remained out of sight unless needed.

"Lady Helena," Nathan said. "Won't you join us?"

Lieutenant Sandra Rhom scarfed the last few bites of her food and mumbled, "I was just leaving."

As Helena sat she said, "There is no need for you to leave us alone, Lieutenant."

Rhom glanced from Helena to Nathan. "Gym," she said. "I must go to the gym."

After another moment of awkwardness, Rhom rose and headed for the door.

"That was odd," Helena said as she keyed her order into the table. Another salad sounded good to her.

"She thinks we're—"

"That's just silly," Helena said when she understood Rhom's hasty departure. Ever since Caledonia, the crew had made their assumptions about Helena and the captain.

"I know, right?" Nathan said, though his desires were easy to read.

He wanted her in a way that made his heart burn. Shocked, she retreated from his mind as quickly as she entered. For a reason she couldn't describe, she didn't want to invade his personal thoughts so casually.

"I'm here to report back for duty on the bridge," she said.

"Oh. Right. Thanks for your help in the medical ward. Dr. Manningham sent along his admiration of your skill. From what I hear, the doctor isn't easy to impress. I appreciate your willingness to help my wounded crew."

"I'm most at home in a hospital," she said. "It was my pleasure."

"Well," he said as he accessed the table's holographic projector and datalink, "the past few days have been very positive. Your sisters succeeded in destroying all Proxan communications along the front lines. As you predicted, the strike was swift and decisive. The Proxans have retreated to their strongholds and they are licking their wounds."

"Licking?"

"Oh," Nathan said, "it's just a figure of speech. They are recovering from the assault."

"Ah."

"We've stayed put here at the beachhead," he said. "The final ship we have – the *Bastion* – remains in orbit near Terra to defend our core worlds. As you know, none of your sisters are stationed aboard the *Bastion*."

Helena nodded as she examined the data displayed on the hologram. Everything was falling into place. Once the Proxans were destroyed, Helena and her sisters would carry out the second part of the plan which included the destruction of the Human fleets and the tellium stars.

"You know," Nathan said, "the gym doesn't sound like a bad idea. Care to join me?"

"I'm not-"

"Do you know how to box?" he asked quizzically.

Confused, Helena said, "Box? Oh yes, I think I saw a match on the wave while I was at the Human Embassy. Violent sport."

"It's not so bad," he said. "Many of the officers enjoy it as an outlet. It's a great way to blow-off some steam. I can teach you."

"I'm not sure that's safe-"

Nathan smiled. "You won't get hurt, I promise. It really is-"

"No," Helena said playfully, "I didn't mean for me. I meant, well, after the chess match and volleyball... I'm not sure your manly psyche could handle another defeat at my hands. I'd be devastated."

A few of the nearby officers caught the exchange and snickered. Apparently, Captain Nathan Connor had a reputation for winning and it amused them that Helena was the one person to hand him so many defeats. Humans sometimes enjoyed laughing at the misery of others.

Such a curious race, Helena thought.

"We don't need to hold a match," Nathan said. "I mean, this isn't like chess where you can outthink me. I've been boxing for years. It wouldn't be fair."

"I understand if you don't want to challenge me again so soon after Caledonia," Helena said.

Why was she goading him into this? What could she possibly gain? Her decision to distance herself from him was a wise one as she seemed to unravel every time she talked with him. She wasn't herself.

"Yeah, Captain," one of the officers said from his table, "we understand too if you are afraid of her. We won't tell anyone."

Now everybody in the lounge was watching. Helena would have felt pity for Nathan if she didn't know him as well as she did. He could handle himself.

Straightening, he said, "Okay, My Lady. I didn't intend to turn this into a competition, but since you insist. I'll see you in the sparring ring in fifteen minutes."

Helena glanced at the time display on the table and said, "Very well."

News of the match spread throughout the *Jupiter* and almost every off-duty Human crowded into the gym to watch. Helena allowed Nathan to teach her how to don her boxing gloves and secure them to her wrists.

"See what you've done?" Nathan asked as he finished securing her gloves. "I'm not even sure everyone here is off-duty."

Lieutenant Sandra Rhom assisted Nathan with his gloves and rang a bell. "Round one!" she said.

Nathan advanced and asked, "So you know the rules?"

"Rules?"

Sighing, he said, "Just don't hit below the belt."

"Fair enough," she said as she swept his feet from under him with her leg and pounced.

Rhom rang the bell a few times and everyone burst into laughter.

"Bet you weren't expecting that, Captain!" someone yelled from the crowd.

"You lose again!" someone else shouted.

Helena stayed her elbow and realized she had violated the rules.

"May I just get the rules from your memory?" she asked.

"Please do," Nathan said.

Moments later, they were both on their feet again and Helena understood the sport better than when they started. Apparently, she was only allowed to use her gloved fists. How boring!

Rhom rung the bell again and Nathan advanced on her again.

"Mind your feet," he said. "While on the defensive, position your feet like this."

Helena knew all about footwork. She was a renowned fencer in her youth and she doubted the Humans could offer her any new insight. However she allowed Nathan to direct her.

"Good," he said. "Now, if you want to throw some jabs, position your feet like this."

He shuffled forward on the balls of his feet and threw a few mock punches.

"See?"

Helena nodded.

"You'll need to mind your hips and shoulders for a more powerful punch," he said as he demonstrated a few options.

"I think I get it," she said.

They kept their distance from each other for a few moments and the crowd grew restless.

"I think they want us to start hitting each other," Helena said.

Nathan smiled and obliged by throwing a few weak punches in her direction.

"You're not moving at full speed," she said.

"I just don't want to hurt you," he said.

"You won't."

While he hesitated, Helena decided to force the matter. She stepped forward and attacked with a few swift punches. Nathan blocked a few but was soon cornered under her assault. She landed some punches to his ribs and the side of his face and he pushed her away. For some reason, that was allowed by the rules.

Sufficiently goaded, he advanced and launched some full-speed punches. Helena was already in his mind reading his attack and calculating trajectories. She was able to bob, weave and block her way through his assault and she prepared her counterattack when the bell rang.

"You didn't even touch her!" someone yelled from the crowd.

"Helena for Captain!" someone else yelled.

Defeating him in chess with her mental abilities was warranted. But she wasn't sure she could humiliate him in front of his crew. The match could be fairer if she allowed.

She walked to his corner of the ring and whispered in his ear. "I'm sorry," she said. "I'll stay out of your mind for this one. If nothing else, you deserve a fair fight from me. For once."

He raised his eyebrows and asked, "Are you sure?"

Helena winked and returned to her corner. She had never given him the credit he deserved. Without her advantage, she wasn't sure she could have beaten him in chess. She respected him too much to pry her advantage in front of his crew.

The bell rang again and they met at the center of the ring. This time, Helena relied on her reflexes and vision to anticipate his attack. He advanced and landed a few punches to her midsection. She wasn't sure if he was holding back again, but her ribs burned from the beating.

She whirled to avoid being cornered and landed a devastating roundhouse. Taking advantage of the blow, she assaulted his face and body with swift jabs and barely legal uppercuts. He blocked one such uppercut with force enough to throw her off balance. She realized too late his follow-up would knock her over. She turned her face to avoid the brunt of the blow, but she did end the exchange on her back.

"Damn," she breathed.

"Are you okay?" he asked as he kneeled next to her.

She pushed herself upright and said, "I'm fine."

"You're bleeding. I shouldn't have-"

"When can we start again?" Helena asked, eager to correct her mistakes.

"When you're ready," Nathan said.

Helena immediately renewed her attack but soon found herself cornered by Nathan's superior technique and strength. Though she guessed he was still holding back, she couldn't break through. The bell rang again and she decided to admit defeat before she got hurt. Humans seemed to be a tad more durable than Antaran princesses.

"I concede," Helena said to Nathan and the crowd. "Your skill at clobbering another person is remarkable. Does anyone have a towel to throw?"

"No need," Nathan said with a wide smile.

Helena felt content as she walked with Nathan and Rhom to the locker rooms. The crew showered Nathan with praise and connected with their new captain for the first time. He was their hero and Helena felt like he needed that win.

"You know," Helena said, stopping the group. "I think I'm going to hit the pool for a few laps."

"You have a bathing suit under there?" Nathan asked.

Helena nodded. "It was part of my plan and then we punched each other for twenty minutes. I guess I forgot. Yeah, I need to take a swim for sure."

"Have fun!" Nathan said.

As Helena leisurely lapped the pool she detected a conversation between Rhom and Nathan. Their words carried to her as if she was in the same room with them.

"Captain, the sexual tension between you two is pretty obvious," Rhom said as she shed her clothing in front of him.

Humans had no sense of propriety.

Doing the same, Nathan said, "I don't know what you mean, Lieutenant."

"C'mon, Captain! What happened down on Caledonia?"

"Seriously, nothing," he said. "Helena is a perfect lady."

"I see the way you look at her," Rhom said. "I wasn't sure the feeling was mutual as she's a hard one to read. But after watching you two today, you may as well been having sex in the ring."

"I think you're seeing things-"

Rhom shook her head. "I don't know. You two are awfully chummy lately."

"Is that so bad?"

Helena marveled at how casual the two spoke to each other.

"No, I like her," Rhom said. "I just don't want to see you demoted again."

"And what is she's 'the one?'"

Rhom groaned. "Not that *destiny* crap again," she said.

Nathan winked and ducked into the showers. Though she enjoyed watching the naked Human through Rhom's eyes, Helena severed the mental link. She decided she couldn't indulge herself too much.

After her refreshing swim, Helena returned to her quarters and rested her head on the soft pillow. Her sleep was interrupted when the intercom crackled to life.

"Lady Helena?" Lieutenant Sandra Rhom said through the speaker.

"Yes, Lieutenant?"

"We just received word of a Proxan counterattack," Rhom said. "The captain requests your presence on the bridge."

"Tell him I will be right there," Helena said.

A counterattack? So soon? The move didn't make sense. The Proxans either had a surprise for them or were acting upon some bit of information unknown to her. Helena wrinkled her nose in disgust at both possibilities.

Chapter 31

The bridge buzzed and swirled with activity. Officers and crewmembers called information to each other. Consoles displayed scrolling information. Lights flashed. A quick scan on everyone's surface thoughts revealed they were preparing to depart.

Helena found Nathan at the main tactical display. He was studying a playback sent to them by the *Bastion*.

"My Lady," he said. "I have something to show you. The *Bastion* is defending a planet which was the target of a heavy Proxan counterattack. We're prepping to leave now, but I want to get your input."

Helena watched as the holographic scene played. The *Bastion* defended the planet and surrounding stations from three Proxan battleships. It appeared as though the Human captain was holding his own against the invaders, though the situation would not remain in their favor for long.

"What's so important about their target?" Helena asked.

"I'm not sure," Nathan said. "There's a research facility there. But militarily, it's not very strategic."

"Three battleships. The Proxans must find it important," Helena said. "What kind of research?"

"Pulling that up now," Nathan said. "Looks like commercial polymers and compounds. Nothing military or secret."

"What else is there?" Helena asked. "There has to be a reason for such a large assault force."

"Here, I'll send it to your screen," Nathan said.

"We're ready, Captain!" Lieutenant Rhom said.

Helena blocked the chaos in the room and focused on the data readout of the planet. Why would the Proxans attack here? Nathan was correct – it made little strategic sense. So, if the goal was not a tactical one, what was behind the attack? Helena poured through screens of data as the *Jupiter* hurtled through space. Nothing of significance presented itself.

Moments later, the *Jupiter* dropped from high warp and the tactical holo-map immediately flickered to life. The *Bastion* was almost crippled and only two Proxan battleships remained. The image of a Human captain winked open at Nathan's terminal.

"*Jupiter* – we are glad to see you!" the other captain said through the holo-communicator.

"What's the situation, Captain Hoode?" Nathan asked.

"The Proxans came in heavy and attacked several civilian targets," Captain Hoode said. "Then, we arrived and two more Proxan battleships joined the fray. I think they just meant to draw us out."

"Where is the third ship?" Helena said.

"Who is that?" Captain Hoode asked.

"This is the Lady Helena," Nathan said. "My senior tactical advisor."

"I see. The Antaran?"

Nathan nodded.

Captain Hoode disappeared for a moment as he barked an order to his crew. Then, he returned and said, "The third ship jumped away, but not before capturing a passenger liner."

"Can we get the passenger manifest?" Helena said. That liner must have been their target.

"Sending it over to you now," Captain Hoode said.

"Okay, *Bastion*," Nathan said. "We're still a bit battered, but we're joining the fight."

"Glad to have you with us," Captain Hoode said.

Helena studied the tactical situation. The *Bastion* was in trouble and the Proxan ships seemed unconcerned with the *Jupiter* for the moment. Reaching out to the Proxan minds, Helena sensed that their mission was complete. The liner was, indeed, their target. The *Bastion* was just an added bonus if they managed to destroy it.

Once the *Jupiter* advanced, the Proxans decided it was time to leave. Helena weighed her options. This was the perfect opportunity to see the destruction of the one Human battleship which didn't have one of her sisters aboard. Could she afford to make this large a 'mistake' in front of the captain? Would he view it as a mistake and not intentional?

Helena made her decision.

"Come around the other side of the planet," she said.

Nathan narrowed his eyes and said, "That'll take longer."

"They are retreating," Helena said. "This will give us the chance to run the closest one down."

"And risk the destruction of the *Bastion*?" Nathan said. "I don't think so."

"Tell Captain Hoode to maneuver to kappa-nine," Helena said, hoping Nathan wouldn't recognize the blunder. "That should buy them time."

Nathan examined the holo-display for a few moments. He eyed Helena and said, "That's not a good move. I don't like it."

"Trust me," Helena said, her voice and gaze even.

Nathan kept his eyes on Helena. His heart was conflicted, but he yielded.

"Lieutenant, tell Captain Hoode to maneuver to kappa-nine," he said. "Helm, swing us around the bottom of the planet. Mark gamma-one, full burn."

"Aye sir!"

Helena watched as the ships lumbered into their new positions and the *Jupiter* swung low. The Proxans sensed the mistake and resumed their assault on the *Bastion*. As Nathan called for more speed, Helena's heart thumped against her chest. Would the *Bastion* hold? Would Nathan see through her actions?

Stugardt burst from the lift and ran to the tactical station.

"I'm sorry, Captain," he said. "I was in the engine room. What's our situation?"

Nathan glanced at Helena and said, "Tenuous. The *Bastion* is in real trouble."

"Two Proxan battle fleets, I hear?" Stugardt said.

"Yeah," Nathan said. "They sacked a passenger liner."

Moments later, the *Jupiter* emerged on the other side of the planet and the *Bastion* was gone.

The bridge fell silent as everyone looked from the tactical display to the forward viewport. Shock and grief filled the room. Helena's heart shriveled as she *felt* the pain from everyone aboard. Thousands of deaths were on her hands.

"Sir! I have a firing solution on the closest battleship," a weapon officer called.

"Take it down," Nathan said, his mood turned dark.

What did she just do? What was this sinking feeling of despair she felt in her heart? Why couldn't she repress the emotion? Was she strong enough to destroy the *Jupiter* when the time came?

Stunned, Helena stood like a still image as the bridge crew of the *Jupiter* shouted orders and reported their status. Alarms blared and lights flashed, but Helena's mind remained locked in the moment of the *Bastion's* destruction.

"Helena!" Stugardt yelled. "Are you with us?"

Helena blinked and pulled herself from her reverie.

"We're getting hammered!"

Helena glanced at the tactical display and then sought the Proxan minds on the two battleships. The closest ship was hers for the taking, but they would probably have to retreat from the second one. Perhaps.

"They are firing torpedoes along kappa-four, thirty-seven degrees," she said. "Come to mark two and discharge aft-port batteries nine through twelve."

As the crew followed her orders and the immediate danger was avoided, Helena said, "Come to twenty four degrees and fire a full broadside on my mark."

Nathan raised one of his eyebrows and said, "A *full*?"

"We won't be able to fire again for three minutes," Stugardt said.

"I know," she said. "Twenty seconds until my mark."

Nathan pulled Helena aside and whispered, "Listen, I know how it feels to make a mistake and you want to make up for it as soon as possible. We will be defenseless for three minutes if I allow this order."

Helena looked into his eyes and found less there than before. She was diminished to him because of her actions. Time froze as she wrestled with the conflict in her heart. Why couldn't she separate herself from the violence she needed to unleash upon the Humans? Was she too close to her enemy?

Clearing the unwanted thoughts, Helena exhaled and said, "Trust me. I'll keep us safe for three minutes. They'll either retreat after we deal this decisive blow or they'll pursue. I'm sensing they will withdraw."

Nathan searched her eyes for an answer to his questions. Was he right to put his heart out in the open? Was his own vision clouded by his feelings for this alien? How could she fail so completely?

Helena's heart stung with each doubt and regret she read on his mind. How much damage had she caused? Her people won a great victory today with the destruction of the *Bastion*, but she endangered her mission. No, that wasn't the weight on her heart. The real damage had been done in Nathan's eyes. His doubts stung like a fresh wound.

"Admiral, carry out Lady Helena's order," Nathan said. "Full broadside on her mark."

With only a second to spare, Helena said, "Mark!"

Moments later the Proxan battleship flared and imploded. Halfhearted cheers escaped from a few of the bridge crew as everyone watched the massive vessel disintegrate.

"The other battleship is withdrawing," Admiral Stugardt said.

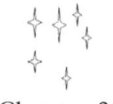

Chapter 32

Helena discovered doubts in her heart as she cried herself to sleep. Meditation was impossible. Her guilt over destroying that many lives – enemy or not – burdened her heart. Was her father's path an evil one? How would history remember the Antarans? Would she be able to return to her life once this was over and the blood gone from her hands? No. She decided her hands would never be clean.

Forgoing food, Helena remained in her quarters the next day. She couldn't face the crew. What did they think of her now? Did they still trust her? Did she endanger her own mission? Helena reviewed the previous day's events in her mind and if she was to ensure the safety of her people, her decision was valid. Math and duty… was that all there was to her?

Her door chimed and she heard Nathan's voice.

"Lady Helena?"

Helena took the time to inhale and exhale three times. This trick calmed her nerves to a more manageable level.

She opened the door and forced a smile. "Yes, Captain?"

Before he spoke, Helena sensed his surprise. She wasn't wearing her Gima tattoos! Helena turned away from him.

"I… I came to check on you," he said. "It's late, and we were wondering where you were. May I enter?"

"You shouldn't see me like this," Helena said. "It's not proper."

Nathan stepped into the room behind Helena and put his hands on her shoulders. That wasn't proper either!

"Listen," he said as the door closed behind them. "We've all made mistakes. It comes with the territory, with what we do."

Helena pulled away, even though her heart flipped over in her chest in response to his touch. Unsure what to do, she sat on her cot. Even with the distance between them she wasn't able to turn her face towards him. She hoped he didn't sense that her mood was not from what he perceived to be a tactical failure.

"I... I am sorry," she said.

Nathan joined her on the cot and lifted her chin with his index finger. He looked into her eyes and said, "Nobody blames you. The move was an aggressive one. This is war, and people die."

Helena heard his words, but her attention was on his lips. Would one taste be so wrong? Could the heir to the throne indulge her own heart? Was she allowed happiness?

"You know," he said as he leaned backwards in the cot, "my first mistake caused many deaths as well. But it also led me to you."

Puzzled, Helena asked, "How do you mean?" Though she could have probed his surface memories, she found her concentration unreliable around him. He flared emotions she'd never felt.

"In that skirmish above Antares, I misjudged my enemy," he said. "It cost me my ship, most of my crew, and it cost many Antaran citizens their lives when we crashed into your city."

"I... I didn't know."

"As much as I regret that mistake," he said. "I am also thankful that I was brought to you."

"Me?"

"Can't you read my heart?" he said, leaning towards her.

Helena concentrated, but found that she was unable to sense his feelings. She sensed her own emotions and she knew at that moment that she loved this Human. Despite her duty to her people and her mission, she couldn't deny her own heart. The feeling blinded her senses and judgment. She realized she needed to regain control.

Helena stood and turned away from him. "I think you should leave now," she said. "This is not allowed."

"Allowed?" He rose and placed his hands on her shoulders again. Helena's skin erupted in Goosebumps. "Why do you hide that beautiful face?"

"You cannot talk to me like this-"

"Like what?" he said. "You mean, I shouldn't tell you that time stands still when I see you? That gravity itself retreats from the area and you appear in slow motion as my heart stops? That your luminous eyes consume me? Why can't I tell you these things? I need to-"

Everything was crashing around her. His words, his closeness was dangerous.

"I... I-"

He whipped her around and kissed her. Helena's world exploded into a cacophony of pleasure, guilt, and yearning. She needed him too.

Helena returned the kiss, remembering Marcella's lesson. She ran her hands through his brown hair and pressed her body against his. Her walls crumbled and she allowed herself a moment of vulnerability and joy. What choice did she have? Her heart was in control.

He pushed her to the cot and covered her as he trailed kisses down to the base of her neck. With a growl, he removed her nightgown. She didn't protest. This wasn't as tender as she read in her Antaran books, but Humans apparently had their own set of rules.

With each kiss, her skin felt as if it was on fire. She squirmed in delight when his mouth roamed. Moaning, she lifted her body in response.

Then, he stopped.

They stared into each other eyes for a few moments and Helena felt a connection unlike any she had ever known. He smiled and kissed her tenderly as she felt his body against hers. Helena wondered for a moment where his pants had gone, but her musings quickly fled as she was filled with anticipation. This was the moment she had denied herself for far too long.

When it was over, she was encompassed by a new sense of peace and wholeness. The love of a partner was more than platitudes and dedication. There was also *this* part. She realized her task had become more difficult, but she didn't allow herself to focus on that eventuality. At that moment, she chose *love*.

Chapter 33

Helena awoke in an empty bed. She yawned and couldn't remember falling asleep. Why didn't she sense Nathan when he awoke and left her? Helena shook the fog from her head and saw the note:

Helena,

I would have enjoyed waking by your side, but duty calls. If you awaken before 0900, I will be in the officer's lounge for breakfast. You are more than welcome to join me.

I meant what I said last night – my world stops when you are near. You have my heart.

Helena paced her quarters with the note in hand as her adrenaline rushed throughout her body.

What was she thinking last night?

"You weren't thinking and that's the problem" she said aloud as she stopped and studied her face in the mirror.

Did she really think she was justified in her actions? Her heart was in control? What kind of a justification is that?

Now, separated from the rapture of the moment, she regretted. Though she believed her feelings for Nathan were as real and immediate as her feelings for her people, she needed to bury her desire.

But how?

Helena shook her head and felt lost for the first time since her mother died. She had nobody to turn to for answers.

Marcella told her to enjoy the captain. Valeria already disapproved, and she didn't know the whole story. Prisca. She needed Prisca.

"Where are you right now, my sister?" Helena asked into the mirror.

Her reflection held no answers.

Realizing she had time for a shower, Helena slipped her nightgown over her head and started the water. She smiled as she remembered Nathan's aggressiveness in removing the garment from her body the night before. As the memory dominated her consciousness her fingers and toes tingled.

No! she scolded herself. Keep those thoughts out of your head.

After her quick shower, she donned a simple blue dress and headed into the busy *Jupiter* corridors where repair crews worked. The ship was a mess as the recent battles had taken their destructive toll.

Helena arrived in the officer's lounge and she felt Nathan's excitement at seeing her. His mind strayed to the memory of their lovemaking and her thoughts weren't far behind. Where was her control?

"Good morning, Captain, Lieutenant," she said without betraying any emotion on her face.

"Lady Helena," Nathan said, "I hope this morning finds you well?"

She nodded and sat across from them.

"Hello, Lady Helena," Lieutenant Rhom said with a smile.

"Lieutenant."

"You can call me Sandra when we're off-duty."

Helena nodded and said, "As you wish, Sandra."

"Did you sleep well last night, My Lady?" Nathan asked. His mind was full of mischief. He enjoyed the secrecy.

"Very well, thank you, Captain," Helena said.

Helena's airy mood crashed when she sensed Rowe enter the room. Her back was to the door and she cursed herself for her carelessness. She found his mind difficult to read again. In his position, he was well-skilled in subterfuge, so her troubles made perfect sense. She was confident she could break through his barriers with more time.

Rowe strode to their table and said, "Did you two have a fun night last night?"

Helena remained calm while she sensed Nathan's panic and Sandra's confusion.

"The Lieutenant and I did not see each other last night," Helena said forcing him to play his hand if he wanted to.

Stepping to face her, Rowe glared into her eyes and said, "You know what I'm talking about, you whore."

Nathan shot out of his seat and his chair crashed to the floor. Everyone in the officer's lounge stopped and watched.

"I'm going to assume I misheard you," Nathan said. "You should leave. Now."

Rowe pulled a chair underneath him from the adjacent table. "Sorry, Captain," he said. "I have orders to watch this… outsider. That's what I intend to do."

"It's okay," Helena said, attempting to calm Nathan's rage. "Insults from such a petty, insignificant man mean little to me."

Instead of inciting him, Rowe simply shrugged and said, "I could say the same for you."

"Careful," Nathan said. ""I can only forgive so much."

"No, Captain, *you* should be careful," Rowe said. "Don't you have a regulation against fraternizing on your own vessel?"

The secret was out. Already.

Sandra's eyes widened. A few of the closer officers stopped in mid sentence, trying to decide if they correctly heard the accusation.

"Now," Rowe said, "I'd be surprised if your crewmates would think well on you sending me to the brig. Sending me there to protect your alien whore would cause-"

Helena sensed Nathan's violence before he swung, but she didn't stop him. Nobody on Antares would dare call her or one of her sisters 'whore.' Though Rowe was a despicable creature, she still felt the sting of the word. Was she a whore? Was she simply taking control of the captain so she would be in a better position to destroy the *Jupiter*? Helena wanted to believe that her emotions for Nathan were real, but she couldn't be certain. This was new territory for her heart.

Nathan landed a fearsome punch squarely into Rowe's jaw, sending the assassin to the ground. The crew watched, stunned.

"I won't send you to the brig," Nathan said, "but each time you insult her, you risk a broken jaw. Understood?"

Rowe remained on the floor, amused by the turn of events. "I should have your marines arrest you," Rowe said.

Nathan stepped forward and said, "Ask them, and see how far that gets you."

Helena stood and placed her hand on Nathan's arm. "Please, that is enough. You do not need to waste your energy on this man. He is of no consequence to me."

Holding his jaw, Rowe stood and said. "Perhaps I should head to sick bay so they can properly log the captain's violence."

Rowe exited the lounge and Nathan's breathing returned to normal. He sat and said, "I'm sorry. That was a childish thing to do."

Returning to her chair across from him, Helena said, "Doesn't it feel good? Hitting him?"

Sandra said, "If you want, I can hold him down so you can get a punch in there too, My Lady."

Helena shook her head and warmed as the memory from Terra resurfaced. "No need, I've already done that."

Nathan chuckled and rubbed his fist." Yeah, it did feel pretty good."

♦

After breakfast, Nathan and Helena shared the same lift to the bridge. She eyed him as the lift ascended. No, the previous night wasn't a mistake. She needed this. She needed him. As long as she was close to him, she decided to heed Marcella's advice and enjoy her time.

She stopped the lift in between decks and locked her eyes on his.

"How long until they think something's wrong?" she asked as she moved towards him, surprised by her own aggressiveness.

"I've thought of nothing but *you*," he said breathlessly as he scooped her into his arms and attacked her with his lips.

She invited him into her mouth and trembled at the rush of pleasure. Their tongues separated for a moment as he pushed her against the wall of the lift and held her there. He spread her legs and pushed her dress upwards. She didn't stop him.

The ecstasy came as quickly as before and Helena wondered why Humans rushed their lovemaking like they rushed everything else in their lives. Marcella taught her that these moments should last for *hours*, not *minutes*. However, Helena was too hungry for him – too eager to feel the rush of her own body against his. No, this suited her just fine. She didn't need or want the marathon sessions for which her sister was famous. She enjoyed the cloak and dagger affair that had started with the captain. She was walking along the razor's edge and she found she craved the danger of it.

Helena straightened her hair and retouched her tattoos as Nathan resumed the lift's ascent. He tucked his shirt into his pants and attempted to calm his own racing heart. Apparently he was equally exhilarated by their arrangement.

Maybe she was just feeding off his emotions? Helena shook her head and tried to focus on her duties.

♦

The *Jupiter* kept on the move for the next few days while the crew repaired the damage from the recent battles. Helena's sisters had begun the attack upon the Proxans and nobody suspected their plot. During the downtime, Helena poured over information from the attack on the *Bastion*. Pushing aside her guilt over her hand in so many deaths, she repeated the questions in her mind. What were the Proxans looking for? What was so important about that passenger liner they captured? She studied the passenger manifest again and noticed something odd.

"Dr. Jamie Moore?" Nathan asked as he reviewed Helena's findings. "Never heard of her."

He secured the door to his quarters and brushed a kiss behind her ear. Helena's skin responded with Goosebumps. Her concentration slowly regained its focus as he returned to his desk. Pushing his work aside, he focused on her. His mind buzzed with the possibilities as they weren't expected on the bridge for another hour.

"You probably wouldn't," Helena said as she attempted to rein her galloping heart. "I did some digging, as you Humans call it. Dr. Moore is a nanobiologist."

"Nanotech?"

"Yes," Helena said. "Microscopic cyborg organisms designed to perform all manner of tasks. Part living, part machine, the study of nanotechnology was outlawed by your church a few centuries ago. It has since faded into your history."

"This doctor was studying rouge science?" Nathan asked.

Helena sat across from him, retrieved her datapad and tucked a strand of silvery black hair behind her ear. "There's more," she said. "The Proxan's biology is symbiotic with nano organisms. Some of your history books hint that the Humans created the Proxans, as an offshoot of their own evolution, using nanotechnology. They cannot survive without nanos."

"They wanted her for her research?"

Helena felt a twinge of regret over diving straight into business with Nathan. If she had delayed telling him everything, perhaps they could have enjoyed some time in his cot. Now, the moment had passed.

Helena punched a code into her datapad and turned it towards him. "They're dying," she said.

"What?"

"Everything makes sense now," she said. "When I am in their minds, I feel their sense of urgency. I never knew where it came from until now. They are a dying race and they need breakthroughs in their science to continue their existence."

Now came the difficult part – she needed to lie again.

"Dying? How?" Nathan asked.

"I must speak with my sister Prisca to discuss my theories in detail," Helena said, "but I think there is a genetic disease within the nanos that they cannot cure. It laid dormant for millennia until something triggered it."

And the lie: "They were planning on attacking Humanity if we didn't rekindle the war," she said. "They reasoned that if they could defeat their only rivals, they could focus on reversing their extinction event."

Nathan studied her and said, "If they were planning a major offensive, we didn't catch wind of it. Are you sure about this?"

"Well, it doesn't matter now," she said. "We started things up for them. Trust me. All the disjointed thoughts in their minds make sense now. They captured the doctor because she made some underground breakthroughs in nanotechnology. The Proxans are desperate."

Nathan returned his attention to the data feeds on the surface of his desk. "Well, the good news is coming in now," he said. "Lady Valeria reports major victories all along the front line. We're already pushing them back."

The thought of slaughtering a dying race twisted in Helena's stomach. Somehow everything had gone sideways. They hadn't known about the Proxan's state. Was the Antaran plot even necessary? Were the Proxans on the verge of surrendering before her father intervened?

Dangerous thoughts, she cautioned herself. Such theories were the workings of her heart which desperately wanted to find an alternative.

"Thank you for the update," she said.

Her words were empty as she struggled with the new information about the Proxans.

"I'll get your report to High Command," Nathan said. "And I'll arrange a meeting with the *Jupiter*, so you can talk with Lady Prisca about this."

Helena examined him and knew that he would do almost anything for her. How could she betray him? The alternative was betrayal of her people and that wasn't an option.

She settled on his lap and ran her fingers through his brown hair. Instead of talking, she held his head to her chest and journeyed through his thoughts. His mind was alive with opportunities between them. When the war ended, he hoped she would stay with him. Marriage. Children. A life together. He knew he foolishly wanted everything, and a part of him feared her response to such thoughts. He loved her with his whole being. Startled by the depth of his feelings, she retreated from his thoughts and blinked tears back into her eyes. Could she follow through if it meant destroying him?

Silence settled over the room and between them. He appeared lost in his thoughts about their future and she wallowed in doubt. Her mission wasn't supposed to be this difficult.

The door chimed and she flinched. The admiral.

Helena rose from Nathan's comfortable warmth and placed her palm on the wall reader. The door slid into the wall and Stugardt smiled as he entered.

"Good day, Admiral," she said as she passed him.

She was alone with her thoughts as she returned to her quarters. Already responsible for hundreds of deaths aboard the *Bastion*, now she faced the realization that she was slaughtering a dying race.

As her doubt and guilt mounted, she decided her heart was too active in her thoughts. She needed to corral her unwanted feelings, but she hadn't settled upon a solution. If she wasn't careful, she predicted her emotions would be her downfall.

Chapter 34

"My sister," Prisca said as they clasped hands together. "Does the day find you solitary in mind and body?"

Helena nodded as she translated Prisca's coded message in her mind. She was asking if they would be allowed to speak alone.

"Indeed, my sister," Helena said.

"Good day to you, Captain Nathan Connor," Prisca said. "It is a pleasure to see you again."

Nathan nodded slightly, as previously instructed by Helena. "The pleasure is mine, My Lady."

Helena realized her sister was probing his thoughts and she quickly grabbed her arm. Nathan's recent memories would be like low-hanging fruit for Prisca. Embarrassing fruit.

"We have much to discuss," Helena said as she whirled Prisca towards the hangar bay lift. "I will return in seven hours."

"Take your time," Nathan said, scratching his chin. He likely detected Prisca's invasion.

"That was foolish," Helena said as she led Prisca to the captain's yacht.

After they had boarded and closed the ramp, Prisca turned to Helena and smiled. "I see you have found some measure of happiness with the captain," she said.

Helena paused her initiation sequence and exhaled. "Those are private memories."

Prisca sat in the navigator's chair and examined her. "Private? Since when do you value privacy? I think the Humans are wearing on you."

Still cautious of listening devices, Helena said, "I'm sorry. It has been a trying few weeks."

Prisca lifted one of her brown eyebrows. "Indeed."

The docking clamp refused to budge and Helena couldn't find the source of the malfunction. Then, Rowe's voice crackled through the intercom.

"Another unauthorized jaunt?" he said. "I think not. Lower your ramp. Since the captain won't let me ground you, I'm going with you."

"Not a chance," Helena said through the intercom. "We were promised privacy."

"So you can plot against us?" Rowe said. "Not on my watch. Lower your ramp."

Helena released her finger from the intercom switch and said, "I hate that man."

"Hate? Another Human emotion?" Prisca asked.

Ignoring her inquiry, Helena sent a text message to Lieutenant Sandra Rhom.

Release the docking clamp in hangar bay three, please. Rowe is making a scene.

After a few moments, the clamp released.

"No you don't," Rowe said through the intercom. "If you leave, I'll arrest you when you return. This isn't authorized!"

"Strap in," Helena said with a wink.

She rammed thruster forward and the yacht shot from the hangar bay. The *Jupiter* twisted behind them as they curled towards the planet surface. Tan expanses of desert awaited them and Helena reminisced of the test she gave to Terentia. Maybe their mother dreamt of this world and modeled the test upon its lands and people.

"That would be a fun adventure," Prisca said, sharing Helena's thoughts as they so often did.

"Terentia passed," Helena said. "She passed better than any of us did."

"I know. She's so special."

Helena swept the nose of the craft towards the spot she picked and keyed in new destination coordinates.

"Father sees it too," Helena said. "I just hope-"

Finishing her thought, Prisca said, "-she survives this ordeal." She examined Helena again and said, "You *hope*? Since when is that word in your thoughts? The Humans have changed you, sister."

Helena nodded and withheld her tears. "That is true."

Nathan dominated her thoughts and she sensed Prisca's disapproval.

"It wasn't supposed to go that far," Prisca said. "Can you control your feelings?"

Helena glanced at Prisca and said, "Of course."

Smiling, Prisca said, "I see your strength. Please forgive me for doubting you. As you mentioned, it *has* been a trying few weeks. Longer for you."

Helena eased the yacht to the ground and initiated the shutdown sequence. Flying was easier than she thought it would be. Unfortunately, everything else was far more difficult.

They settled on a green patch of grass near a fertile oasis. The sun bore down upon them, but their hoods and eyeguards kept the harmful rays at bay. Certain they could not be heard, they finally relaxed.

Prisca spoke first.

"You seem weary," she said, her hazel brown eyes full of concern. "Share with me."

They joined hands to enhance their words. Helena always felt at peace when she was close to Prisca. They shared a passion for science and always had something to discuss. Now, however, the topics were grim and heavy.

"I don't know what to do," Helena said. "My feelings for the captain and some of the other Humans have clouded my judgment. I love him, Prisca, and I cannot allow that."

"I see," Prisca said, evaluating Helena's words and thoughts together as a comprehensive whole.

"You see how he makes me feel?" Helena said. "Have you ever felt like that?"

Prisca shook her head. "Never. For all her improprieties, I don't think Marcella has either. What you feel is rare, by my calculation. Even amongst the Humans."

"I cannot control it," Helena said. "I thought about trying a hormone suppressor or other medical solution, but they all hamper my ability to concentrate. I cannot afford either!"

"I see your despair. Allow me to meditate upon your dilemma for a few moments."

They released their hands and Prisca moved closer to the water to assume a meditative pose. Unable to focus, Helena failed again to meditate upon a solution. Her fate was in her sister's hands. Prisca must find a solution.

The bright yellow sun moved across the clear blue sky and Helena grew uneasy. What if Prisca couldn't solve her problem? Could Helena return to the *Jupiter* and execute her plan? Could she kill Nathan when the time came?

The same doubts swirled in her mind as she watched her sister. After what seemed like days, Prisca rose and dusted sand from her dress. She looked into Helena's eyes with a sorrow Helena had only seen one other time – when their mother died.

"I know what you must do," Prisca said.

Helena embraced her sister and said, "Tell me. I feel so lost."

Before Prisca spoke, Helena sensed the solution. The terrible and necessary solution.

"No," Helena said. "I… I may never recover."

"That is a risk," Prisca said. "But to ensure your heart doesn't overwhelm your mind, you must. I see no other way."

So clouded was her mind, Helena had forgotten about the mental exercise taught to them by their mother. The act, if successful, would sever all emotion. It was meant to be a last resort to avoid interrogation or another equally unpleasant ordeal. With all her emotions blocked, she would be free from her feelings towards Nathan. Only her duty would remain.

If not executed properly, she risked the permanent loss of her heart. The joy of spending time with her sisters, the comfort she felt with others and her contentment in her career as a physician – all gone. Forever.

The love for Nathan would also be stripped from her.

"That's the point," Prisca said as she read her sister's thoughts again. "Since you cannot control it, you must remove the object of your desire. It's too risky to kill him before we attack Proxus and reassigning you, if even possible, would look suspicious. This is the option that retains our chance of success. Anything else lowers the numbers. Do the math, you will see it in perfect order."

She had already run the calculations. Prisca was correct. This was the only way.

Helena touched her forehead to her sister's, closed her eyes and said, "If I fail, and I don't recover-"

Prisca gasped, surprised by her sister's strong feelings. Then, she relaxed and smiled. "You love us. We know. We love you too, sister."

"Rest easy. I will do this," Helena said.

"You will succeed."

They sat and watched the mirror-like surface of the water ripple gently after each breeze. If she wasn't in the middle of a war and surrounded by so much self-doubt, Helena guessed she would have found the locale quite peaceful. Instead, she struggled with her haunting thoughts.

Despite her bravado, she wasn't sure she could succeed. The process to sever all emotion wasn't a trivial task.

When her mother taught her the technique, a younger Helena didn't realize the price she would need to pay. Helena hadn't discovered the all-encompassing love she now felt towards Nathan. Her most difficult obstacle was losing her connection with her sisters – a worthwhile price to pay for whatever goal required such extreme measures.

Now, she was uncertain of the price. Was it too steep? If the process rendered her heart dead then she wouldn't even realize the truth. She would be condemned to a prison of her own making, never knowing the joy she felt when she was with Nathan.

"Such is the price of duty," Helena whispered after many hours of silence.

Prisca nodded as she shared her sister's grief. All seven of them were altered in significant ways, like a stream altered by a falling boulder. Helena wondered at the changes they now caused to many generations of Antarans. Humans and Proxans too. They were changing the course of history.

"Your adversary, Rowe, is causing quite the ruckus on the *Jupiter*," Prisca said, her head cocked to the sky.

Helena frowned when she concentrated on her shipmates. Rowe was making life difficult for Nathan and the others.

"We should return," Helena said. "I accomplished what I came here to do. As always, my dependable Prisca has saved the day."

"I live to serve," Prisca said.

Helena recognized that it had already started – Prisca was making the transition to an empty heart easier for her.

Dependable Prisca.

They exchanged farewells before boarding the captain's yacht. No need to show the Humans any more than they had to, Helena reasoned. The trip was silent as Helena maneuvered into the *Jupiter's* docking bay.

"I will see you soon," Helena said as Prisca departed for her own shuttle destined for the *Saturn*.

"When this is over," Prisca said and she turned towards her waiting crew with all the regal splendor of an Antaran Princess.

Rowe stormed towards Helena the moment Prisca was clear.

"I've already contacted the Church," he said.

Without acknowledging him, Helena strode towards the lift.

"They will override the Council," he said. "Then your little game will be up."

Finally turning to him, she said, "Do you have anything of value to say to me? I have duties to attend."

"The Church has power," he said with a sneer. "Your days are numbered, witch."

"If I'm not mistaken," Helena said, "witches were spiritual leaders and well respected, according to your ancient history. It wasn't until men like you felt threatened that they were unlawfully hunted. Are you complimenting me, Rowe? Or are you one of those shortsighted men who fears what he cannot comprehend?"

After a pause, he said, "Your words are like poison! Know that I am not fooled, witch."

As the lift closed, she said, "I see you are the latter."

She sensed him fuming as she rode towards the officer's deck. He was dangerous so Helena decided to keep tighter mental tabs on him. Religious zeal had a way of turning people dangerous. Well, she reasoned, Rowe was an assassin and zealot so he was twice as unpredictable.

More complications.

The *Jupiter* repaired her wounds while the rest of the Human fleet pushed forward into Proxan space. Helena reviewed the reports on a daily basis to ensure her sisters were safe. The uncertainty and anxiousness would have been unnecessary if Helena could have found the strength to remove her feelings. Instead, she frequented Nathan's bed and procrastinated.

After several weeks, Helena decided to attempt meditation again. She had never gone this long with such a cluttered mind. Alone in her dark room, she lit some candles and allowed her doubt and guilt to wash away from her. She acknowledged each concern and then let it pass though her. Once her mind was clear, she examined her current situation.

Nobody suspected her real motives concerning the *Bastion*, so she was safe there. The reality behind the state of the Proxan race still disturbed her. Did they choose the right side? No, it didn't matter. Their goal was to destroy *both* enemies.

The war effort moved forward as her sisters engaged the enemy and won several key battles while the *Jupiter* underwent repairs. Her sisters were alive and well. Nobody had detected their plot. The only audible opposition came from the Human Church. They cautioned the Human populations against the "witchcraft" of the Antaran people. So far, that movement had gained little ground. Only a few news outlets featured Church zealots.

The last topic on her agenda was her heart. Perhaps Prisca's solution wasn't necessary. Helena attempted to view her love for Nathan as a vacation – a temporary state of being for her. She knew she must concentrate on the war and on her mission. If she remained conflicted, she would be forced to employ the emotion-severing technique taught to her by her mother.

That path was dark and she didn't see her future in it. Helena shook her head and examined her face in the mirror upon the far wall.

"What will you become?" she asked aloud.

The intercom in her room buzzed. Lieutenant Sandra Rhom's voice carried through the speaker. "Lady Helena?"

After a pause, she said, "Yes, Lieutenant?"

"The captain requests your presence in the war room," Lieutenant Rhom said. "The strategy session is about to begin."

She had lost track of time during her meditations. That was a positive sign. Perhaps she could discover an alternative.

"Thank you, Lieutenant."

Helena walked the corridors of the *Jupiter*, nodding and smiling to the crew as she passed them. Some of the awe was gone, replaced by disappointment and uncertainty. Perhaps the railing of the Church had gone farther than she calculated. Or, perhaps they lost some of their admiration after the *Bastion* fell. Digging deeper, Helena found a mixture of those two thoughts and a third: their distrust over her relationship with the captain.

Rowe waited for her outside the war room. He eyed her as she passed and she found she couldn't penetrate his thoughts. No matter, he was leaving soon. Nathan had finally won his battle with the Council and the assassin was being reassigned.

Her face betrayed no emotion as she passed him. He eyed her from beneath his dark bangs, but she didn't give him the pleasure of a glance.

"Lady Helena," Stugardt said. "Everyone is ready."

Admiral Leighton's face appeared on one of the holo-displays. "Lady Helena," he said. "Thank you for joining us."

"Admiral," Helena said, nodding towards his image.

"We are going to begin the main offensive," Leighton said. "You and your sisters have proven to be an invaluable tactical aid. The Proxans are reeling from each defeat. I'm sure they are wondering how we're beating them so soundly."

"It's probably best they wonder," Helena said. "It means we still have the advantage."

"Agreed," Leighton said. "Anyway, let's get into the details so we can push this thing forward."

Nathan flicked his eyes towards Helena and said, "We're ready to begin when you are, Admiral."

Helena smiled in response to his glance in her direction. So much for controlling her emotions! Was there any way to avoid that dark path? As Helena sat in front of her console, she realized the necessity of her resolution. She caught Nathan's eye again and her heart fluttered like a humming bird.

Necessity. Duty. Responsibility. Survival. Her people needed her. Why did she doubt? The darkest path was the correct one in this case.

The meeting plodded forward at the crawling Human pace Helena had come to expect. She reviewed the plan with them again and made corrections where she saw fit. If nothing else came from the Antaran gamble, the Proxans would fall. The part after that wouldn't be as easy.

A few days passed and Helena found herself reflecting on her recent concern over the Human Church. Why did they concern her so much? Then, as if in answer to her mental question, the day's news feed turned sour.

"How could this happen?" Stugardt said as he watched the newscast.

Everyone on the bridge was fixated on the broadcast screen as the Human Church was publically denouncing the Antarans and their witchcraft. The Cardinal, speaking on behalf of the entire church, called for the immediate detainment of Helena and her sisters. Everyone knew about their mental powers now.

"Admiral Leighton has ordered us to attack two days early," Nathan said. "We can't afford the Proxans time to review this information. It's only a matter of time before they know too."

Helena wondered for only a moment who leaked the secret about her abilities.

"I know who did this," she said. "Rowe."

"Rowe?" Nathan said.

"He is a religious fanatic," Helena said. "He recorded conversations and he vowed to destroy me."

"Well, the Church has no hold over the military," Stugardt said. "The secret is out but we can deal with that. Nobody's coming to arrest you or your sisters. I, for one, don't believe in witchcraft or the Church's stand here. And neither does the Council."

Helena's blood rose in temperature and she clenched her fist. "I'm going to talk with Rowe," she said.

"Wait," Nathan said. "Let me make all the preparations for our departure and I'll go with you. I'd like to hear what he has to say. If it was him, then we'll throw him in the brig for treason."

Helena sensed Rowe in one of the nearby hangar bays. He was leaving. "No. He's stealing a ship!"

"Wait!" Nathan said as Helena dashed for the lift.

Lieutenant Sandra Rhom followed Helena into the lift and pulled her sidearm.

"The captain ordered me to go with you," Sandra said. Helena nodded. As the doors closed, she heard Nathan order some marines to intercept. They would be too late.

The lift halted in the hangar bay and the doors opened. All was quiet as they entered the bay and Sandra checked a console. Besides their own movements, the chamber was still. Long shadows crept between the piled crates. Helena detected his presence but she couldn't pinpoint his location.

"He fused the main doors shut," Sandra said. "The only way in is through the lift we just took."

Then, Helena sensed Rowe and his imminent violence.

"Get down!" Helena called.

Rowe, hidden behind some barrels, fired three shots from his pistol. Two bullets impacted Sandra's back and the third hit the wall with a violent spark. The Lieutenant crumpled to the ground and was motionless.

Helena rushed towards Rowe and focused on his mind. Though it was more difficult than before, she gained entrance and discovered he laid this trap for her!

He raised another pistol, loaded with needle-darts.

"Let's go on a little trip," he said as he depressed the trigger.

Helena calculated the trajectory of the dart and ducked. The dart sailed over her head. Rowe fired two more times. She deflected the first one with the palm of her hand, but the other one sunk itself into her leg. She tumbled to the ground from the pain and numbness. Poison. Rolling to her feet and keeping her momentum, Helena jumped and caught him in the face with her foot. He fell backwards and his pistols scattered across the floor.

Helena's world lost focus for a few moments as the poison flowed through her bloodstream. Then, her gut erupted in pain as Rowe bludgeoned her with a metal pipe. She regained clarity long enough to block his next attack with her forearm and deliver an open-palmed strike to Rowe's shoulder. She was aiming for his throat. He countered with an elbow to her chest and she fell to the ground. The hangar spun. Her leg burned. Her head felt heavy.

Before she lost consciousness Rowe said, "Sweet dreams, witch."

Chapter 35

Helena awoke in a white room with several beds – the *Jupiter's* medical ward. She turned her head and saw Lieutenant Sandra Rhom on the bed next to her. The Lieutenant's face was covered with an oxygen mask and her eyes were closed. Intravenous tubes pinched at Helena's arm and her head ached. What happened?

One of the ship doctors smiled and approached. "Just get some rest," he said.

Helena drifted in and out of consciousness for days. She floated to her home, where the memories were sweet. Safe with her family, and far from the war, she basked in the glow of her dreams. Her mother was with her again and she floated in the carefree days of her youth.

Slowly, the present solidified around her. Like a climber reaching the top of a mountain, she strained to remain conscious through the last few moments of drugged sleep. She sensed a quiet room with only two beds. Sandra smiled when Helena opened her eyes.

"There you are," Sandra said.

"What… what happened?" Helena asked.

"You were right," Sandra said. "Rowe was the one who informed the Church. He wanted to take you with him, but the captain saved us both."

"The captain?"

"Yeah. Rowe disabled the lift after he shot both of us. Then, the captain and several marines crawled through the shaft and captured Rowe. Following protocol, the captain jettisoned Rowe in a pod with a beacon. The authorities may or may not pick him up and take him back to the nearest planet to face charges. I hope he runs out of air."

"My head feels so heavy-"

"The doctor said you were poisoned with something that would have put you in a coma. Good thing the captain got to you quickly, otherwise it could have been much worse."

"I'm sorry... tried to warn you-"

Sandra smiled. "I know. Thanks."

"How long?"

"Three days," Sandra said.

"Three?" Helena said. "I need to get to the bridge."

The doctor entered and said, "Not anytime soon. You need rest."

Helena sat in her bed and collected her scrambled memories. No. The attack was probably already underway.

"I'll be fine," she said.

Despite the doctor's protests, Helena disconnected herself from her tubes and made the trek to her quarters. She donned a simple dress and her Gima markings. After a brief meditation session to center her mind and body, she ascended the lift and stepped onto the bridge. Dizziness threatened to overtake her several times, but she kept her balance.

"Helena?" Nathan said, forgetting to address her in the proper way.

"Captain," Helena said. "I am ready to resume my duties."

"The doctor called. He's not too happy with you," Nathan said.

"I'm fine," she said. "What's our situation?"

Nathan pulled her aside and searched her eyes. His concern was imprinted upon his face. "You need sleep," he said. "We can handle things up here."

Helena shook her woozy head. "I'm not going to spend the war in the medical ward," she said. "I'm fine, really."

She sensed many eyes on them. The bridge crew was still curious about their relationship.

"Listen," he said, lowering his voice to a whisper, "are you alright? Really?" His eyes searched for an answer.

She met his gaze and said, "Yes, I am fine, Nathan."

He studied her for a moment and said, "Alright, I think I even believe you. But... it crushed me to see you in that bed. I almost lost you."

She smiled and touched his arm. "Thank you for saving me," she said. "Lieutenant Rhom tells me you were quite heroic."

"Keeping Rowe onboard for as long as we did was my decision and it was a costly one," he said. "You have nothing to thank me for. I should have sent him away a long time ago. I'm sorry."

Helena shook her head. "You couldn't have known-"

"Captain?" a science office said. "Can you take a look at this?"

Nathan sighed and broke all protocol by hugging her. She felt the collective shock and some jealousy amongst the bridge crew. Only Admiral Stugardt seemed pleased.

"When this is all over, I promise to show you my home in New Detroit. It's a bit rainy, especially in the fall, but I think you'd like it. You know, to visit that is."

Helena smiled. "I would like to visit your home someday, Captain."

"Perhaps Caledonia again, too?" he said as he fingered her glowing hair accessory.

"I will always hold Caledonia dear in my heart," she said.

Nathan scanned the bridge and said, "Admiral. Take over for me here."

Admiral Stugardt nodded and resumed his discussion with the science officer who interrupted them.

"Let's just-" Nathan said as he led her into the captain's office. After closing the door behind them he embraced her again, this time pressing his body against hers.

Then, Nathan looked into her eyes and smiled. Realizing she was already lost in his presence, Helena pushed away from him and gazed out the small viewport into the empty stars.

"What's wrong?" he asked.

"I... I must not see you anymore," Helena said. "Not like this."

"Why? Our relationship isn't causing any harm."

She couldn't meet his eyes. "I think there is a time and place for *us*," she said, "and now isn't it. Until the war is over, we must redefine our relationship."

He approached her from behind and pushed her hair off her shoulder. "I don't think I can do that," he said. "Can you not sense how important you are to me?"

As if she could shield herself from his emotions, she squeezed her eyes closed and attempted to ignore the shared feelings between them. If she told him that he was as meaningful to her as she was to him she guessed she'd break down in front of him. Driving pains lanced through her heart when she realized the truth.

She didn't have the strength to separate her feelings for him from the rest of herself.

And that meant...

He wrapped his hands around her and each breath from his nose grew goosebumps on the back of her neck. She softened her closed eyes and slightly parted her lips. How could he affect her so completely?

Before her desire could take control she stepped from his embrace. After monumental effort, she said emotionlessly, "We should return to the bridge."

Prisca's plan was the only path left to her. She realized needed to start the process to remove her emotions. The death of her heart would mean life for her people.

Resigned but hopeful, Nathan said, "As you wish."

Keeping her back to him, she exhaled as she walked to the door. Control. She must remain in control until she was able to meditate and start the process.

"Excuse me, Captain," Admiral Stugardt said as he intercepted them on their way back to their stations. "We're picking up some fluctuations from within the cloud."

As Helena and Nathan returned to the tactical command station, Helena asked, "What's happening?"

"We're providing support for the *Saturn*," Nathan said. "She's scouting a nebula right now. We think the Proxans have a hidden communication station in there."

Helena marveled at the red and orange cloud of gasses and dust which dominated the front viewport. The space anomaly reminded her of her gaseous globed jewelry which scintillated with almost the same pattern and colors. The *Saturn* winked in and out of view on the holographic tactical display as the nebula interfered with sensors.

"What else-?"

Helena's words halted in her throat when both the viewport and holographic display erupted in a brilliant flash of light. The cries of thousands of people echoed in Helena's head and she grasped the handrail to avoid from falling. Among those voices was Prisca. Helena searched the escape vessels and the new Proxan battleships with her mind. She scanned the nebula and the debris from the *Saturn* with every cell of her being, but her sister was gone. Prisca and most everyone onboard the *Saturn* was dead.

Chapter 36

Helena fell to the ground as the bridge crew scrambled for their stations. Two Proxan battleships and a swarm of smaller vessels broke through the cloudy nebula and attacked the *Jupiter*. The ship rocked and the noise level in the room escalated. Everyone was shouting. Helena felt empty.
Prisca was dead.

"Helena!" Nathan said. "We need you!"

"Torpedoes in the water," someone yelled.

"Move to bravo-nine," Admiral Stugardt said.

The *Jupiter* shook again.

"Direct hits on our port engines," one of the officers said.

The voices jumbled together until someone pulled Helena to her feet. It was Nathan. He calmly looked into her eyes and said, "We need you."

She searched his eyes for answers but realized none were there. Prisca was gone. Dependable Prisca. What happened?

"Please," Nathan said.

Time halted for Helena as she exerted all of her skill and determination into one instant of focused thought. The bridge froze in mid calamity but Helena didn't examine anyone's face. She dared not look at Nathan again. Instead, she closed her eyes and pushed time aside in a bubble around her. She looked inward and, out of necessity, began the process her mother taught her to sever her emotions.

The meditation was designed to be completed over many weeks. But Helena didn't have the luxury of time. She pushed the limits of her ability to cause the ripple around her while she drifted towards a desert plain – the same desert upon which her mother gave her the test.

Eons had passed in this world between worlds since the last time Helena had visited. Like before, she found herself on a scorching wasteland wandering for days on the brink of dehydration and exhaustion. Then, she stumbled upon a vibrant city. People bustled about their tasks and everybody seemed cheerful. This was different from what she remembered.

"Mother," she said aloud, "what is this place?"

The answer came to her before she finished forming the question. This was the same place she had visited many times – an internal representation of her own psyche. There was one difference. The people had discovered love.

People rejoiced everywhere she looked. They lived fuller lives. They were complete. At that moment, Helena realized what she was destroying.

For many days she sat on the edge of the city. Her mind was active but her body was an empty shell. She knew the path her mother taught her was a violent one. She must destroy the city. Then the next city and so on until all traces of life were gone from this world. Then, and only then, would a new order arise. An order free from the confines of emotion.

No. Not *confines*. Emotions weren't binding – they were liberating! Why did the early Gima work to suppress emotion? Were they afraid of the decadence that permeated the Humans and Proxans? Were emotions the path to destruction?

Her father believed as much. Her people corralled their emotions into specially approved sections of their lives. Why?

Again, Helena immediately knew the answer.

Look at yourself, she thought. You love the Human captain and that emotion interferes with your duty. You are an Antaran princess and heir to the throne. By what authority do you deem your heart more important than the whole of your people? Kill them all and you will find the strength to both handle Prisca's death and destroy the Humans. Even those you once loved.

The words were her mothers. Or, rather, that part of her mother that still lived within herself. Her grandmother was also there, staring down upon her. And all the way down the Antaran line to the Gima queens of the past. They all stared and waited.

"You know your duty," they said collectively.

Helena looked at the faces of the jubilant people in the city and lifted her spear.

"You will make a fine empress," the voices echoed.

She hesitated. There was another way.

"No other way ensures this," the voices said.

Despite the protests of the voices from her ancestors, Helena toiled for what was a lifetime to her. She recruited the help of people in the city sympathetic to her, but even they died of old age. Perhaps she was working for longer than one lifetime.

When she was finished, she gazed upon her wall in the morning desert sun.

"This will hold," she said aloud. "This must hold."

"A wall is fallible," her ancestral voices said. "You must return to the cities and kill everyone. Only then will you be free from your emotions."

Helena shook her head. "I will keep them safe behind this wall, with me on the other side. I will not destroy them, but I cannot allow them free reign any longer."

"They are like a barbarian horde. They will destroy this wall and you as well."

"Your solution is imperfect," they said.

For the first time since she started, Helena looked upon the faces of her ancestors.

"No," she said, "yours is. This wall will hold."

"You are speaking from emotion," they said. "Even your own calculations don't yield one hundred percent success."

Helena grinned, a gesture of Nathan's she imitated.

"I don't need one hundred percent," she said. "It'll hold."

With a flash, she returned to the chaotic bridge of the *Jupiter*. Time snapped back into motion and Helena almost stumbled.

Nathan caught her forearm and was prepared to ask her for help again. She scanned every facet of his mind, even the dark recesses. He loved her but she wasn't familiar with the emotion. Memories of the past few months clicked by in her mind like a slideshow and she realized her tactic must have been to gain his trust before killing him.

A solid plan.

Like a rebooting computer, she quickly took stock of everything else that had transpired. She only found one interesting item of note: a wall around her heart. Well, she visualized the mental construct as a wall, long and tall against some unseen force. She calculated she must have put that there for a valid reason, but she couldn't recall the exact details.

No matter, she had a battle to win.

Before Nathan could say another word, Helena whirled to examine the tactical display. "Full burn – now!" she said.

The helmsman didn't hesitate and the *Jupiter* lurched forward and between the two Proxan battleships.

"Double-broadsides," Nathan said. "On my mark."

"Double?" Helena questioned. "Are you sure?"

He nodded and said, "Let's try to do as much as we can before passing them."

Helena calculated the risk and said, "That will leave us too vulnerable."

"I'll just need you to time it perfectly," he said. "Trust me."

"Okay, Captain," she said.

To her surprise, she realized she *did* trust him. When did that happen? No matter, the plan was aggressive but appropriate. They would likely survive the maneuver.

The weapons officer shot a glance to the captain. Nathan nodded and said, "On her mark, Lieutenant."

Helena waited and watched the display. Just a few more seconds. "Mark!" she said.

The front viewport was set ablaze with laser and tracer fire. Both Proxan ships reeled from the blow and veered away to get a better angle on the now listing Human battleship.

"Engines are offline. All we have are torpedo bays seven through twelve," the weapons officer said.

"Okay, you were right," Nathan said. "We're defenseless. Any ideas?"

"No, that was a good move," she said as mind worked through a solution. "Have the frigates form a perimeter around us and patch communications directly to me. I'll guide them."

Nathan issued the appropriate orders and he stepped to her side. "What are you planning to do?"

Helena affixed her earpiece and said, "We took out their batteries. All they'll have while we recover are torpedoes."

"I know," Nathan said. "That's not good for us."

"The frigates will shoot down the torpedoes," Helena said. "I'll send them coordinates."

Stugardt looked up from his console and said, "They're firing. Two volleys of torpedoes incoming."

Helena sensed the trajectory and firing solution used by the Proxan gunners. She barked a series of coordinates and angles into the communicator and watched as the Human frigates moved into position and picked the torpedoes apart.

"All bogeys were shot down," Stugardt said.

Straining to keep her concentration, Helena entered the minds of the Proxan commanders and found that another volley was on the way. She recorded those coordinates and fed them to the frigate captains. Again, each torpedo was destroyed. She gasped as her head throbbed and her stomach threatened to empty its meager contents.

"No," she said as she gritted her teeth, closed her eyes, and kept her mind attuned to the Proxans.

"Helena?"

The voice was Nathan's, but she couldn't respond. She had to remain focused on the enemy.

"Engines back online," someone called.

Helena opened her eyes and said, "Move to delta-four."

"What's your plan?" Nathan asked.

"Delta-four," Helena said. "I sent the frigates to harass the second Proxan battleship. We're going after this other one."

"You're moving to attack them?" Stugardt asked.

"We can't run," Helena said. "We must find out what happened to the *Saturn*. This is the only way."

Nathan pondered the order and his mind was conflicted. Could he allow Helena another aggressive move? What if this one ended as poorly as her decision to keep the *Bastion* engaged? Was she right? Was there no escape?

The memory of the destruction of the *Bastion* was a distant spark in her mind. Was there something special about it? That day saw many Humans killed. All Helena recalled was the completion of another task in her list. It was a victorious day for Antares.

After a few moments of silence, Nathan said, "Listen to Lady Helena."

"Coming around," the helmsman said.

"You sure about this?" Nathan said as he leaned close to her.

Helena glanced at him, but she didn't respond. He expected a warmth in her eyes that wasn't there. Why had she changed in his mind? She remembered the wall and realized it was significant, but she wasn't sure why. She mentally shrugged the chatter in her mind. Now wasn't the time for second-guessing herself. She needed to know what happened in that nebula and to Prisca. Helena decided to play out the battle a few thousand times in her head to determine a way to destroy both ships, in case that became a necessity.

She sensed the Proxan ship was about to change course, just like she predicted. "Quick burn on my mark." She waited. "Mark!"

The *Jupiter* shuddered from the strain, but the vessel lanced forward. Too late, the Proxan battleship attempted to correct its mistake.

"No you don't," Nathan said, realizing the brilliant move Helena had just made. "Starboard broadside - fire!" he said.

"Torpedoes too, sir?" Stugardt asked.

"No," Nathan said. "I see what Lady Helena was trying to do."

The broadside scorched the Proxans and, sure enough, the battleship corrected its position again. They had it.

"Fire all forward torpedoes *now*, Lieutenant," Nathan said.

"Torpedoes away."

Moments later, the Proxan battleship imploded and the shockwave rattled the *Jupiter*. Cheers and pumped fists escaped from the bridge crew and the brilliant display unfolded on the main viewport.

"Now, the other one," Helena said through clenched teeth.

"The other ship is heading for the nebula, sir."

"Follow it in," Nathan said.

"Are you sure that's wise?" Stugardt said. "Our sensors will be scrambled."

"Helena?" Nathan said. "Can you find them in there?"

She narrowed her eyes and said, "Yes, Nathan. I can see them no matter where they try to hide."

Why did she disregard his rank and title? Why would she call him by his given name? A quick scan of her memory told her she had been using his name since their trip together to Caledonia. Very well, she thought, best to not raise his alarms.

At her first convenience, she decided she needed to meditate on her actions inside of her own mind. She determined she must have ventured into her own mind for some important cause, but she had to trust her reasoning. Why couldn't she remember?

"Good enough for me," Nathan said. "Helm, full ahead! Lieutenant, bring the frigates in."

The *Jupiter* penetrated the nebula and the gasses parted for the vessel as it shot towards its target. Helena guided the helmsman to where she sensed the Proxans. She relayed a firing solution to the weapons officer and waited.

Then, the Proxan ship was gone.

Helena opened her eyes and said, "There is a wormhole in this nebula. They are no longer here."

"Wormhole?" someone asked.

"Two points of connected space," Nathan said as he looked out the viewport, expecting to see the anomaly.

"I'm not sure," Helena said, "but I believe this would take us deep into Proxan space. I'm keying the location on the tactical display now. It's that area of dense gravity."

All eyes moved to the tactical display as it showed the faint outline of a tornado-shaped area of high gravity.

Then she remembered. Her memories had finally aligned and she recalled her reason for the wall. She needed to remain emotionless throughout the rest of her mission because her emotions were clouding her judgment.

Wise decision, she thought.

She visualized the wall around her heart and recognized the truth of the barrier. It shook from some internal force and dust fell from a few of the bricks. She wondered what could slam against the wall with such great force.

Then, for a moment, Helena didn't care about the wormhole nor the destroyed Proxan ship. Her heart thumped in dread over the loss of her sister.

"Prisca," she whispered. "Where are you now?"

As soon as the terror arrived, it was thrown back over the wall. Back to where it couldn't harm Helena. Back to where she could forget.

Before serenity returned to her the wall shook again.

Chapter 37

Before he rang the chime to her quarters, Helena sensed Nathan. In fact, she was in his mind when he made the decision to come see her. She remained in everyone's mind aboard the *Jupiter*. How could she have been so foolish before? Why did she respect their desire for privacy? Her mission from her father was of the utmost importance. Though she couldn't recall the exact reasons behind her decision to build her wall, she recognized the prudence of it. She calculated that she must have been on a self-destructive path.

After pressing the unlock code and raising the lighting level, Helena stood and watched as Captain Nathan Connor entered her quarters. The war effort was at the forefront of his thoughts, but he also hoped for another sexual encounter with her. He was just uncertain of how to talk to her after the death of her sister. She pitied him for allowing his emotions guide his thoughts and actions. Humans were flawed.

"Helena," he said.

Before he could continue, Helena said, "You will address me in the proper manner, Captain."

Shocked by her words, he blinked and raced in his mind. After a mad dash of thoughts and doubts, he arrived at his conclusion: Helena was mourning her sister.

How wrong he was. There wasn't time to grieve.

"I'm sorry, My Lady," he said. After a brief hesitation to search her eyes, he motioned to her desk and continued. "I sent new orders to your station here. We're pushing into Proxan space with the wormhole."

"I've read the report," Helena said, her eyes as cold as the space beyond her quarters. "The anomaly connects that nebula with a point very near the Proxan homeworld. The *Saturn's* destruction shall not be in vain, it seems. I've already sent my plan to Admiral Leighton."

Nathan's doubts continued. He wondered if things between them would ever be the same as they were before. He doubted his ability as a Human outsider to remain in her life. Above all, he wondered what she was feeling at that moment. He also grieved Prisca, but mostly because it should have had a profound effect on Helena. He wondered why she didn't request time away from her duties as tactical advisor. He also wondered how much he could talk with her.

He decided to be direct.

"Helena," she said softly as he stepped towards her and put his hands on her shoulders. "I just want you to know that I am here… if you need me. I know what it's like to lose family-"

Helena shrugged his hands from her and glared into his eyes. No, she cautioned herself, you mustn't distance yourself just yet. Keep him coming to your bed so it will be easier to kill him when the time comes.

Trusting her inner voice, she feigned softness and allowed herself to be encompassed by his embrace. The wall around her heart shook and cracks formed along the surface. Ignoring the turmoil within, she kissed him fiercely.

The wall will hold, she thought. Somehow, those words were important to her so she held on to them as she savagely made love to him. He seemed surprised at first but he welcomed her aggressiveness.

She played the part of the secret lover but he sensed a change within her. At first he rationalized it as a response to Prisca's death. However, after he had left her quarters, Helena remained in his mind. His doubts swirled into a maelstrom as he returned to his room. A part of him was screaming that he had lost her, that she was always beyond his reach and he was just fooling himself. He tried to suppress that voice of reason, but it grew louder within him as he agonized over her.

Not much longer, Helena thought as she walked naked to her desk. She keyed her code into the surface and prepared the message to her sisters. Under even intense scrutiny, the message appeared to be a casual note of encouragement. However, Helena hid a secret code in each message instructing her sisters to carry out the rest of their plan once the battle at Proxus was won.

They responded. They were ready.

As the *Jupiter* sat in the nebula, waiting for the command to attack Proxus, Helena thought of her sisters. Ferocious Valeria had become the tigress. Her battleship was on the front lines of the war and had dealt serious losses to the Proxans. Justina managed to collect extensive notes about Human religion and had forwarded them off to Antares. She was also able to deflect much of the Human Church's attack on the daughters of Emperor Agreios. By befriending a priest of the Human's faith, she gained an ally in the smear-war against the Antaran "witches." Rowe's betrayal flared brightly for a few weeks, but then died away. The populace was already in love with Helena and they found it easy to cheer her sisters as war heroes with each victory over the Proxans. Marcella had so completely won her Captain's heart that he would have likely laid down his life for her. She was in complete control. Claudia's ship, the *Minotaur*, served more of a support role and Helena hadn't heard much from her. Terentia had become famous for her *Song of Lunar Lament* which she sung over the graves of fallen Human warriors. The people of Terra made her into a celebrity and she was quite common in Human recruitment ads. Then, of course, Prisca had fallen in the nebula where Helena now sat. Ambushed and killed by the Proxans, Prisca gave her life for her homeworld. Helena found she harbored no grief but the wall around her heart rattled each time she thought of Prisca.

The wall must hold.

A Human officer smiled at Helena as he departed from the lift.

"One more battle, hopefully," he said.

Without responding, Helena ventured into that dangerous part of herself – the area around her wall. One more battle. She felt as if she had lost a part of herself behind that wall. What if she needed that part? Could she carry forward after the war if she was no longer intact?

Helena ascended the rest of the way to the bridge alone with her thoughts. Unwanted thoughts. The wall trembled and Helena focused upon the task at hand. The Proxans must fall. Prisca was the first Antaran casualty in their new struggle. As Helena risked a last parting glance at her wall, she realized her heart was the second casualty.

The doors glided open and Helena strode towards her place at the tactical display. The bridge was quiet on the eve of battle. With the main lights dimmed, each Human face was illuminated by their consoles. They were anxious, nervous and hopeful. Even without her abilities, Helena could sense their tension. Utilizing a trick Marcella had mastered, Helena soothed their minds with thoughts of confidence. They gradually eased.

"We have the order," Nathan said as he manipulated the holographic tactical display between them.

He glanced at Helena a few times as his doubts continued to roil. She pretended to not notice.

"Orders confirmed," Admiral Stugardt said.

Nathan activated the ship intercom system and drew a deep breath.

"This is everything we have trained, hoped and fought for," he said to the entire crew of the *Jupiter*. "One last battle and we will be free from Proxan raids for all time. We will no longer have to worry for our family and friends. We can sleep easy. All I ask is one more day of your dedication and ability. One day to triumphantly defeat our enemy and build a new era of peace. One day to live forever in the histories of our time. One day is all I ask."

Helena felt the confidence rise in the crew. They were dangerous, determined and ready.

The *Jupiter* hurtled through the nebula and wormhole to join the battle already in progress. Helena immediately assessed the situation from their flank and began to issue her orders.

For Helena and her sisters, there was still one fight to finish after this one. The Humans wouldn't be prepared for that one. The seven daughters of Antares had succeeded in their secrecy. Human leaders had no comprehension of the danger that lurked in the shadows. They would regret their actions of the past.

The battle was long and intense. Helena sensed her sisters under the strain of their telepathic marathon during the Invasion of Proxus. The remaining Proxan battleships stood their ground against the superior Human fleet. However, like all battles, the defender had the advantage. Ground and orbital batteries pelted the Human warships as they advanced. Mines and other hazards hindered their approach.

The *Jupiter* rolled on its axis to absorb the brunt of the battery fire from the nearest Proxan battleship. Though battered, the *Jupiter* held together to deliver a killing strike to the enemy vessel.

"The *Minotaur* is going down," Admiral Stugardt said.

Helena acknowledged sorrow over the likely death of Claudia. However, she didn't dare inspect her wall. The time for grief would need to come later. She felt her internal wall shake as a large fireball formed near Proxus, fell to the surface and disintegrated.

"May your journey be swift," Helena whispered, hating herself for what she had to become to fulfill her duty.

Hate. There was no place for it so Helena tossed that over the wall as well. Her mother would have lamented over the loss of her eldest daughter's heart, but Helena knew no other way to complete her mission. Everything must be contained. Controlled. She was like the winter – dark and cold.

"The Proxan battleship on the far side of the planet just jumped," Stugardt said. "The *Mars* is in pursuit."

"Fair speed, Terentia," Helena said, her voice barely audible.

Compassion for her sister? That mustn't be allowed through the wall either. Helena forced those feelings behind the wall. Nothing must interfere with her duty.

The wall strained against its new inhabitants but it held.

"We need to take out those orbitals," Nathan said. "Have the frigates concentrate their fire there."

Orders were given and orders were followed. Helena existed as a tool of strategy, nothing more. She guided the *Jupiter* through the Proxan defenses and they commenced their bombardment of the Proxan surface. How many millions died? Helena didn't want to calculate the number. She was cold and devoid of remorse. That was the only way. She knew Nathan sensed further change in her, but she walled that out too.

"We're receiving word of surrender," Stugardt said.

Helena examined the tactical display and noted two remaining Proxan battleships. "No," she said. "They are planning a trap. *Every* Proxan ship must be destroyed."

With ruthless precision, Helena watched as the *Kraken* and *Waterloo* moved in for the kill. She sensed Valeria and Marcella as they tore the defenseless Proxan ships to pieces. No mercy. This was what had to be done to ensure the safety of her civilization. Helena's face remained a cool mask of nothingness. There was no emotion below or above the surface.

Hours passed. Bombs dropped. Proxans died.

As the sun peeked around the side of the planet, the war came to its conclusion.

Chapter 38

Twenty hours after the fall of Proxus, Helena visited Nathan's quarters. Though he was hesitant, he allowed her to share his bed. Doubts plagued him but he was unable to resist her when she was that close to him.

When exhaustion finally overtook him, Helena sent the signal to her sisters – now was their time. From the captain's console, she executed her code into the *Jupiter's* computer system and the ship's engines churned in preparation for the course Helena had set.

When she rejoined him in his bed, he moved to kiss her and said, "I've missed you."

Helena pulled her head away and looked into his eyes. She realized he wasn't just referring to her short trip to his desk. He missed Caledonia. He longed for the exciting days of discovery between them.

"I do wish things were different," she said.

Large sections of the wall around her heart crumbled as she looked into his heart. What had she done? Why did she resort to such desperate measures to complete her goal? Was she really not strong enough to both love the Human and also her people?

Nathan stiffened when he felt the needle against his skin. "What?"

"Do not move or I will be forced to inject you before I have the chance to set myself right in your heart," Helena said. "I do love you, a part of me always will. You taught me that I can be so much more than daughter and heir. I can be a woman... a *partner*. For that, I cherish you." She paused as the pain mounted in her stomach. "Please understand that my duty is to my people."

"What do you want?" Nathan said. "The war is over."

"We cannot allow Human or Proxan warmongering to ever again threaten our planet, nor can we forgive the atrocities of the past," Helena said.

"I don't understand," Nathan said. "We are allies. You don't need to fear us any longer."

"We fear the potential of your weapons and your imperialism," Helena said. "Though you promise me things today, a thousand years from now my people may not receive the same assurances. Don't you see? This is the only way."

More sections of her wall crumbled and she scrambled to repair it as her own doubts mounted. How could she do this to the man she loved? To the people she befriended? No. Those thoughts weren't welcome. They must return to behind the wall.

This was the only way.

"What about *us*?" Nathan said, his voice uneven. "Was that a lie so you could execute your betrayal?"

Helena shook her head. "I loved you with a part of my heart I did not know existed," she said. "But, it is my *reason* I must follow now. That is the part that tells me we are enemies."

Helena readied the needle and said, "I would have very much liked to see your home, Nathan."

The intercom crackled to life and Lieutenant Sandra Rhom's voice carried over the speakers.

"Captain, we are receiving a distress call from the *Mars*," Rhom said. "And something's wrong with the computer. We need you up here."

Nathan turned to Helena and said, "Isn't your youngest sister, Terentia, on the *Mars*?"

Helena paused. Terentia? No! The war was over, she shouldn't be in danger! Chasing down that last Proxan battleship must have gone awry. Helena performed the math and decided that she couldn't risk saving her sister, though large sections of the wall exploded when she realized the danger Terentia faced.

Memories of raising Terentia from an infant flooded from the destroyed sections of the wall around her heart. She fed Terentia her bottles and rocked her at night when she was upset. Terentia's favorite bedtime story rang in Helena's ears. Oh, how many nights she had read it to her! Helena taught her the mental disciplines and was proud of her ability.

Though she lied the promise to her father, Helena couldn't deal with the death of another sister – not Terentia. She said she would keep Terentia safe and that's what she had to do. Without the wall to contain her emotions surrounding Terentia, Helena made her decision.

"Captain, we both have people we care about aboard the *Mars*," Helena said.

"We do."

"I've seen you go to great lengths to keep your word in the past, would now be no different?" Helena said.

Nathan nodded. "My word is my name. I would never break it... not even to my enemy."

"We are close enough to assist, yes?"

"Yes."

"We will assist the *Mars*," Helena said. "And then you will turn the *Jupiter* over to me."

"And what of my crew?"

More bricks cracked along her wall. She mustn't falter. "I.... I-"

She realized at that moment the imperfections in her plan. Her ancestors warned her that the only way to a true emotionless state was to destroy the capacity to feel. Helena thought she was clever. She built a wall instead. A wall to contain her heart. Now, that wall was failing her. The heart proved stronger and she realized she didn't have much time before the rest of the wall crumbled.

What would happened then?

"Here's my counterproposal," Nathan said. "We assist and then everyone aboard this ship will evacuate to the *Mars*. Is that acceptable?"

"You would give your word on this?" Helena asked, sensing no deception in his heart. Instead, she found love there. Love, after her betrayal. She finally appreciated the power of these new emotions.

"My Lady, you have it. Always."

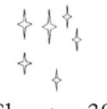

Chapter 39

The *Jupiter* jumped to the spot where the *Mars* had sent their distress signal. The Proxan battleship was attempting boarding maneuvers when they arrived. After a brutal salvo of torpedoes, the Proxan battleship was destroyed. If Helena's sisters were successful, these were the last two battleships in the universe. However, Helena couldn't destroy them both, as she had bargained one for her sister's life.

Nathan evacuated the entire crew of the *Jupiter* to the drifting *Mars*. Though there were many puzzled looks, the crew obeyed the order.

Admiral Stugardt was the last to leave the bridge. He stopped next to Helena and said, "I don't understand… why would you do this?"

"To never again see a war or weapons of this magnitude in our skies," Helena said. "And to punish for Human crimes of the past. You awoke the sleeping tigress, Admiral. Do not cry now that she cut you deep."

"I thought we were friends," Stugardt said. "I looked upon you as I would my own daughter. Nadine loves you. I just don't understand."

"Tell me, Admiral, what lengths would you cross to protect your wonderful family?"

Stugardt shook his head and said, "Not this… not this."

"I'm sorry to have disappointed you," Helena said. "But my duty is to my people."

Admiral Stugardt passed Nathan on his way from the bridge. They exchanged words and the admiral departed.

"They have arrested Terentia," Nathan said. "I thought you would want to know."

Helena nodded as she re-executed her computer attack upon the *Jupiter*. "Shouldn't you be getting to your shuttle?" she asked.

He looked into her eyes. His face was full of pain. Helena couldn't return his gaze for fear of utterly destroying her wall.

"A captain goes down with his ship," he said. "My place is here, on the bridge."

Helena turned to him. "I am destroying this ship. Though it is my duty to destroy you as well, my bargain with you will stay my hand. Please, leave now."

Nathan shook his head. "Just like I kept my word to you, I will keep my oath to the Human navy. I will stay with my ship until the very end."

"That is suicide, then," Helena said. "Your death is not on my hands."

"Do you really believe that?"

Helena didn't answer. She gained control of the *Jupiter's* navigation system and she jumped towards the tellium star. Using the wormhole, the trip didn't take long. Her last act was to disable the computer and propulsion systems. The *Jupiter* would drift into the star.

She looked at Nathan before departing the bridge. "I do wish things were different between us," she said.

His eyes watered and he said, "I love you, Helena."

She nodded and detached the orange globes from her hair. Handing the piece of jewelry to him she said, "I will keep the memory of Caledonia in my heart. I have reserved a special place for it and for you, Nathan. You taught me how to be a *woman*, but now I must be the *Empress*."

"Then keep it," he said. "So you won't forget me-"

"No, I cannot."

Before the fortress around her heart crumbled, Helena dropped the globes in his hand and rushed to the lift. She paused midway and spoke, but she found she couldn't look him in the eyes.

"I know this may not reconcile what I have done," she said, "but the walls we sometimes build around our hearts are both terrible and necessary to fulfill our duty. I regret my betrayal to you... and only to you."

Before risking more words, she entered the lift. Her heart felt like lead in her chest. What was she doing? This was all wrong!

She reached for the *halt* button as her emotions rallied against the remaining sections of wall around her heart. She could incapacitate Nathan and spare his life. She reached with her mind to find him. He was frantically trying to disable her ironclad code. His mind was embattled too as his heart yearned to follow her and abandon his post. Yet he remained as resolute to his duty as Helena had to hers. Her finger hovered near the button, but she didn't press it. Moments later, she arrived in the hangar bay where the captain's yacht waited to take her home to Antares.

She risked one last glance at the lift that could bring her back to the bridge and to the place in her heart where she found joy. Helena again considered *forcing* Nathan to come with her. Perhaps he could forgive her in time. She reached for the button.

"No," she said aloud.

Could she risk him never forgiving her? How would that place in her heart heal if he didn't love her anymore? His duty was to attempt to save his ship after she was gone. As fruitless as that would be, it was his duty. He kept his word because he was a man of honor. Helena decided that was how she would remember him. She hurried up the ramp to the yacht and powered the engines.

The yacht sped from the doomed ship and Helena severed her connection to Nathan's mind. She couldn't bear to be linked to him as he died. She turned her vessel away from the *Jupiter* and sped towards home.

"Good bye, my love," she said. "You will live forever in my heart."

Chapter 40

"I am sorry," Emperor Agreios said, "I have failed my daughters and I have failed Antares."

Helena watched from her father's balcony as the Human ships descended to the surface. The emperor quickly surrendered when the Humans threatened to bomb the planet.

"This is not how I wished this to end," Agreios said. "With my planet occupied and my daughters shattered."

"Emperor," Valeria said. "I heard a rumor that Justina was killed by her crew. She couldn't bring herself to execute the plan. That leaves two battleships with the Humans. We failed."

"And Terentia is captured," Helena said as she strapped her sword to her waist.

"Helena, Valeria and Marcella," Agreios said. "Is this all that is left of my family? Is there no one else?"

Helena stepped to her father and put her hand on his arm. "Father," she said, "you know Claudia and Prisca were killed in action. We are the only ones to make it safely home. Though I guess Antares will not be our home for long. We destroyed both tellium stars, but we grossly miscalculated one variable – *emotion*."

"Emotion?" Agreios said. "We knew Humans were governed by their hearts-"

"Not them... *us*!" Helena said, "*We* are not devoid of that spark of life which flares brighter than all else. We thought we were, but our math was wrong."

"The plan was sound-" Agreios mumbled.

"They will scatter us," Marcella said. "To ensure we are never a threat again."

He nodded. "Yes, I can sense that is their intention. Also, my life is forfeit."

Helena embraced her father, though her love was but a distant and intangible memory. She hadn't even begun to recover from building the wall around her heart to fulfill her mission. The reality of her mother's warning echoed in her mind – *you may never recover*.

"I'm sorry Father, but that is the Human penalty for what we have done," Helena said. "Do we deserve less than this?"

Agreios flinched when he touched the sword. He looked to each of his three remaining daughters. Marcella holstered pistols underneath her jacket and Valeria inspected the edge on her own sword.

"Where... what are you doing?" he asked.

Helena cupped her father's face in her hand and said, "We know Terentia is alive, maybe Justina too. We intend to rescue them."

"And kill as many Humans along the way as possible," Valeria said as she rammed her blade into its scabbard.

"Terentia-" Agreios said. "I would very much like to see her again. She reminds me of your mother."

Helena removed her hand from her father and stared into his eyes. He was not the same man who started this series of events, but he was responsible for the most dramatic destruction of two superpowers the universe had ever seen. He would be remembered as a zealot, a terrorist. Helena wasn't sure that was far from the truth. His actions had changed them all and brought about the fall of Antares.

"Unfortunately, Father," Helena said, "You will never see Terentia again. They will bring you back to Terra and they will want to kill you. However, the fate of all Antarans will *not* be the same, as you hoped. I will rescue Terentia and I will carry the crown of Antares for as long as I am able. We will gather whatever refugees we can and we will find a home. I promise you the Antarans will live as we always have – free from the imperialists of this universe. If they dare interfere again, I will remind them of what happened the last time we were provoked. And they will remember."

"My Empress," Valeria and Marcella said in unison.

"I am sorry, Father, but you have indeed failed your people," Helena said. "For that, I remove you of your title. You are hereby excused from your duties."

Agreios's eyes widened as he realized what his daughter was doing.

"The Humans will know that *I* am the ruler of Antares," Helena said. "So it is me who must answer for these crimes and not you. The Human press will also know of this, so if they try to execute you, they will be breaking their own interstellar laws. And they are not strong enough to do that anymore. The other civilizations of our universe will hold them accountable."

"But they will hunt you down," Agreios said. "You will not be safe. What if they capture you?"

"Then my fate will be more dreadful than that of my people," Helena said. "And that is how it should be."

Epilogue

"You know, I did a little research of my own," the Human, Smythe, said. "You ladies have quite a price on your head."

Valeria stepped towards Smythe and said, "If you are thinking of betraying us, your death will not be a quick one."

Placing a restraining hand on her sister's arm, Helena said, "We are in his domain, now is not the time for threats."

Smythe pointed a thick finger at Valeria and said, "You should listen to her. My guys will take you down, do you hear? Take you down!"

Though the room was small and dimly lit, Helena knew every corner and exit. Two of the four thugs smoked cigars. The other two fingered their automatic weapons. Helena sensed these men had seen many deals go sour in this very room. Though Helena had hoped to avoid killing Smythe, it was now clear that he had betrayed them.

There was no other alternative.

"You have information!" Valeria said. "Tell us what you know. We have the money."

Smythe leaned backwards and his chair creaked in protest to his girth. "You see, there's the problem," he said. "I'm not sure you have enough."

Valeria glared at the Human and said, "We have already agreed upon the price."

"That was before I knew how much you were worth," Smythe said. "I'm a reasonable man, however. Pay me triple and we'll have a deal. I'll let you fine ladies walk right outta here."

"Triple?" Valeria reached inside her longcoat and Helena sensed the thugs tense.

Helena restrained her sister and said, "Alright! Triple." She just needed more time, though she knew Smythe didn't intend to let them leave. He had already made his deal.

"See? I knew you were reasonable women," Smythe said. "Now, where's your other sister? I'll only make the deal with the three of you."

There was the confirmation. He intended to turn them over to the Human bounty hunters. After five months of searching, they finally had a lead to find their imprisoned sister – Terentia. Now, this piggish Human wasn't going to keep his word.

"Marcella?" Valeria said as a grin tugged at the corner of her thin lips. "My sister is right behind you."

With blazing speed, Valeria and Helena drew their swords and dispatched the four guards. Their surprise died in their throats as they only had time to widen their eyes in shock. Helena felt as if this wasn't the last time she would be forced to draw blood.

Smythe's eyes bulged as Marcella appeared behind him with a dagger to his throat.

"Are the others dead?" Valeria asked as she wiped the gore from her blade on Smythe's jacket.

"Yes, my sister," Marcella said. "But we don't have much time. More are coming."

"Alright, alright!" Smythe said. "I'll give you the information. Just don't kill me!"

Helena placed one of her boots against Smythe's chest and said, "It is too late for that. Betrayal is met in-kind and the only hope you have is for a quick death."

She pulled a vial from her coat and continued her bluff. "This is one of the most painful Antaran poisons," she said, though she held a simple antidote for travel nausea in her hand. "You will suffer for weeks as you feel like your organs are burning from the inside. The Human doctors will attempt to keep you alive to cure you, but they will fail. Trust me when I tell you Marcella's blade is a much more welcome end to your pathetic life. You have information? We want it. Hand it over now and we will show you some measure of mercy."

Smythe thought for a moment and Marcella tightened her grasp. "Okay!" he said. "I was going to meet a guy who knew where your sister was being held. Everything's in the safe over there in a brown envelope. The code is-"

Helena was already in his mind, which was unreadable moments before. Like Rowe, this man was accustomed to lying. His memories and thoughts were difficult to penetrate.

"I know the code," Helena said as she approached the safe.

"Anything else?" Valeria said as she replaced Helena in front of the frightened Human.

"Everything's there," Smythe said as Helena manipulated the keypad. "Meeting time, location, everything."

Helena pulled the brown envelope from the safe and emptied the contents on a nearby table. With a *clink*, something familiar fell from the package. At first, the memory was hazy, like a ship too far from shore. Then, the final brick around her heart crumbled as the memory of Captain Nathan Connor regained its hold. The glowing globes he gave her on Caledonia rested at the center of the table. She returned the jewelry to him when they parted aboard the *Jupiter* because she couldn't bear the pain of her betrayal to him. He died aboard the *Jupiter* as Helena sent the vessel into the tellium star.

But no, he didn't die. He was alive. And he knew Helena and her sisters sought Terentia. Like before, Helena knew her task had just become more difficult.

Matthew C. Plourde is a cancer survivor and native New Englander. He is a husband and father of two children. His family called Vietnam "home" for a month while they adopted their son. Though writing is his passion, he currently works as a compliance consultant for large enterprise corporations. His shorter fiction has appeared on many different e-zines and he continues to write novels.

For all the latest, visit his blog:
http://matthewcplourde.wordpress.com/

CPSIA information can be obtained at www.ICGtesting.com
Printed in the USA
LVOW01s1614020913

350637LV00028B/626/P